THE REAL THING

Marina Simcoe

To My Captain

1

Marina.Simcoe@Yahoo.com

Facebook/Marina Simcoe Author

Cover Design by Naomi Lucas and Cameron Kamenicky

Edition 2019

Spelling: Canadian

Editing by Nikki Groom, The Indie Hub

Proofreading by Anna Bloom, The Indie Hub

The Real Thing is a paranormal romance. It contains sexual situations, graphic descriptions of intimacy, and some violence. Intended for mature readers.

Chapter 1

MARCUS

Through the slits of his mask, he watched the blonde's head bobbing in his lap, up and down, in a perfect rhythm. Way too perfect, actually. He was mere seconds from coming already.

Only he couldn't do it, could he? He was in a hotel room in the middle of Manhattan. Too many people, tall buildings, too dangerous . . .

He needed to get a grip and stay in control.

With an effort, he forced his attention to anything else other than the amazing sensation of the girl's mouth on him.

Her hair. Was it naturally this luminous blonde?

He didn't remember her name. Most of the time, he didn't even bother asking their names. He recalled, though, she mentioned she was from Turkey. Or was it Brazil? Either way, her smooth skin, the colour of coffee heavy on the cream, supported her claim. He wasn't sure about her platinum blonde hair, though.

Were there natural blondes like that in Brazil? He had no idea—this was one of the few countries he hadn't visited yet. And why the hell not? He should go to Brazil, if only to satisfy his curiosity and find out if there were any blondes with blue eyes there.

Were her eyes blue? He didn't remember that either, and he couldn't see them now because of the position she was in.

Again, his focus shifted to the slick heat of her mouth gliding up and down his dick, and his control wavered.

It was time to take the matter into his own hands. Or his mouth, to be precise.

"Babe."

"Mmmm?" She lifted her gaze without releasing him from her mouth.

Fuck, she looked hot at this angle!

He had to stop this—quickly—before it was too late.

"My turn," he croaked, his throat dry, and shifted his hips. His erection sprung free from her mouth and into the cool air of the room. Grabbing the girl's hips, he flipped her on her back.

"Marcus. Are you sure? I could have finished . . ."

Silent, he pushed her knees apart and dove in, shutting her up instantly. Experience had taught him this was the most effective way to make any woman forget about anything she might not have *finished* for him.

After he gave her a few orgasms, she would leave here deeply satisfied, happily blabbing to everyone that he was truly Marcus the Magnificent in bed and that she had the best sex ever. She'd completely forget the fact that there had been very little of actual fucking involved, and she would never notice that the condom he tossed in the trashcan after a night of passion was empty.

This was his modus operandi, which he had perfected over the years.

Except that the girl didn't want to leave so easily this time, even after he made her come again, or maybe because of it.

"Oh, Marcus." She stretched on his hotel bed lazily as the streetlights from the window played on her perfect skin. "You completely wore me out, baby."

This couldn't mean anything good for him at this point. He was still painfully hard and beginning to grow irritated.

It was time for *Marcus the Jerk* to take over.

"I'm sorry, babe, but you'll have to leave now. I have a show tonight and need to rest," he offered as an explanation, feeling somewhat guilty for kicking her out when she clearly didn't want to leave.

"But it's New Year's Eve, baby." Her cherry-red lips, swollen after sex, rolled out into a most delicious pout. "We can take a nap together and then have dinner."

What was that like? To have someone to take a nap together? No sex, no expectations, no painful tension. Just the warmth of another human being at his side.

People did it all the time.

Not that he would ever find out. The more time he'd spend with anyone, the more risk there was for them to start asking questions.

The blonde in his bed misunderstood his pause.

"We can order some champagne." She got up on all fours and crawled along the mattress seductively. "Champagne makes me do crazy things. I may even let you fuck me in the ass." She wiggled her backside playfully.

"Not today," he replied firmly.

Energy buzzed just beneath his skin, the fire taking over, making him restless and increasingly anxious. He knew it'd get worse, the agony driving him mad.

Thankfully, he had a show tonight. Performing was one of the only two things that helped him to cool off—performing and sex—real sex, whenever he could have it. Not tonight though.

"I don't sleep well if there's someone in my bed, babe. You do need to go." He got up, hoping she'd follow his example.

"But when can I see you again?"

"How about tonight?" He tossed her clothes on the bed for her and strolled to the bathroom, wearing nothing but his mask. "Times Square. Make sure you look up if you want to see me." He grinned. "Way up."

Chapter 2

"COME ON, ANGELA! MOVE your ample behind."

Oh, little brothers. Our joy and pain. More pain than joy, actually. Especially if we were talking about my brother, Evan. He would never just call my biggest asset *your fat ass* like normal people would. No, he made sure to use fancier words because he knew that, for some reason, I found them more offensive.

No wonder I didn't like Evan very much. I couldn't help but still love him, of course. He was my brother after all.

"I'm coming!" I yelled at his back, putting my best effort into catching up with him and Lily, his girlfriend.

We were in New York, almost in the middle of Times Square now. Evan moved forward like an icebreaker, parting the crowd with his wide shoulders and pulling Lily by her arm in his wake.

My best friend, Emily, and her fiancé, Mikey, were so far ahead of us already that I could no longer see them.

"Don't get lost!" Evan threw over his shoulder. "I'm not going to spend New Year's Eve searching for you in this city."

"As if you would," I muttered under my breath, ignoring the annoyed look Lily hurled my way. "At most, you'd probably just put up some *"Lost Sister"* posters two days later."

To be fair, I knew Evan cared about me. Despite occasional disagreements, we were close. When he lost his job and got kicked out from his apartment, he showed up at my door instead of going to live with our parents. I let him stay with me for months, putting up with his "recreational" drug use that got him in trouble in the first place.

My parents and I finally talked him into trying a rehab program. Shortly after he got out, he met Lily, who was firm in her stance against any substance abuse.

Highly intelligent, she held a well-paying job with the provincial government in downtown Toronto, but lacked severely in social skills. She tended to communicate in brisk statements that were mostly offensive and out of place. Still, I believed she was the best thing that ever happened to my brother.

Lily was driven and organized, which seemed to be rubbing off on Evan. In the year that they started dating, he finally completed his college program and managed to hold down a job with a theater production company.

Evan was right, though, it was way too easy to get lost in the crowd in Times Square on New Year's Eve. It seemed just as easy to get crushed or trampled to death, especially if you were a woman of average height with average muscle tone, like me. The four-inch heels of my fabulous boots weren't helping my speed, either.

Without having a strong manly back to part the crowd for me, I had to rely on my very own elbow power, which wasn't much. I didn't want to admit that I actually missed Matt, my ex, for the first time since we broke up last month. Well, maybe I didn't miss *him* specifically, just having someone special by my side to share the moment with.

I'd known it wouldn't be easy to go on this trip as the fifth wheel with two couples, but Evan and Emily were my best friends and, lately, my only friends. They and their significant others were the only people I'd see whenever I could squeeze any social life between my two jobs.

I didn't regret coming along but couldn't help feeling a little lonely surrounded by couples in love. And it would only get worse once the ball dropped and everyone started kissing, but the alternative was to celebrate New Years in my apartment with only Lannister, my cat, for company.

Finally, using my own shoulders and elbows and tossing a good curse here and there, I made my way through the crowd and caught up with Evan and Lily right across from the huge billboards. Mikey and Emily were already there, squeezed by the crowd from all sides.

Grabbing Emily's sleeve, I took a moment to catch my breath, feeling a bit overwhelmed by the surroundings. I lived, worked and studied in downtown Toronto and was used to living in a big city. However, the crowd, the lights, and the noise right now equaled all my experiences multiplied by a hundred.

"There he is! Look!" shouted somebody in the crowd, and I tilted my head way back, searching the night sky high above.

The biggest of the billboards across from us shimmered with lights, and his masked face appeared on the screen.

Marcus the Magnificent, the up-and-coming magician—or *illusionist* as I heard they preferred to be called—the newest internet sensation, according to my brother.

Marcus was the opening act of this year's celebration in Times Square. He was going to walk between the rooftops of two buildings, on nothing but air.

The crowd stilled. The noise had subdued, and I squinted to see a figure standing on the edge of the roof, hundreds of feet above us.

From down here, I could only make out his silhouette backlit by several spotlights—the long mane of his dark hair and the ends of his coat whipping in the wind.

The giant screen above us, however, displayed a close-up image.

He wore all black—leather pants and heavy boots, in addition to his long trench coat. His straight jet-black hair must have reached past his waist. The longs strands lashed across his face with the gusts of wind. A black half-mask covered the upper part of his face.

Dark and mysterious, he commanded attention and enticed imagination, without saying a word.

There was no introduction. Marcus didn't seem to care whether all attention was fully on him yet. Slowly, he moved his foot forward and stepped off the roof into the abyss.

The crowd gasped as one physical entity. The breath caught in my throat, too, as I half expected him to plummet to the ground in a bloody mess.

My heart skidded to a halt, and I jerked forward as if I could catch him before he hit the pavement at my feet.

But he didn't fall. Instead, he remained suspended in the air, halfway between the sky and the earth.

He took another step forward, slowly but without hesitation. Then another step. And another.

Unhurriedly, he was making his way across the sky, with the thousands of people gaping at him far below. The gusts of winter air caught the ends of his trench coat, flapping them violently against his boots. Hair flew across his face, completely obstructing it at times.

Nothing seemed to faze him. He kept walking with confidence on nothing but air for support.

The crowd below seemed to have found its voice again. People shouted encouragements and offered their guesses on how the illusion was accomplished. Most snapped pictures and took bad videos with their cellphones.

"Isn't it cool, dude!" My brother yelled.

"He should've put his hair into a ponytail," came the aloof voice of Lily. "It's a mess. How can he see where he's going?"

"He is so hot. Angela, isn't he hot?" Emily hugged my shoulders.

"It's the mask," boomed Mikey's deep voice just behind me. "Everyone looks hot in a black mask. Even I would if I wore one."

"Sure you would, honey." Emily laughed and got on her tiptoes to place a quick kiss on Mikey's chin. She couldn't reach any higher—at well over six feet tall, Mikey towered over all of us.

I said nothing, my gaze fixed on Marcus as he walked across the sky.

It was a perfectly executed illusion. So perfect, in fact, that it didn't even seem like an illusion at all. It felt real. Wonder and awe rose inside me, as if in the presence of real magic, and I was afraid to breathe lest I scare it away.

I watched his face carefully, trying to make out his expression behind the mask. What was he thinking at that moment? What would it feel like to create a miracle in front of thousands of people?

The camera zoomed in on his face then, and I got a clear view of his eyes through the slits of the mask.

Suddenly, I knew exactly what he was feeling. His eyes said it all. He was bored.

His head tilted slightly to the side, the vacant expression in his eyes was that of someone stuck in traffic or standing in a grocery checkout line, waiting for the time to pass.

How could Marcus not feel what everyone else did at that moment?

My own skin buzzed with excitement for him. He literally stood on top of the world right now and should be enjoying the highest high possible in his occupation. Surely, weeks or even months of planning had been spent to bring him to this point. He was pulling off the perfect illusion in front of hundreds of thousands of live spectators and numerous TV cameras.

Why did it seem like he'd rather be anywhere else but here?

Chapter 3

MY GREY TABBY CAT SAUNTERED into the hallway to greet me when I returned home.

"Hi, Lannister. Did you miss me?"

The cat was as cuddly as a rabid porcupine, and I believed he had no chance of being adopted when I found him as a stray. So, even though I could hardly afford to have a pet, I ended up keeping him myself. Something about him reminded me of the cunning and backstabbing personalities of the Lannister family from *Games of Thrones*—hence his name.

"Is your pet feeder running low on food or something?"

The cat strolled to the kitchen. Tossing my travel bag in the corner, I followed him.

It was insane how much food Lannister could eat, considering he was an indoor cat now and spent most of his time napping. The cost of cat food added a sizable expense to my already stretched-to-the-limit budget.

After getting my degree, I was lucky enough to get a job in operations with a major transportation company. However, my expenses always managed to run slightly ahead of my salary.

Instead of quitting the part time job at a shoe store that I had while in school, I ended up keeping it, too. It helped with student loans and other things that my regular salary didn't cover. The forty percent employee discount on already reduced shoes was a huge incentive for me, too.

I topped up Lannister's food dish and logged onto my laptop to check my email. I knew that a message from my mother was long overdue, and there it was.

She never asked me for money in person or by phone but preferred to do it through email. Maybe because it was easier for her to ask without facing me or hearing my voice. Or maybe because this way, she felt she gave me the choice to delete and ignore her message. If I replied, it was because I wanted to, not because I had no other option.

Was there any other option, though?

I knew my parents had to remortgage their house to pay for my brother's rehab treatment. Long before that, they already struggled to pay their monthly bills.

My father was a retired Math Teacher. Unfortunately, his math skills remained purely academic, rendering him either unable or unwilling to deal with their financial situation. Instead, he gave my mother free reign of their accounts and credit cards, and now they could barely afford to keep the house where my brother and I grew up.

The house was one of the reasons why I couldn't ignore my mother ever so subtly asking for money. It was my childhood home, the place where my family gathered every holiday. I would hate to see them having to sell it.

The other reason of course was that they were my family. I wanted to help any way I could, whether it was letting my brother stay with me when he had no place to go, or scraping every last bit from my checking account to make a mortgage payment for my parents.

This was why I worked two jobs, why I watched every penny I spent, and why I closed my personal savings account long ago because there was nothing extra to put away.

I opened my banking page and sent whatever money I could spare to my mother. This should buy me another month of a happy mother-daughter relationship, free of any money-problem talks. This alone should be worth it, shouldn't it?

Closing my banking page, I lingered in front of the computer. The eyes of the mysterious masked man—who had walked across the sky—came to my mind as if from another life.

Surely, Marcus the Magnificent had a very different life than mine. *His* must be full of fun, glamour, and excitement. He wouldn't have to deal with trivial things like money or family problems.

His days must be filled with magic and his nights shrouded in mystery.

I typed his name into the search bar of my browser, wishing to see his face uncovered. Was it still as handsome and mysterious, or was Mikey right and the magic was in the mask?

Plenty of images came up under his name. Most of them were promotional posters, though, artfully designed and professionally photoshopped. In them, he was even more handsome than I remembered from the giant screen in Times Square.

In the posters, he was portrayed like a true magician—levitating in the air over the stage, with his arms spread wide, rays of light radiating from his fingers. In all the photographs he was wearing a mask, and his eyes—of an unnatural cerulean blue—glowed through its narrow slits.

I searched for candid shots of him in everyday setting, but there were none, just as there weren't any of him without the mask, either.

A few grainy images from online tabloids showed him arriving at a party. In those, he was dressed in what appeared to be his usual outfit—leather pants, a black t-shirt with a band logo, and a long trench coat. The ever-present mask was covering half of his face. Two incredibly beautiful women flanked him from both sides, smiling readily in the camera. Marcus was neither smiling nor frowning in the pictures. Actually, he again appeared bored.

Bored on his way to a party? With a gorgeous woman on each arm? Why?

The question nagged at me.

Why didn't Marcus the Magnificent seem to enjoy his work *or* his life?

Chapter 4

OVER THE NEXT MONTHS, it had happened slowly. So gradually, I didn't even recognize my obsession with Marcus for what it was right away.

Working two jobs and being constantly broke, I didn't have much time or means for entertainment.

Ever since I had broken up with Matt, or more precisely, since we drifted so far apart that breaking up was just a formality to end our non-existent relationship, I hadn't dated anyone. Just thinking about how much time, energy, and money dating would require made me put any thought of it on hold.

I would come home after a late shift at the store—too late to go out, too early to fall asleep right away. Grabbing an apple from the fridge or getting a bowl of cereal, I would turn my laptop on and browse the web in search of everything there was to know about Marcus, searching for answers and only gaining more questions.

Frustratingly, there wasn't much information about him. I wasn't even sure if Marcus was his real name. All of his social media accounts must have been managed by an assistant, who posted promotions and announcements, no personal photos.

Over time, the fame of Marcus the Magnificent had risen. Shortly after his performance in Times Square, it was announced he'd signed a Vegas contract and would be starting his new show in March.

There were more pictures of him on the internet now, but I still couldn't find any without the mask. He wore it everywhere he went—to clubs and parties, to every performance and interview. I wondered if he ever took it off at all, even at night.

Well, at least his nightlife didn't appear to be that much of a mystery. Most of the pictures of him in public had him accompanied by beautiful women, and I had yet to see any one of them twice—none seemed to stay long enough.

Of course, just because my own personal life was non-existent didn't mean that everyone else had to practice abstinence or even restraint, as Marcus's case appeared to be.

I couldn't deny that his apparent good looks—mysteriously concealed behind the black mask—fed my imagination, but Marcus was also mesmerizingly good at what he did.

He often gave free impromptu performances, right out on the streets, and people adored him for it. The location would be announced on social media, with sometimes as little as one hour before the start of the act.

Not surprisingly, Marcus had an ever-growing number of followers on the internet, stalking his every move, hoping to get to his next free show.

There were hundreds of amateur videos taken all over North America when he was touring and then from Las Vegas when his contract began.

Watching the videos, I'd seen Marcus walk on air between skyscrapers, mountain peaks, and national monuments. He marched effortlessly up vertical walls, moved through solid panes of glass and massive brick walls, or levitated over lakes and rivers. I watched him make a number of things disappear—from an elephant to a national monument—in front of many witnesses.

I knew all magic tricks were smoke and mirrors, of course. However, as I compared the acts of other illusionists to those of Marcus's, I began to see the difference.

The acts by others could be explained as being staged and pre-recorded. Their professional videos were taken from one or two carefully selected angles, and the illusions were done in front of relatively few people who could've been hired actors.

Marcus always performed openly—almost carelessly—in a public place in front of a crowd of complete strangers. His unplanned shows ran with no rehearsals and took place in a new location every time.

Watching many times every illusion he'd ever performed in public, I wondered how he managed to execute each of them so flawlessly.

How did he do it? And why didn't he seem to enjoy what he did so well?

I stared at the computer screen, into the impassive eyes in the slits of his mask. There was a secret hidden deep inside their overly saturated blue colour—I sensed it. I could almost feel the restrained energy behind his expression of boredom.

The next moment, the illusion of understanding would vanish again, always so close, yet forever out of my reach.

⸻ ◉ ⸻

"ANGELA, YOU JUST CAN'T say no!" Emily literally screamed, grabbing the attention of everyone on the patio of the coffee shop.

It was a sunny afternoon at the end of April. I had a rare Sunday off, and Emily talked me into spending most of the day outside with her. We did fun things like window shopping and walking in High Park, and now we were having coffee and desserts.

This completely trampled my plans of doing laundry and cleaning my apartment, but I wasn't angry with her in the slightest—it felt good to do things I *wanted* for once, instead of things I *had to*.

Emily and Mikey had set their wedding date for this June, and she asked me to be her maid of honour the minute they got engaged. Now Emily had informed me that she wanted a bachelorette party in Las Vegas and she absolutely needed me there.

Of course, the little detail of my financial insolvency wouldn't stop someone like Emily in her grand plans—she and Mikey offered to pay for my trip to Las Vegas.

Emily insisted it was merely a loan that could be paid back anytime. However, we both knew it wouldn't be soon.

"I still owe you money for the trip to New York for New Years," I reminded her in a loud whisper, wishing people would stop staring at us and mind their own business.

"Oh no! New York didn't count." Emily vigorously shook her head, making what must've been at least a million tiny dark braids bounce around her face. "We still would've paid the same for the hotel room, whether we had you sleeping on the couch there or not. You just . . . kinda filled the space that was already paid for." With her fingers spread wide, she gestured in the air between us energetically, illustrating the paid space she had mentioned.

"Still—"

"No *stills*, no *buts*, Angela," she cut me off, then made a one-eighty, changing her tactic from pushy to pleading. "Please, you have to come."

Emily asking nicely was much harder for me to resist than the pushy Emily. Much, much harder. Her big, chocolate-brown eyes opened wide as she leaned forward across the table. "You have to do this for me. I want a bachelorette party in Vegas. I've always wanted one. Ever since I was a baby."

"Really?" I sincerely doubted it had been that long.

"Yes!"

But then again, who was I to argue with Emily?

"And even then, I already knew you had to be there."

Well, that for sure wasn't true. Emily grew up in Vancouver. And although it felt at times as if I'd known her forever, we actually didn't meet until our first year of university.

We clicked instantly and bonded over our mutual unhappiness with our living arrangements at that time. I had a long commute to classes from my parents' house in the suburbs, and Emily fiercely despised her roommates in the student residence.

We ended up putting our heads and our finances together and found an apartment in an area where we could afford the rent.

The place was in one of the worst parts of town, wedged between an intersection of two busy roads and a crossing of two even busier railways, with the local fire station next door. There was always noise, day and night. A number of old abandoned factories made the neighbourhood even scarier because it attracted all kind of suspicious activity. Coming home late at night, I'd often had to pass by prostitutes soliciting their services. Walking to my classes early in the morning, I had to take extra care not to step on the occasional used condom on the sidewalk.

After the graduation, Emily moved in with Mikey, and I stayed in the apartment alone, which was cheaper than finding something else.

She proved to be a fiercely loyal friend and earned my absolute loyalty in return. I would do anything for her. I'd give up a kidney if she needed one.

Except that Emily wasn't asking for my kidney at the moment, was she? All she wanted was for me to come to Las Vegas for her party next month and for me to accept that she, the bride-to-be, would pay for my trip.

"Please say yes, Angela! How am I supposed to have a bachelorette party without my maid of honour? It won't even cost that much. Mikey is flying us there on standby using his work benefits. We'll be sharing the hotel rooms. It'll be next to nothing, really."

Mikey was an airline pilot. Flying standby on his benefits would cost very little, but it would still cost something . . .

I never talked to Emily about my family's financial situation. This was something I couldn't discuss even with her. However, I was sure that she suspected something wasn't right. She'd seen me cutting down on my fun times with friends because even the cheapest things cost money.

"Come on, Angela. How am I supposed to deal with Lily if you're not there? Who is going to deflect all her remarks? Remember she told me at my engagement party that interracial and intercultural couples faced additional challenges in marriage? And then went on to list the said *challenges*? At my engagement party!"

"Lily doesn't really think before she speaks." I felt the need to explain. "She often simply repeats what she heard or read somewhere, which is not necessarily her own opinion."

It certainly felt that way with Lily, as though she tried to break any awkward silence in company with other people by reciting whatever random thing rose in her memory at that particular moment.

Emily scoffed. "As if I didn't have my own parents as an example of a happy interracial couple." She bounced in her chair once. "That's it . . . If you're not coming, I won't go, either. It would never be the same without you, anyway." She was obviously pulling out all the stops, using her most effective weapon—guilt. "I just won't have a bachelorette party then. There are plenty of brides out there who do fine without them, I'm sure."

How could I deny my best friend what she'd always wanted?

I'd have to find a way to come up with the money to pay her back, even if it took me years, even if I ended up eating Lannister's food from now on myself.

"Okay. Please don't cancel the party. I'll go . . ."

"Yes!" Emily yelled triumphantly and launched forward to hug me across the table, knocking over my empty coffee mug.

"You. Are. The bestest. Friend. Ever!" She kept giving me hug after hug, squeezing me harder and harder each time until I could barely breathe.

"No, Emily, you are," I managed to reply, squished in her arms. "The bestest friend ever." Definitely worth a kidney.

———⬩———

I SWEAR I DIDN'T THINK about it until I got back to the office on Monday and logged on my computer. The last page I viewed before I left on Friday was still on the screen. It was my favourite picture of Marcus.

He wasn't on stage in this one, neither was he levitating or shooting light rays from his fingers. This was still a promotional studio picture, only a more casual one.

Dressed in a black button-down shirt, Marcus stood in a relaxed pose, his hands in his pockets. The few buttons open at the top of his shirt exposed his collarbone.

He stared into the camera with the eyes of the same photoshopped cerulean-blue. I could still read the usual bored expression behind his mask. However, the underlying tension in him was more obvious to me here. Some hidden energy seemed to be churning just beneath his composure, ready to burst out. His long, black hair unbound, he reminded me of a wild horse, captured and restrained.

Then it hit me in a rush—I was going to be in Vegas next month, the same city where Marcus had a show. Was this my chance to see his performance again?

Of course, Emily and her party were my unquestionable priority on this trip, but maybe, just maybe, there'd be enough time to see his show, too. Maybe Emily and the rest of the girls would like to come with me.

My heart swelled with an unexplained longing as I stared at the picture on my screen, remembering the feeling of awe and wonder when I watched him walk across the night sky in New York.

What was it that had kept him in my thoughts all this time?

Was it the nostalgia for a miracle—something we all believed in as children—that attracted me to him? Or the mystery I couldn't solve about him that refused to leave my brain?

Maybe if I saw his performance on stage—much closer than up in the sky or through the computer screen—the illusion of magic would be less beguiling? Then my strange obsession with Marcus The Magnificent would possibly fade away?

I touched the screen, tracing one long strand of his hair that must have been blown across his chest by the studio fan, and wondered if his hair would feel silky to the touch or thick and coarse, like a mane of a horse. Did the girls he took home at night get to run their fingers through it? Did he like it when they did?

I had yet to find any pictures of him unmasked. There were none from backstage or his home, as if there was no man behind that mask at all. He only seemed to exist as *Marcus the Magnificent* and all but disappeared outside of the spotlight.

Yet after spending so much time with pictures and videos of him, I'd began to feel like the little bits I've learned about him here and there had gradually melted into a person, with his own quirks and habits, gestures and expressions.

His interviews seemed always too short and scripted. I noticed that he always sat with his right ankle resting on top of his left knee. When seemingly nervous or impatient, he tapped his thumb against his thigh or against the arm of the chair.

He never smiled. Ever. And I wondered if that was an act, too, a part of his onstage persona. Or were his smiles always so rare that they never made it to the photos and videos?

If I did get a change to see him live on stage, would I be able to catch one of his smiles after all?

I opened the website selling tickets for his Vegas show to see if there were any available for the days I was going to be there. One glance at the ticket prices—and I closed it again quickly. There was no way I could add this expense to the money I was already going to owe Mikey and Emily.

It wasn't the first time I had to say "no" to things I really wanted, especially during the past couple of years. And I knew it wouldn't be the last.

"CN Rail is still on strike, Angela." Barb, my manager, materialized out of nowhere right in front of my desk, yanking me out of my daydreaming.

I blinked, startled, but managed to minimize Marcus's picture in time. It wouldn't do for anyone, especially my boss, to catch me gazing at pictures of mysterious hot men during my work hours.

"Yes." I made an effort to sound enthusiastic, ready for anything she threw my way.

"One of those shipments that are stuck in Vancouver needs to be here ASAP." Barb tapped her finger against my desk for emphasis. "The client needs it for the upcoming flyer promo."

"Sure." I nodded. "What is it?"

It absolutely didn't matter what it was. I asked just to maintain the illusion of a dialogue, because most conversations with Barb tended to be one-sided—she talked and others were supposed to listen and nod, then do what they had been told.

"Paper towels." Barb lifted her eyebrow. "Why?"

"No reason." I shook my head, regretting my asking. "I'll get right on it."

Opening a spreadsheet, I searched for the minimum quantity required and lifted the receiver of my phone to call our Fleet Supervisor. Now, I needed to talk him into finding a truck for me.

Another problem to solve. Another crisis to avert. This was what made my job interesting for me. Something I was good at—saving the world, one shipment of paper towels at a time.

Chapter 5

AMONG THE MANY NEW things I learned in Las Vegas over the past couple of days, the following two were the most important right now.

First, unlike Toronto, the weather in Vegas was already incredibly, unbearably, inhumanly hot in May.

And second, my favourite candy-apple red peep-toe pumps with a cute bow on the back were not designed for sprinting along the Vegas Strip. Even though they were the perfect match with my vintage—aka secondhand—red polka-dot sundress, I wished for a pair of running shoes instead as I dashed down the Strip in the sweltering afternoon heat.

It didn't help that my head was still a little fuzzy from all the partying we did last night and from all the window shopping we did this morning.

Emily, Lily, and the other two girls in our party were all asleep in our hotel, recuperating. I, on the other hand, had so much adrenaline pumping through me that if it wasn't for the blisters on my feet, I would've flown along the Strip with the speed of a bullet.

Like any self-respecting celebrity stalker, I followed every one of Marcus's social media accounts. Just about twenty minutes ago, I got a notification about an unscheduled performance near the fountains of the Bellagio.

My heart soared.

I will get to see him perform, after all.

For free. If I made it to the fountains in time.

We were staying in a small hotel off the Strip, and taking a cab was out of the question for me. So, here I was, running as fast as my kitten heels would carry me, and sweating through the polka dots on my dress.

I knew better than anyone in this town that Marcus the Magnificent didn't do lengthy introductions or pre-shows. If I wanted to see him at all, I had to be at the fountains on time.

Straining my eyes, I tried to catch a glimpse of the fountains in the distance. Not seeing the water jets, I realized as I got closer that they were shut off.

A fairly large crowd had already gathered along the railings surrounding the fountain pool, and I made my way through it, unceremoniously using my elbows. This was my one and only chance to see Marcus perform up close, and I wasn't going to waste it by staying politely at the back.

I had just made it to the railing as epic music suddenly blasted from a speaker somewhere, making me jump. Anticipation ran up my arms, prickling my skin.

A group of gorgeous women, dressed in gladiator costumes, exited the tour bus, which was parked along the Strip. Dressed in leather-looking armour, with one arm fully covered and a breastplate not larger than a bra, the showgirls moved in pairs, holding long spears decorated with gold ribbons.

Perfectly choreographed, the first two marched their stiletto sandals to the edge of the fountain. Then the pairs split up, stepping away from their partners to form a corridor from the railing to the black limo parked next to the tour bus.

Two men dressed in suits hurried to the fountain, carrying a shiny-looking ramp. Propping it on the stone railings, they extended it all the way into the water in the pool.

The next moment, the music volume lowered and a male voice shouted through the speakers, "Ladies and gentlemen! Marcus the Magnificent! One time only! The miracle of a man walking on water."

My focus shifted to the limo, and I saw *him* as he strode along the corridor formed by the beautiful gladiators.

Marcus wore his usual leather pants and heavy boots, but traded his trench coat for a black leather vest, which was open in the front.

His eyes were not of that intense blue from the posters after all, but from this distance I couldn't tell exactly what they were.

Also, his skin turned out to be much lighter than the golden tan on the posters. The pale, almost ivory colour of it formed a stark contrast to the black leather of his clothes.

The rest, however, was exactly as I had expected, if not better. He was tall, fit, and undeniably handsome, with hair that fell down his back in a sleek, heavy wave.

Marcus moved with purpose, unsmiling as always. His shoulders visibly tensed, hands balled into fists, he seemed to force himself to slow down, which brought the image of a restrained wild stallion to my mind once again.

Suddenly, I realized he was heading in my direction, as I stood by the stone railing next to the ramp.

The person who had occupied my thoughts daily for the past five months was barely a few feet away from me now.

Something inside my stomach fluttered violently, and I gripped the edge of the balustrade behind me, my fingers digging painfully into the hard rock.

The warm spice of male and leather teased my nostrils as he came closer. Unable to resist, I inhaled a lungful, savoring it like one would the smoke of a fine cigar, then caught myself leaning forward, just to snag another tendril of his scent.

The uninvited fantasy of his masked face lowering over mine rose in mind, washing me with a heat that had nothing to do with the weather.

I froze, mortified that he'd hear the sound of my heart thundering against my ribcage and would somehow be able to see the illicit images of the two of us in my brain.

Marcus remained completely unaware of my existence, though. His gaze shifted to the ramp. One hand on the railing, he jumped up on it then walked down to the water.

Quickly, I took a few deep breaths, recovering from the unexpected effect his proximity had on me. The months-long obsession with Marcus proved to be definitely unhealthy. Either that or my even longer abstinence had wreaked havoc on my hormones. How else was I to explain my sudden reaction to him?

Meanwhile, Marcus hopped off the ramp into the fountain pool.

Oddly, the water didn't splash from under his feet. His boots hardly seemed to touch the surface at all.

He paused for a moment, giving the crowd a chance to gasp and applaud, then slowly headed towards the middle of the pool.

Since watching Marcus at Times Square, I'd learned a fair amount about his occupation. I knew that the act of walking on water was accomplished by placing plexiglass fixtures on the bottom of the pool. Fully submerged and filmed at a certain angle, they were practically invisible even as a person stepped on them.

I'd seen videos of this act performed by other illusionists. They did it in a controlled environment, with cameras filming from a certain angle and with hired actors who played the spectators.

Now, I carefully watched Marcus perform the same act, determined to confirm this explanation. From whatever angle I looked, though, I couldn't spot any plexiglass in the water.

How did he do it?

Was there one large sheet of it under the water, with no edge for me to see? But would it be possible to cover a section of the fountain with one solid piece? When and how could it be done without anyone noticing? And wouldn't the movement of the water in the pool be different if there was a large sheet of plexiglass just beneath the surface?

Questions and possible solutions turned inside my mind like the multicoloured squares of a Rubik's cube—not unlike my process of solving problems at work every day.

Surely, I could figure out this one, too, if I watched Marcus closely and thought hard.

Meanwhile, he stopped on his way and turned around, raising his arms in the air to greet the cheering crowd.

"Jesus, man!" screamed a man next to me, waving a two-foot-long glass filled with a neon-coloured drink in the air. "Marcus! You are like Jesus, man . . . Walking on water!"

The guy was obviously drunk already and slurred his words, happy as could be. His friends cheered him on, also with enormous drinks in their hands.

Marcus waved at people gathered on all sides around the pool then continued on his way back, towards me and the ramp at the railing.

Not a shadow of a smile appeared on his face, but he seemed content now, more relaxed.

I forgot all about the puzzle I was trying to solve, and greedily took in everything I still didn't know about him. How he shook his head to the side to toss his hair away from his face. The way he hooked his thumbs in the belt loops of his pants. How he'd sweep the crowd with his gaze, without stopping it on anyone, including me, the familiar expression of boredom and indifference in his eyes.

He ascended the ramp then jumped from the railing in one fluid motion, waved at the crowd one more time, and swiftly walked back to the limo waiting for him.

Just like that, it was over.

I watched him move away and waited for the inescapable feeling of sadness and disappointment to rush me next.

Except that . . . something was missing here. Something wasn't right, and I couldn't put my finger on it.

Slowly, I followed Marcus, separated from him by the line of the Amazonian women, as if I'd been attached to him by an invisible line, which I was unable to break off too soon.

"Marcus!" the drunk behind me yelled on the top of his lungs. "Hey, man! Turn the water into wine now. We'll have a par-tay!"

His friends bellowed as one in their loud support of this idea. Other people cheered, too, the crowd growing wild and rowdy. Somebody stepped on someone's foot in the process and got yelled at and punched in return.

Trouble seemed to brew behind me now.

The Amazonian gladiators broke their perfect order. Holding their prop spears up, they retreated back to the bus. From the corner of my eye, I noticed several men in black suits rush around the women and in the direction of the drunks.

And then it hit me what was missing.

Footprints.

As Marcus strolled from the pool to the limo, there were no wet tracks left on the pavement behind him. Not one single footprint.

He had just walked halfway across a pool of water. Even if the whole fountain were covered with plexiglass end to end, the soles of his boots would've still been wet from the water on top of it. It was impossible to keep feet dry while performing the act in the traditional way.

Only, nothing Marcus did was *traditional.*

Just like that, one square of the Rubik's cube fell into place, and the others followed.

Everything I'd learned about his work in the past months made a perfect sense if I allowed myself to believe in the impossible.

Marcus was not an illusionist.

And his acts were not illusions—they were real.

No one could ever notice his props, because there were none. No ropes, no harness to hide. That's why he never had to worry about camera angles and the number of spectators.

That could also explain why he often seemed bored while performing. There was no elation on his face or satisfaction of a job well done because he didn't spend weeks and months planning and practicing his acts. All of his open-street performances, like the one I'd just witnessed, were indeed impromptu.

My heart jumped to my throat from the realization, making it hard to breathe.

Marcus the Magnificent was the real thing.

Not an illusionist, but a true magician.

The solution to his mystery was incredibly simple and right under everyone's noses. It was so obvious yet so unbelievable that no one would ever think of it.

It took a crazy, obsessed person like myself to figure it out.

Yet, even I had doubts about such an out-of-this-world concept as true magic. If I took a moment to think about it logically, I was sure that common sense would prevail.

That was exactly why I didn't let myself dwell on it for long.

Instead, another crazy idea came to me—I had to confront him to know for sure. All attention was still on the drunks behind me. Now was the perfect moment.

Completely abandoning all caution or common sense, I followed the impulse.

"Marcus!" I raced after him, ignoring the blisters on my feet.

"I don't sign autographs," he tossed over his shoulder when I caught up with him at the limo.

"No," I rushed out, afraid he'd get in the vehicle and shut the door before I had a chance to finish. "I just want to ask you—why are you hiding it? Why don't you tell them your work is real? Your magic, I mean."

There were several ways for him to react—ignore me, laugh at my craziness, or agree that he was indeed a true magician, like any good showman would have done.

None of these things would've confirmed my guess for me, but Marcus did none of them.

Instead, he stopped so suddenly I nearly bumped into him from behind, then spun around to face me.

Midnight blue.

That was the true colour of his eyes. Dark and cool, like the pool at the bottom of a mountain waterfall. And, I was about to drown in their abyss, faced with the chill of the obvious resentment swimming inside.

"I . . . um," all I could manage, immediately regretting my blazing decision to come this close to him.

Without saying a word, Marcus grabbed my arm above the elbow and unceremoniously dragged me to the bus.

The door of the limo behind us flew open, and a handsome blond man leaped out.

"Marcus? Is there a problem?" The man's voice was filled with energy and concern.

"Not yet," Marcus gritted through his teeth. "Excuse me, ladies," he addressed the group of his Amazonian gladiators gathered by the front door of the bus. "A minute of privacy, please." He shoved me through the door, following me in.

The chilled air inside the bus was a big change from the outside heat. Shivers ran through me, as the sweat on my skin cooled.

Marcus shut the door behind him with force, cutting off all outside noise at once.

"What do you want?" he bit out.

"What do you mean?" I blinked, stunned by the undisguised hostility in his voice.

"Money?"

"What? No!" I stared at him, mortified. Did I give him any reason to believe I was some kind of an extortionist? My face heated with indignity from his accusations. "I don't want your money."

"So, you want to know *how*?" His voice was still gruff, but with his head tilted to the side, he appeared to be more curious than angry now. Staring through the slits of the mask at me, he narrowed his eyes in visible concentration.

Funny, he seemed to be trying to figure *me* out, as if I, myself, was a mystery.

I nearly snorted at this notion—there was nothing mysterious about me.

"Did you come to demand I tell you how it's done?"

"No." I shook my head. "I'm pretty sure I already know *how*. What I don't understand is *why*?"

"*Why?*" He crossed his arms over his chest and leaned against the back of one of the seats. The mask didn't completely hide the frown on his face.

Obviously, this conversation wasn't going well, but what did I have to lose at this point? He already thought me capable of blackmail. As far as I was concerned, there was no way but up for his opinion.

"Yes." I gestured at the door. "Why don't you tell them that you are the real thing? I would've shouted to the whole of universe if I possessed any magic." The burning need to know more almost erased the earlier unease in me. I leaned closer to him, straining to read his expression behind the mask. "Why don't you blow their minds the way you just blew mine, Marcus?"

In anticipation of his answer, I tried to hold his gaze, but it slid past my shoulder, unfocussed.

"The only *how* questions I have," I continued, since he didn't reply. "Is *how* did you get to be what you are—where did you get the ability to defy all laws of physics? And *how* do you live in this world being the only one like that?"

Although there was no way for me to know for sure he was the only one of his kind, I knew enough about his profession by now to be certain that there was no other performing magician like him out there.

His mouth pressed into a firm line, Marcus remained silent. And as the seconds trickled by, it had become apparent he was not going to answer any of my questions.

Disappointment slithered inside me, but it was greatly overshadowed by the sudden awareness of us being alone on this bus. I realized I was leaning too much into his personal space, breathing the air filled with his scent of male and leather.

Quickly, I drew back, wiping my suddenly sweaty palms on my skirt.

"Marcus?" Someone began to pound on the door, and I believed I recognized the voice of the blond man from the limo.

Marcus stirred, his brow furrowed above the mask. Lifting his hand, he brushed his hair away mechanically, as if still lost in thought.

I watched his fingers run through the black, glossy strands and fought the sudden wish to do the same. Would his hair really feel like a horse's mane to the touch? He was so close—all I'd have to do was stretch out my hand.

The banging on the door came again, and the silence between us grew awkwardly heavy.

He paid me no attention. It seemed he was no longer aware I was here at all. No matter what, though, I already got the answer to my biggest question.

"I should go," I mumbled and attempted to slip past him to the door.

"That's it?" he asked quickly, his intense dark eyes snapped to mine again. For once, there was no bored indifference in them, but I couldn't name their unfamiliar expression.

Was it a spark of interest? A shadow of regret—a glimmer of hope even—that I'd glimpsed? I wasn't sure. Brittle and raw, it disappeared immediately, as the door of the bus finally opened and the blond man's worried face came into view.

"Marcus? Are you okay?"

"Really, Simon?" Marcus shifted his attention to him, and the spell his gaze seemed to have put me under was broken. I was free to leave.

Quietly, I squeezed past Marcus, trying hard not to breathe in too deeply when I came close enough for the skirt of my dress to brush by the leather of his pants. I could've sworn I felt the warmth emanating from his bare chest, and the alarming desire to press against him only made me move away faster.

As spacious as the bus seemed to be, its walls appeared to be moving in on me, squeezing all air out of my chest.

The physical reaction of my body to this man was unnerving and—considering that he was the unattainable celebrity with all signs of leading a playboy lifestyle—inconvenient and undesirable.

"Who are you?" The blond man, Simon, fixed me with his glare at the door. "And why are you here?"

"I'm leaving." I made an attempt to slip past him.

"Wait." Marcus's voice stopped me, prompting me to glance back at him. "How did you know?"

"Know what?" Simon asked, obviously confused.

But I understood what Marcus was referring to, even as I had no clear answer to give him. There was no way in hell I'd confess my many-months-long obsession to him at this point—no need to add stalker to my reputation of an extortionist in his eyes.

"I . . . um, I guess I've just paid enough attention." I shrugged, giving him an honest answer, without actually coming clean. "Don't worry, I'll keep your secret." I turned around to leave again, and no one stopped me this time. "Goodbye, Marcus. Maybe I'll come to see your show one day," I added, simply because the mere *goodbye* sounded so depressingly final.

Still, it felt like a giant weight had lifted off my chest when I stepped off that bus and back into the heat of the Strip. The suffocating coldness inside it had felt oppressive.

The insanity of what had just happened, as well as my incredible discovery, would need some time to really sink in. However, now that I got my most important question about him answered, I hoped that the hold Marcus had over my life would finally let go.

I just needed to put some considerable distance between us, I decided, as I hurried back to our hotel on my sore feet. Then the time would help me to get the images of his chiseled chest out of my brain and his intoxicating scent out of my system.

"I PARTIED MORE IN THE past three days than during my entire life prior," Lily said, sitting next to me on the plane. Knowing Lily, her statement was most likely absolutely true.

We were on our way back home to Toronto. I never told anyone that I went to see Marcus, not even Emily.

His secret was now mine to keep, and somehow even my going to see him perform had become a part of it in my mind. I realized this would forever connect me to him, whether either of us wanted it or not—he'd be the one true magician in the world, and I'd be someone who knew that true magic existed.

"I am sooo tired! I'll need a week to recuperate." Emily yawned on the other side of me and stretched out as far as the economy class legroom would allow.

"Too bad." Sarah, Emily's friend from work, turned over from her seat in front of us, a teasing note in her tone. "I'm sure Mikey's been missing you terribly. I don't think there'll be much time allowed for your *recuperation* once you get home."

"There are some sexual positions that allow for minimal energy expenditure," offered Lily thoughtfully, and added, "especially for the female participant."

The conversation came to a screeching halt, as it often did when Lily spoke.

Completely exhausted, I welcomed the silence, ready to catch some sleep during our five-hour flight.

Chapter 6

LILY PULLED HER YELLOW Toyota into the driveway of my parents' house in the western suburbs of Toronto. This was where I grew up, and visiting still felt like coming home.

It was July's long weekend, for Canada Day. For as long as I remembered, we always got together for a BBQ on this day. Of course, things changed slightly from year to year. It was our second Canada Day with Lily, and last year I was here with Matt.

"Hold on, Evan! I'll carry the truffle, you already almost dropped it once." Lily jumped out of the driver's seat and rushed to the trunk where Evan unloaded their things.

I grabbed my purse and got out, too. Unlike Lily and Evan, I wasn't staying overnight and didn't have any bags to unload. I needed to be back in Toronto later tonight, to work in the store two days out of three this long weekend.

The huge rose bush in front of the house was already covered in big, pink flowers—my mother's pride and joy. I inhaled their warm, sweet smell. Roses were not my favourite flowers, but their smell always reminded me of home.

"Well, hello there," my father greeted us.

He had his apron on, ready to man the BBQ grill. It was only early afternoon, and he probably wouldn't start grilling for at least a couple of hours yet, but he must've had that apron on since breakfast as a reminder to himself that today was going to be a fun day.

"Oh my dear, dear children!" my mother sang from the kitchen when she heard us enter, and rushed out into the hallway to hug all of us.

It was good to come home.

"SO, HOW ARE YOU DOING, kids?" Dad leaned back, after finishing his dessert. "How is your job, Evan?"

"Um, it's kinda boring." Evan licked his spoon.

"Why?"

"How?"

Both of my parents seemed to be immediately on the verge of panic. At that moment, I really hated Evan for making them so jumpy. After all, it was his addiction and his past lifestyle that taught them to expect the worst from him.

"I don't know." He shrugged, "Just boring. I wanna quit and look for something else."

"That's not how it works, baby," Lily stated matter-of-factly. "You find a new job first then you quit this one."

Mom gazed at her with clear gratitude.

"Yeah. Sure, babe," Evan replied. "But I want to start looking now."

"I thought you liked working as a stagehand with the theater," Dad said, still seemingly confused and slightly panicky.

"It was okay for a while," Evan agreed. "I get to see a whole bunch of shows for free. That's cool. But I want to use my head more, you know? Be more involved in sound and stage production, and stuff. Maybe do something different, like TV or movies."

"Well, that's admirable to aspire to use your head," Dad said carefully. "But is there a chance for you to get in a movie production?"

"Do you think there is a job that you would absolutely love?" my mother asked, hesitantly.

"Um, I don't know . . ." Evan grew increasingly restless in the spotlight of their attention. As usual, he quickly resorted to his tried and true method of defence, switching the topic of conversation to me. "Hey, Angela has two jobs. I'm sure there is at least one for me out there."

"That makes no sense, Evan. We're not even in the same industry!" I protested, but it was too late, their focus had turned to me already.

"You still haven't quit your job at the shoe store?" Dad faced me.

"Not yet. It's not like I can give up the employee discount, right? How else would I buy shoes?" I joked, but it came out rather flat.

"I would think you make enough at the office to be able to buy a pair of shoes, don't you?"

"Oh, Dad, a woman needs more than *one* pair of shoes."

In fact, even with the discount, I couldn't afford to buy any shoes at all lately. All of my footwear was at least a year old, and I was able to buy them only because of my small shoe size that was not very popular with shoppers—the store ended up discounting it several times in a year.

"You're working too hard, honey." My dad shook his head.

"Do you even have time for dating?" my mother chimed in.

I knew it would come down to a public discussion of my private life. Sooner or later, most of our family conversations ended up there.

Stalling my answer, I diverted my eyes to the elegant light-green placemat in front of me and fidgeted with the matching napkin ring. These must be new. My mother seemed to have chosen summer as the theme for this dinner—green grass-woven placemats, flower-print napkins, bright centerpiece arrangement with a paper Canadian flag to mark the holiday.

"No, I don't," I replied finally. "You know I don't have time for anything." I didn't mean for it to sound accusingly. After all, nobody forced me to help them financially and it was not my mother's fault that I could only have the means to help them by working two jobs.

Still, I caught my mom flinch at my words, and I rushed to salvage our happy dinnertime even if it meant throwing myself under the bus. "I just can't find a decent man," I mumbled, staring at my half-eaten dessert.

The truth was that even if I had all the time and money in the world, I seemed to be unable to kick a certain Vegas magician out of my head long enough to even think about finding a date.

It'd been nearly two months since Emily's bachelorette party. Enough time had passed since my brief and, let's face it, not even friendly conversation with Marcus. Yet the thoughts of him still occupied my mind way too often.

"Oh, baby, I'm sure there are plenty of decent men in Toronto." Mom waved her hand at me.

"Hardly!" Lily scoffed and smoothed her blonde hair pulled into a neat bun. This was not the first time she took my side in an argument with my parents, although, I never was sure if it was intentional on her part.

"You simply need to give a man a chance," suggested my dad.

"Exactly!" Mom enthusiastically agreed. "If you just stopped being such an . . . um, *ice queen* with them! Try to be a little more approachable. Men like to feel feminine warmth."

Was I really some kind of cold-blooded ice queen with men? Could that be why things didn't work out with Matt? He was looking for *feminine warmth* and never found it in me.

". . . men need to see a nurturing, loving wife in a woman, the mother of their future children," Mom continued, as if encouraged by my silence. "They like to know that they will be taken care of."

"Don't they all have their own mothers for that?" asked Lily, eyeing Evan suspiciously.

Mom ignored her question but leaned in closer.

"You know, Angela never cries," she told Lily, as if revealing a big secret.

"She has a fairly thick skin," Dad chimed in and added quickly, "which is not a bad thing to have. Especially in business, working for a large corporation and such."

"Even when she was little, she would scrape her knee and just bite her lip, but there'd be no tears coming from her."

Uncomfortable goosebumps crept along my *thick skin*, but I kept quiet, thinking about Mom's words, even though I'd heard her telling people the same scraped-knee story many times before.

True, I hated crying in front of anyone. It didn't necessarily mean I was insensitive or that I didn't *feel* like crying at times. It's just that the very idea of baring my weaknesses in front of other people terrified me. Showing strong emotions in public felt like exposing myself to potentially more hurt.

Did this make me an ice queen?

"Evan was always so much more sensitive as a child. He cried at the drop of a hat," Mom went on.

"Is that true, Evan? Did you cry a lot?" Lily gazed at him with adoration, as if there was anything endearing about him being a whiny kid.

Evan squirmed under her attention.

"Hey, Angela, I was thinking the other day, sitting on the toilet . . ." he blurted out, completely out of the blue.

"Okay." I wondered where he was going with it.

Clearly, the topic of the conversation had turned awkward for both of us, and Evan was trying to change the subject the best way he could think of.

"Does the demand for toilet paper go up before Christmas, too, just like everything else?"

"Yes, Evan. It does," I replied quickly, welcoming the chance to shift everyone's attention elsewhere.

"Why?" asked Mom.

"No, really, why?" echoed my brother.

"Is it because people eat more over the holidays and poop more?" Lily ventured a guess.

"Not really." I remembered Barb's musing on the very same topic last Christmas season. "It's because they have company coming over for visits and stuff."

"But wouldn't that mean that there would be less toilet paper consumption in those places where the visitors came from?" Dad wondered. "At the end, the demand across the country should still remain stable."

"Unless, they have visitors from out of country, Henry," Mom argued.

"No," replied Lily, "because some of the Canadians travel abroad, too, to Europe and to the States during Christmas."

"So, unless there is a large difference between the number of people leaving the country and the number of people visiting it, there still should be a balance . . ." This was my dad again.

The discussion had turned rather odd, especially for a dinner conversation, but I was happy the focus moved away from me and my personal life.

As soon as I tuned out the toilet paper discussions, though, my own thoughts drifted back to Marcus, the way they often seemed to do.

As it turned out, my obsession with him didn't end with my guessing his secret, but the nature of it had changed.

Still unable to break away from the old routine, I followed any updates in his schedule and searched the internet for new pictures and videos of him whenever I had a chance.

Only now, instead of watching for any glimpse of props in the videos and trying to figure out how he did what he did, I simply enjoyed his performance and . . . the sight of him. The grace of his fluid movements. The ease with which he seemed to command the crowd, without ever saying a word.

Eventually, I had to admit that seeing him in Vegas was a mistake. I should have stayed separated from him by the computer screen and the thousands of miles. Because now, the images of Marcus were complemented with the memories of him in my mind. His scent. The warmth of his body I'd managed to sense somehow, without touching him. The dizzying, intoxicating sensation of having his eyes lock with mine.

How much time would it take to clear someone like him from my system? I was beginning to fear I would never be completely free from him at all.

Chapter 7

MY HAND ON THE COMPUTER mouse, I hovered the cursor over the browser *close* button.

I had just finished doing my banking, answered my emails, and checked the news quickly. There was nothing I had to use the internet for anymore. With less than an hour before my usual bedtime, I could watch a show on TV or, even better, read a book.

Yet, I lingered.

It was September already. I'd been trying to quit *everything Marcus* cold turkey and lasted for three days without searching his name, but now I had a strong feeling I was failing already.

The need to see his face again—even if photoshopped, on a poster, through a computer screen—had been itching in me since day one. By now, it had grown from irritating to intolerable.

Oddly, the lack of any personal details about his life and his limited presence on the social media only fed my infatuation. It felt as though he had become an old friend and I craved to know how he was doing. Was he happy? Content with his life?

How many people of those surrounding him did he let in on his secret?

The concern on the blond man's—Simon's—face had seemed genuine. Was Simon a friend, an employee?

Since that day in Vegas, I noticed his face in many pictures taken of Marcus. Although mostly in the background, Simon seemed to be always around—unlike any of the numerous girls in Marcus's life. What if Simon was his true lover? How close were they?

Were there others like Marcus, with the same abilities? I doubted it. If so, how did it feel for him to be the only one of his kind in the world?

What if that fragile emotion I'd glimpsed in his eyes was a sign of loneliness, and the hold he had on me through the most of this year was the result of one lonely soul recognizing another?

Giving up the fight with myself, I moved the cursor to the search bar and typed his name, then clicked on his website. The image of the familiar masked face greeted me, his eyes lit with their usual vivid blue in the bright rays of the spotlight directed at him.

For someone who was as protective of his privacy as Marcus seemed to be, spending this much time in the spotlight would be unnerving, I imagined.

I clicked the *Contact Me* button. Surely, Marcus had a team of assistants to handle all his correspondence, emails including. But the word *me* gave the illusion that I'd be writing to him directly.

With a capitulating sigh, I typed *Hello, Marcus,* and paused.

There was so much I could write to him, so many things I could ask and tell him, but probably shouldn't.

The email would most likely never reach Marcus anyway, no matter what I wrote. In the rare chance that he'd actually read it, who was to say he'd even remember me. Seeing him perform and learning his secret might have been a mind-blowing experience for me, but for him, meeting me couldn't have been more than a flitting episode in the course of a day.

What did I want to achieve here, anyway?

I should do it for *my* benefit, I decided. By sending the email, I could pretend I'd reached out using the only avenue I had available. Maybe something would then close in my brain, allowing me to let him go for good.

Keeping it all in mind, I chose for the message to be brief and impersonal but kept it a question, possibly in some faint hope for an answer.

'Do you ever plan to do a show in Toronto?'

Hitting *send* made me feel better already, giving me some odd sense of satisfaction at a task accomplished.

Maybe I could do it after all? Maybe I could get over the man who was never even mine to begin with.

Chapter 8

MARCUS

It was the end of his week off. Another party. He sat in a white leather chair in Simon's suite in their hotel. Simon was there, too, of course, as well as some of their production crew and about a dozen or so showgirls.

Judging by the girls' different outfits, it appeared as if Simon had sent a limo down the Strip to pick up one from each venue. Many still had their stage costumes on. A few wore their regular clothes which left just as little to the imagination as the feathered glittering bikinis of the costumes.

Like a flock of exotic birds, the girls filled the room with noise, colour, and life. He leaned back in the chair and soaked in the vitality that burst around him.

Since his early years, he had been perfecting the art of being alone even when surrounded by people.

Growing up in a number of foster homes, he made sure to stay away from everyone. Other kids learned quickly that his punch packed "superpowers," giving him a wide berth.

Deep inside, however, he'd always hated the isolation. Even now as a fully-grown man, he couldn't stand being alone, especially at night when the loneliness was felt more acutely and the dark memories came from the shadows of his past to torment him. He kept them at bay by having people around whenever possible.

Walking up to his hotel room with a woman on each arm, he felt like he won a few hours from the night again—its shadows retreating. By the time the women finally left his room in the early hours of the morning—giddy, thoroughly satisfied, and exhausted—he was tired enough to pass out, too, sinking into the dark pit of a blissfully dreamless sleep.

"Marcus, are you all right, man?" Simon passed by his chair. "You seem kinda off lately."

"I'm fine." He tipped his chin at the closest group of showgirls. "Just enjoying the view."

"Okay, then." Simon sauntered in the direction of the women. "Theresa, baby, have you met my friend Marcus yet?"

"Not yet." The gorgeous brunette, who had been eyeing him a few minutes earlier, turned his way. "But I'm going to fix that right now." Her lips wrapped around each word seductively as she strolled towards him, hips swaying side to side.

A whiff of expensive perfume swirled around him as she approached. He lifted his hands from his thighs to make room in his lap for her. She lowered her toned ass, barely covered by the silver dress with a high slit, and slid along the leather of his pants closer to his crotch.

His dick stood to attention at once—it'd been way too long since he'd had any action.

Since moving to Vegas, his sexual encounters had significantly decreased in frequency, and lately had come to a complete stop. His usual principle of *new city-new girl* no longer applied here. Living in one place carried a bigger risk of running into the same person more than once.

Yet, no amount of jerking off could compare with the bliss of having a woman in his arms. Even as it could never come to a blissful end for him.

He splayed his hand on the bare skin of the girl's back, soft and silky, and slipped his other hand through the slit of her skirt, up her naked thigh.

She moaned in response and crossed her legs, leaning closer. Beautiful and willing. Exactly like someone he'd take up to his room. Normally.

"I love your mask. So hot," she murmured into his ear and traced the edge of the mask with her finger. "Do you keep it on when you fuck?"

It was too easy. '*There is one way to find out,*' was all he had to say to ensure a warm female body in his bed for the next couple of hours.

Except that he was fairly certain he'd seen Theresa at some party before. There was a strong chance he'd see her again after tonight, too, somewhere. If he took her upstairs now, there was no guarantee she wouldn't want to come up again, next time she saw him.

A relationship of any permanence would inevitably lead to questions one day. Questions, he wouldn't be able to answer.

He shifted his hips under her to minimize the contact of her ass with the straining erection in his pants. The movement only made it worse, intensifying his arousal.

"What's wrong, baby?" Theresa cooed and skimmed the shell of his ear with the tip of her tongue. "Tell me. I'm a very good listener. You can tell me anything."

Could he really? Even if he allowed it to be more than a one-night stand, could he ever let Theresa or anyone else in? Were any of them capable to understand and accept everything about him?

The problem was, he could never *try* to confide in anyone. Once the secret was out, there was no way to take it back. It was impossible to foresee all consequences of coming clean. As a result, hiding had become a life-long habit he saw no way to end.

"What if I told you I fuck without the mask?" he challenged.

Her glossy lips pouted with a practiced perfection as she leaned back.

"No, keep it on, please," she demanded, gliding her finger along the edge of the mask again. "Hot and mysterious. Just the way I like it."

Just the way all of them did. Every woman he ever took to his bed wanted Marcus the Magnificent—fame, mask, and all.

He had no idea what it would be like not having to hide from at least one person in the world.

Not that it was that difficult to hide. Half the time, he didn't even have to explain anything if he made a mistake and accidentally exposed his abilities. People often came up with answers for him—their brains were so pre-conditioned to explain away the unexplainable.

The bright stage lights turned out to be the best place to conceal the truth. He'd been hiding in plain sight for years, and no one knew.

Except for her. The girl in the red dress had guessed his secret. Somehow, she was brave enough to see through his act.

He'd been so confused—scared even, shocked into stupor—when she demanded answers to the questions no one had asked before, he hadn't even thought about finding out her name until she stepped off the bus and it was too late.

Only when lying in bed that night, he was able to fully process everything that happened, and the realization he was no longer the only one carrying the burden of his secret hit him like a freight train.

Even now, months later, he still felt the heady rush of thrill at the thought of another soul somewhere out there, who *knew*. The odd sense of camaraderie with her—just because of that—made him feel less alone.

Eventually, giving in to the desire to find out more about her, he'd made Simon do a search, using the footage of the nearby security cameras. Like most people on the Strip, she turned out to be a tourist.

Simon was able to confirm the hotel where she'd been staying, but she was long gone by then. The name the rooms had been booked under turned out to belong to someone else. All he learned was that she came from Toronto, Canada. Not only from another city, but from another country as well.

That day, he didn't even take a good look at her to memorize her face. In addition to the blurry images from the security videos, all he had were the memories of her bright red lipstick and that it matched her dress. He also vaguely remembered her brown, shoulder-length hair that was pinned up from both sides in a fashion reminiscent of 1940s, but it was mostly a memory of a feeling, not a clear image.

Theresa's cool hand landed on his cheek, just below the mask, bringing him out of his thoughts.

"Baby, you're burning with fever! Are you sick?" She shrank back.

Sure. If being rock hard could be considered a sickness.

No matter what his brain might tell him, his dick seemed to be completely enchanted by the close contact with Teresa's perky ass.

His next show at the venue couldn't come soon enough. He needed a release, badly, but Theresa was not the one capable of giving it to him.

"I'm fine." He lifted his hands up, signaling for her to get off him. "But I think I'll call it a night."

⎯⎯⎯◆⎯⎯⎯

BACK IN HIS OWN SUITE, he vanished his clothes and headed straight to the bathroom wearing only the mask. By now, it had become almost a part of him, not simply an article of clothing or a prop.

Turning the shower faucet all the way to cold, he let the icy water run down his heated body. As expected, the relief was short lived—the chilly rivulets turned to steam just moments after they hit his scorching hot skin, settling on the tiled walls in a thick layer of condensation.

It was clear he wouldn't make it until the show tomorrow. The increasing pain would cripple him overnight if he did nothing. He needed to head to his ranch house outside the city and take care of the matter in the most basic way—by making himself come.

The best part about the ranch house he bought shortly after moving to Vegas was the sprawling property it stood on—acres and acres of land, with no neighbours in sight. For the first time in his life, he had a safe place to *chill out* whenever the fire under his skin became unbearable.

The anxiety was slightly different this time, though, hindering his focus. Turning the water off, he got out of the shower and walked out to the open patio, steam rising in curls off his damp hair.

It was still sweltering hot during the day in Vegas, but at night the air cooled off already as the year headed well into the fall.

He stretched on the couch outside, leaning his head back, wishing he could just stay here and maybe read a little before going to bed.

The light breeze against his naked body was soothing, but it didn't bring much relief from the burning pain rolling through him in swells.

He made his phone appear in his hand and texted Simon.

'I'm sleeping in until noon tomorrow.'

Now Simon would make sure no one entered his suite until then. So, when Marcus returned, he wouldn't run the risk of materializing in front of the hotel maid or anyone else.

Thankfully, Simon never asked why it was important to keep people out of Marcus's room. He just did what he was told.

This was the nature of their partnership ever since it was formed back when Marcus was still in high school, performing in parking lots and gas stations. As long as Marcus continued to do what made them both money, Simon supported him in everything and didn't ask questions.

No one ever did.

Except for her.

The girl in the red dress was the first one to ask him all the right questions, straight to his face.

And he had frozen, not knowing how to handle it.

Not that he hadn't been approached by people who claimed to know the truth about him before. There had been all possible kinds of weirdos, from the extreme end of the human spectrum. Many acted just plain crazy, and most had a number of demands for him, too.

The girl in the red dress looked and talked differently than all of them. She didn't want anything from him—another new one. He didn't know how to take her right away and ended up screwing it up.

The more time passed, the more he regretted not making a proper conversation with her. After all, she was the only person in the world who knew what he was, and he didn't even remember her face or her voice.

He never forgot her words, though.

"Blow their minds as you blew mine."

He took them as a challenge, not to make his secret public, as she'd implied, but to use more of his abilities during the show in an attempt to give it more life. He spent weeks thinking about how to let his own magic shine through the acts of others, which he'd simply shamelessly copied until then.

Several weeks ago, he came up with an act that was all his own. Of course, he never told anyone, but his new closing act which he named Phoenix was his tribute to the girl in the red dress. He planned and produced it himself, taking great care to create a truly magical experience for the public, without exposing his secret. And he was rather proud of the result.

He didn't need the rave reviews praising his work that came out the morning after the debut to know it was good— more than good—but he desperately wished that *she* had a chance to see it.

"Maybe I'll come to see your show one day."

Spoken over her shoulder on her way off the bus, the words couldn't have meant a firm promise. Yet he had caught himself straining his eyes during the show occasionally, searching for a flash of her red lipstick from the stage.

What if she really came to see his show one day? The burning desire to have another chance to talk to her was suddenly almost more intense than the liquid fire coursing under his skin.

Was there a way to make it happen?

After all, doing the impossible was what he did for a living.

He lifted his phone again to send another text to Simon.

'See what it'd take for me to have a show in Toronto.'

The reply came in right away.

'Does it have anything to do with the email Stacy mentioned this morning?'

Marcus tried to remember if he even spoke to Stacy that day. She was one of the many assistants who helped Simon run Marcus's life on stage and beyond.

'What email?'

'Someone asking if we were planning to do a show in Toronto.'

'Never heard of the email. But it must be a sign. Make it happen.'

It was a long shot, but he would make it easier for her to attend his performance by bringing it to her hometown. He butchered their last conversation, but maybe he could have another one?

All he wanted was another chance to talk.

He, the man who could have everything, simply wished for a conversation with the girl in the red dress.

Surely it wasn't a big thing to ask for.

Chapter 9

"HEY, LISTEN, I NEED to ask you something." Evan's easy tone came through my office line.

"Make it quick. I think I can hear Barb's voice in the hallway. She mostly comes in our cubicle maze when she needs something from me."

"When is your next shift in the store?"

"Tonight. Why?"

"No. Tonight wouldn't work. She has a meeting."

"Who? Lily?" I guessed.

"Yeah. She's a bridesmaid in her co-worker's wedding this weekend. The dress is pink, and she needs some shoes to go with it. Shit like that, you know."

I smiled, sensing his obvious discomfort at talking about pink dresses and shoes. Definitely not an easy topic for Evan.

"She's been stressing out about it," he added.

It wasn't clear what exactly distressed Lily—the lack of appropriate footwear or the fact that she was in the wedding party. Knowing Lily, I imagined it was both.

Before she met my brother, Lily's lack of social life could have very well rivaled my own. She ran into him at the only party she'd been to in two years.

After watching Evan chug his fifth double-bourbon that evening, Lily gave him a long lecture on perils of alcohol. My brother must've found something appealing about her lecturing him, because he asked Lily for her phone number and they'd been inseparable ever since. It'd be hard to imagine two people more different than Evan and Lily, but somehow they seemed to make it work.

From what I knew about Lily's wardrobe preferences for monochrome colours, just the necessity to wear pink must have been stressing her out, too.

"Would Thursday work? Or Saturday."

"Thursday is cool."

"Just send her in any time after six. Maybe tell her to email me the picture of the dress beforehand, so I know the style."

"Thanks. I owe you one. Hey!" he exclaimed suddenly, so loud I had to move the receiver away from my ear. "Do you want a ticket to the show this Sunday? They gave me one for Lily, but she has some big presentation on Monday and needs to prepare. You know how she is."

"I know," I agreed. "Thanks but I work on Sunday, too. What show is it?" Not that it mattered, since I couldn't come anyway, but Barb's voice had moved away by now, and I could multitask—chat to Evan while formatting a spread sheet.

"This is gonna be great!" Evan's tone filled with excitement. "You know Marcus the Magnificent?"

With a loud thud, my heart felt like it dropped straight down into my lavender pumps at the sound of his name, and my hand froze on the computer mouse.

"Remember? The magician we saw in New York on New Years?" Evan prompted, since my mouth felt too dry for me to reply right away.

"I remember," I croaked, swallowing hard.

How could I forget?

It was October already, but my obsession with him had hardly eased. Sending that email didn't help. After weeks of struggling to get him out of my head, the most I'd achieved was setting limits on my *Marcus screen time.* By allowing myself to check his news and social media accounts only on the weekends, I found it slightly easier to hold off during the week.

The last time I checked for his updates was Sunday. There was no news on any shows in Toronto then. This must be really last minute.

"You know, he's really big now?" Evan's animated voice continued to ring in my ear. "He's got a Vegas show and stopped touring."

The brief, polite response I got to my email the morning after I'd sent it stated that no shows were planned outside of Marcus's Vegas performances.

"How is he coming to Toronto, then?"

"Beats me. Maybe he needed a break from the Vegas heat?" Evan didn't sound overly concerned about Marcus's motives to visit our city. He was obviously just too thrilled to have him here. "Anyway. It's this Sunday. One show only. Super short notice. No idea how he'll pull it off."

"He will," I whispered and rubbed my arm with my free hand, as if the air-conditioned chill of the bus, mixed with the warm masculine scent, was prickling my skin once again.

"He's using all local crew. Who does that? For a magic show? Anyway, I'll be working during his performance."

"You will?"

"Yeah. I'm psyched! I'll get to know all his secrets."

"You won't." By now I knew that the only way to figure out Marcus's secret was to believe.

The effervescent sensation of wonder curled through my chest again, echoing the feeling I had in Times Square.

"Can't wait!" Evan's enthusiasm was boundless. He didn't seem to pay much attention to my replies. "So, you don't need the ticket?"

Didn't I? Going to see Marcus perform would be like feeding my addiction.

But I'd asked for it. Marcus coming to Toronto definitely had nothing to do with my email, but it happened. He was going to be here.

It was my chance to see him live. And this time, I wouldn't be wasting it watching for props—I already had my answer. I could simply relax and enjoy the magic wielded by the man of my dreams.

"I'll give it to someone else on the crew, then."

A surge of panic yanked me back to our conversation.

"No! I'll go."

"It starts at seven. How about your work?"

My shift at the store ended at six forty-five. Fifteen minutes wouldn't be enough to get to the theater.

"I'll figure something out." I'd covered enough shifts of pretty much everyone in the store, to be fairly confident I would find a replacement for my hours on Sunday.

"Great. I'll meet you in the front at six thirty with the ticket. Don't be late, I'll have work to do."

Evan telling me to be on time. That was something new.

"I'll be there."

The receiver slipped out of my shaking, sweaty fingers as I put it down. My thoughts fluttered inside my head like a flock of spooked birds as my stomach quivered with anticipation.

I had no intentions to confront Marcus again or approach him at all for that matter. The first and only conversation we had went bad enough.

The anticipation of merely being in the same room with him, of experiencing the feeling of wonder in the presence of pure magic was enough to make my heart soar—the condition I was fairly sure would last all through the week now.

Chapter 10

MARCUS

From backstage, he listened to the music closely, waiting for his cue to appear on the stage of the old theater in Toronto to start his show.

He had an odd feeling that his magic was a perfect fit with this place. The red velvet of the chairs and curtains and the ornately gilded balconies held vintage charm, so different from the modern glitter of Las Vegas. The air inside smelled of dust from the decades past, heavy with memories of great performances and the many emotions they had evoked.

The theater had double the capacity of his venue in Vegas. Nevertheless, it was packed—the show was sold out. A miracle on its own since there had been practically no time for advertising.

Simon turned out to be the true magician here, capable to organize it all in an extremely short time.

After Marcus sent him the text that night, Simon showed up in his hotel suite precisely one minute after noon the following day.

"Is there anything I need to know?" he demanded, taking a seat on the couch in the living area and breaking the unspoken rule of not asking questions. "Do you seriously want to do a show in Toronto?"

"Yes." Spending that morning at the ranch house had brought the expected relief—Marcus felt relaxed and collected. The painful burn of restless energy was gone, reduced to an occasional flutter of vibration surging through his muscles now and then, which was rather pleasurable.

Having a show in Toronto still seemed like a good idea.

"It won't be easy, Marcus." He frowned. "Actually, more like impossible. It'd cost us an arm and a leg."

Marcus was well aware that Simon hated to lose money. He expected the objections. They irritated him nevertheless.

"I'll do it during my week off." He plopped down into the white armchair next to the couch.

"That won't help." Simon's frown didn't ease. "The contract doesn't let you do anything outside of Vegas. We had to negotiate hard to allow for your occasional street acts, remember?"

"I'll stop all impromptu performances if that's what it takes." Irritation from not getting his way rose to the surface. He simply was no longer accustomed to hearing *no* from others. Most of his restraints and limits came from within.

"That's not the point, Marcus. I knew you needed to get out occasionally, so I made sure the provisions were there when the contract was drawn up. A show in Toronto is something else entirely."

"Are you telling me you *won't* do it? Or you *can't*?" Marcus asked wryly, changing his tactics.

Years of living on the road together, cramped in an old van, made them learn each other's weaknesses well—enough for him to sense which of Simon's buttons to push in this case. He was well aware that Simon hated admitting he couldn't do something, possibly even more than he hated losing money.

"What is it all about, Marcus?" Simon exhaled heavily. "You can't expect me to dive head first into this type of expense—not to mention the logistics to organize something like this—and not provide any kind of explanation. What's going on with you? Getting stir-crazy, staying in this city for this long?"

Absently, Marcus rubbed his cheek just below the mask. He'd increasingly spent more time with it on than off, even when it was not necessary, like in Simon's presence. By now, it must have been at least three years since his long-time manager last saw his face unmasked.

Admitting to Simon that the girl in the red dress was the reason for the Toronto show felt like exposing too much of himself, not unlike removing the mask.

"I have my reasons." He kept his voice firm, hoping it alone would be enough to stop any further questions.

Marcus had known Simon for much longer than most people realized. They met when both were still in middle school and lived on the same street. Marcus ended up staying only a few months in that foster home before a house fire had destroyed it. Then he was moved to another one and then to a series of others, all across the county.

He didn't see Simon again until a few years later. Marcus was in high school by then and had already started his parking lot magic acts.

Even then, he wore a version of a mask, if only during his shows. At first, the anonymity that it provided helped him fight the initial stage fright. Then he found that people didn't expect him to do much talking when he hid behind it. With the mask on, he could be the silent, mysterious magician, who performed without saying a word. The mask also made it easier to ignore the inappropriate remarks and rude comments from the parking lot crowds and just focus on his magic.

Because magic tricks were all he could do to earn a decent living. He never did well in school. Moving at least once a year didn't exactly facilitate his academic progress. It was a true miracle that he'd even graduated high school at all.

Simon accidentally ran into him during his performance in a shopping mall parking lot. Because of the mask, he didn't recognize Marcus right away, but Simon happened to be just the right mix of bold and practical to realize the potential of what the two of them could achieve if they worked together.

"Do you need a break or something? Change of scenery?" Simon continued undeterred, bringing Marcus's focus back to him. "Why the show in Toronto?" He placed his feet on the coffee table in front of him and folded his arms across his chest. The pose demonstrated he was not moving until he got his answer.

Despite Simon's obvious enjoyment of the lifestyle that Marcus's ability afforded them both, Marcus believed money was not the main reason Simon stuck with him through thick and thin for all these years. By now, he'd become the closest Marcus had to a friend.

At the very least, he decided, Simon deserved an honest answer to the only personal question he'd ever asked. Actually, Simon might be just wild enough to handle it.

"I want to find a girl." Marcus leaned back in his chair and propped his bare feet next to Simon's shiny Italian loafers on the coffee table.

"A girl?" Simon's voice rang with confusion as his eyebrows rose almost all the way up to his sandy-blond hair. Obviously, this was not the answer he'd expected.

"She's from Toronto." The memory of the girl in the red dress had become too personal by now to openly talk about her with anyone, even with Simon. With his thumb, Marcus tapped the smooth leather of his pants stretched over his thigh, fighting the unease. "I figure she is more likely to come to the show if I have one in her city."

It did sound crazy—hardly logical and even silly—when he said it out loud.

"All this to find a girl?" Simon narrowed his eyes at Marcus, as if searching for ulterior motives in whatever expression he could glimpse behind the mask. "Wait a second." The understanding spread across his face. "Is it the same girl I had to do the security search on? The one at the Bellagio?"

Marcus nodded. There was no reason to deny it at this point.

"I just want to talk to her."

Surprisingly, Simon didn't end up yelling or swearing. He didn't laugh, either. Instead, he went silent for a moment, leaning back with his hands behind his head.

"What happens if you don't find her?" he finally asked.

"Nothing." Marcus shrugged, resisting the cold emptiness that threatened to take over at the thought of such an outcome. "I'll do the show and come back to Vegas."

"Okay. Fine." Simon nodded quickly, and Marcus couldn't believe that the truth was all it took to make him agree. "I don't promise anything. It will be a shitload of work." He shook his head. "But I'll see what I can do."

Simon rose from the couch, brushing down the pants of his custom-made suit. He strolled to the door on his way out then paused, as if thinking of something.

"What happens if you *do* find her?"

That was the question Marcus didn't dare to answer. Even in his imagination, he'd never gone past actually finding her first.

"I have no idea."

Chapter 11

I ENDED UP HAVING TO bribe one of my coworkers with my homemade cookies for her to agree to take my shift on Sunday.

And here I was now, in the seat right in the middle of the orchestra. It didn't happen to be the first row but still close enough to the stage for me.

Excitement vibrated through me simply from being in the theater. I couldn't remember the last time I went to see a movie, let alone a show or a play. The fact that I was about to see Marcus live set my skin alight with nervous anticipation.

All thoughts moved to the background as soon as the first strains of music began. My attention fully focused on the stage.

Powerful, orchestral music filled the theater as a large cloud of silver smoke appeared in the center of the stage. Then a dark figure emerged, surrounded by bursts of fire.

The black silk cloak unfurled from around his shoulders, revealing Marcus in all his shirtless glory.

Fingers clutching the armrests, I swallowed hard at the sight of him. Black leather pants held low on his trim hips by a wide studded belt. The cape of his raven-black hair streamed at his back. His tall figure commanded the stage as he strolled across it in long, confident strides, shoulders rolled out wide, arms raised in greeting to the crowd.

Being in the same room with him felt like meeting an old friend I hadn't seen for a while. His gestures, the way he moved—so familiar to me now. Watching him in his element, I simply reveled in his presence. Peace and contentment took over me, as if this was where I was meant to be—near him.

Most of the magic tricks he performed I'd seen many times already, done by others. The one most obvious difference was that Marcus didn't use assistants.

Sure, there were beautiful showgirls carrying props and handing him things, but they weren't a part of the actual act. Instead, a number of animals took the place of human assistants in his version of the famous magic tricks.

Marcus used a full-size, live horse in the classic act of sawing a person in half. He made an African elephant disappear with a wave of his cape. And in another instance, he had Siberian tigers escape from locked cages in plain view of everyone in the audience.

The animals didn't appear to be bothered by whatever seemed to be done to them. The horse that had been sawed in two, looked completely unfazed by the fact, and happily chomped on the apple that a showgirl fed to its front half as its other half swished its tail from the opposite side of the stage. After waiting patiently for Marcus to reunite its two parts, the horse then trotted back and forth across the stage in the apparent demonstration of his wellbeing and vitality.

The lights dimmed suddenly, and I felt a pang of disappointment. Was it over already? The show seemed too short, and I wasn't prepared to say goodbye yet.

Then the music changed to a slow, foreboding melody, and I realized that something else was about to happen.

The stage had sunk into complete darkness, as if the whole theater, including all of us in the audience, suddenly became a part of the current act.

The air had chilled, filling with a moldy smell of a crypt blended with the smoke of burning candles. In the suddenly menacing atmosphere, even my seat no longer felt safe.

Black chandeliers lowered from the ceiling. The thick burning candles in their twisted wiry arms provided the only light in the theater now.

An eerie, icy gust of air swept through the room, swishing the wisps of cobwebs that dangled from the chandeliers. Dark shadows moved in from every corner, like an army of undead closing in on life itself.

"Oh, my goodness, this is so creepy," the elderly woman in the seat next to me said in a haunted whisper. A chilly feeling of dread slithered down my spine at her words.

A dark figure—a mere shadow in the candlelight—separated from the side curtain. Then a pale green spotlight flicked on to illuminate Marcus as he moved across the stage.

In addition to the leather pants and boots, he now had a long, black, silk coat on, open in the front to bare his chest and abs. The seemingly endless train of the coat dragged behind him as he slowly approached a tall arch erected in the middle of the stage.

Walking under the arch, Marcus came up to its side and placed his right foot on it. Slowly, he lifted his left foot off the floor, too, and positioned it above the right.

His body shifted parallel to the floor, his coat hanging straight down from his shoulders, held by the sleeves.

A shiver ran through me, and I rubbed my arms through the material of my dress, unable to tear my gaze away from the dark figure walking up the inside of the arch.

He reached the top under the ceiling and stopped in the centre, hanging upside down like a bat by the soles of his boots. His arms spread wide, the black silk coat draped from his shoulders all the way to the ground, billowing in the chilly draft like a long sail of a ship lost in the vast, deadly ocean.

In the watery green spotlight, the pale skin of his bare torso appeared to glow and the black mane of his hair seamlessly blended with the silk of his coat.

A sharp rise of the music made me jump and my insides jolt with unexplained fear. Marcus moved his arms down and clasped his hands together below his head, pointing them straight to the floor. The coat swished close, enveloping his head and shoulders like a cocoon.

Bizarre and graceful, the sight of the continuous line of a man's body and silk extending from the ceiling to the floor was grotesque and beautiful at the same time.

The next moment, a wave of subtle warmth gently caressed my face as it spread through the theater and chased the graveyard chill away. The music picked up, filling the room with glorious symphony, and the air gradually filled with scents of sun-warmed grass and flowers.

A faint glow shimmered from the cocoon that enclosed Marcus's face and arms. Then his silk coat split open in the middle, emitting rays of bright light that flooded the theater, blinding me after the gloomy semi-darkness moments earlier. I closed my eyes for a second and when I opened them again, my breath hitched in my chest.

Marcus had twisted in the air and was now upright, levitating in the centre of the stage, held up by a pair of the most magnificent golden wings.

They were enormous. Open wide, they spread all the way across the stage. Instead of feathers, brilliant rays of orange, red, and yellow ran through the wings like tendrils of liquid fire. Shimmering waves of light radiated from Marcus to the outer edges of the wings, making them appear to be living, breathing creatures on their own.

Marcus's clothes had changed, too. Barefoot and bare-chested, he wore a pair of loose pants made from gold silk. His black mask had turned the colour of ancient gold, too.

Phoenix.

That was what Marcus was portraying on stage for us—Phoenix, re-born from dead and ashes into fire and light. The enchanting symphony continued to fill the air, adding to the feeling of wonder.

"Wow!" I heard the older woman next to me exhale in awe.

"Wow . . . " I echoed entranced, pure joy washing over me in waves.

'Blow their minds the way you blew mine,' I told him once. And that was exactly what he did.

The waves of shimmering magic radiated from the mythical human-bird suspended in the air, reaching everyone in the audience like a tangible, warm embrace. At that moment, I felt connected to every soul in the theater—elated and happy—and everyone around me seemed to be as enchanted as I was.

Slowly, the music faded away. Marcus lowered from the air and gracefully landed in the middle of the stage. His wings folded behind him into a golden shimmering cape, but the theater still remained completely quiet.

Silent, Marcus walked to the front of the stage and swept the audience with his gaze. I knew he couldn't see me, but the intense focus in his posture made me shrink in my seat, nevertheless.

"Hello, Toronto!" he called into the audience, raising an arm in greeting. "How did you like the show?"

As if just having been waiting for his signal, the room erupted into screams and applause, tearing the silence to pieces. The enthusiasm of the crowd was unstoppable, rolling through the space in swells. People jumped off their seats, clapped their hands and screamed his name.

Marcus waited patiently, with his hand up in the air.

"I need a favour from you, Toronto!" he shouted as soon as the noise had subsided a little. "I'm looking for a girl."

Cheers erupted from the audience again, and Marcus grinned.

A real, genuine smile.

I'd never seen him so much as smirk before.

Shocked, I stared at the true miracle that was his smile, committing it to memory. Bright, white-toothed, with a hint of cheeky. I wished he'd take his mask off now, to let me see more of this happy expression on his face. I needed more.

"She might be here tonight." His words brought me out of my enchantment, and finally the sense of them trickled into my mushy brain.

Marcus was looking for a girl.

"She came to see me in Las Vegas once," he went on, "and started a conversation that I'd love to continue. I don't know her name—"

"What if she doesn't want to have the conversation?" somebody yelled from the audience.

"If she came here tonight, I hope she does," Marcus replied. "She was the one who inspired the closing act of my show. At the very least, I'd love to ask if she liked it. Will you help me find her?"

The crowd cheered, swelling with excitement. Everyone seemed to be still high on his show, and no one wanted it to be over, welcoming the unexpected delay of the end.

A large screen appeared behind Marcus.

"I want you to take a look at the person on your right and then at the one on your left. Raise your hand if either one of them is a young woman in her twenties to early thirties." A forest of arms rose from the audience, including the one of my elderly neighbour, who just smiled at me happily when I raised an eyebrow at her.

Marcus was searching for a girl to talk.

Something akin to honest-to-god jealousy scratched inside me. Oddly enough, the fact that his personal life was as bright and multi-coloured as a patchwork quilt hadn't bothered me much before. Seeing him with a new girl or even two on each picture never had the same effect on me as learning that he was interested in a conversation with one particular woman.

The envy for *her* also painfully tugged at my heart.

It became clear—I could no longer deny that I had a problem. Admiration for an artist and his work was one thing. What I was feeling right now showed that my infatuation with Marcus had spread into the "creepy stalker" territory.

My interest in him as a man was not healthy, and could very well turn to be as self-destructing as my brother's addiction.

I needed help, I realized.

Meanwhile, the object of my obsession continued to describe the girl of his interest, "She has chestnut brown hair, just past her shoulders. And she wears it pinned up on the sides like this."

Black and white pictures of actresses from the Hollywood Golden Age appeared on the screen behind him, all of them displaying a version of my preferred hairstyle.

I lifted my hand to my hair in confusion.

What was going on?

Marcus couldn't be talking about me. There must have been dozens of girls he'd met in Vegas since my trip in May. Besides, I hadn't said that much to him, and he'd accused me of blackmail—hardly a conversation one would wish to continue.

Most of the arms in the audience had gone down by now.

"She promised to come to my show one day," Marcus's voice reached me, but I was no longer watching the stage. Instead, I stared straight at the back of the seat in front of me, afraid to breathe, each of his words fanning my confusion. "If she is here tonight, she may be wearing red. Maybe just red lipstick."

I had a grey pencil-skirt dress on. Well, the thin leather belt of it was red . . .

What was it all about, dammit?

I looked up again.

The screen on the stage was showing the theater audience now. The camera moved from one raised arm to another, zooming in on the young women whose neighbours thought they matched Marcus's description.

He smiled and talked briefly to each woman and her neighbour but then always shook his head, sending the camera off to the next girl.

"I'm sorry, man," he laughed, addressing the next person who appeared on the screen with his arm up. "But the woman next to you has a blonde pixie cut. Quite the opposite of the girl I'm looking for."

The woman who came up on the screen was at least twice the described age, too. A wide grin spread on her face.

"I'm his wife." She pointed at the man with his arm still up in the air. "But I don't mind having a conversation with you, Marcus!"

Everyone laughed, including myself, and then I recognized my own face on the screen.

Eyes wide, I glanced at my neighbour, who still had her arm up. She shrugged casually and cheerfully explained, "You are wearing a red lipstick."

Mortified, I moved my gaze to the back of the seat in front of me once again, unable to face Marcus.

I was certain it was a mistake. It had to be. He couldn't possibly be searching for *me*. But what if he remembered me from our not-so-pleasant encounter on the bus? Would he be repulsed to find *the extortionist* instead of his girl?

Every nerve in my body seemed to be abuzz, and my heart galloped so fast it must have been seconds away from jumping out of my chest. Heat crept up my cheeks, as I sensed all eyes diverting to me, including his.

"Found her," he said quietly, and a spotlight hit my face, making me squint.

Applause erupted around me again and then, suddenly, I felt . . . weightless.

"Don't be afraid," his voice whispered straight into my ear.

Chapter 12

MARCUS

It was her!

He may not have remembered her face, but he knew it was his *girl in the red dress* the moment her image appeared on the screen.

Spinning on his heel, he peered into the audience, trying to make out her face in the sea of others. A spotlight illuminated her, guiding his gaze.

Blinking in the light, her brightly coloured lips slightly parted in surprise, she seemed stunned and . . . stunning. Her looks weren't flashy, but she definitely had the vintage elegance of classic Hollywood.

Suddenly, he wanted to see all of her, to commit everything to memory this time. He needed her closer.

Gently, he lifted her from her seat with his thought. Her large brown eyes went wider, her gaze roamed around wildly as she floated up into the air.

"Don't be afraid," he whispered, then sent his words her way across the audience to calm her. Throughout his life, he'd witnessed enough people being terrified of what he could do, and he desperately ly wished she wouldn't be one of them.

Pressing her skirt to her thighs and hips with both hands, she didn't seem to be that scared, but she definitely appeared tense and worried.

Of course, she was wearing a dress.

He couldn't possibly make her float across the whole theater in a skirt. Stopping his gaze from following the gliding movements of her hands along the curves of her body, he gathered his focus and thought back to the costume room in Vegas.

What style would make justice to her hourglass figure?

Her clothes shimmered for a moment before being replaced by a one-piece pantsuit. Held at her waist with a gold-tone belt, the white silk of the suit flowed into wide pants that almost could pass for a skirt.

Obviously surprised by her sudden outfit change, she peered down at her new clothes then lifted a foot a little and cast a curious glance at the golden stiletto sandals, with which he'd replaced her high boots.

Impatient, he gave a mental nudge, directing her towards the stage.

She lifted her head, and her face lit up with wonder. There was still some astonishment in her expression, a little apprehension, but no fear. She was not afraid at all, he realized with relief as she moved closer.

Unlike all of the other people in the theater, she knew exactly what was going on, and she was not scared of him or his magic.

Fearless.

Warmth of admiration spread through his chest.

Finally, her wandering gaze caught his. She spread her arms wide, shook her head and . . . smiled, soaring through the air, like an angel dressed in white.

As soon as she got close, he reached out and caught her small, cool hands in his, eager to pluck her out of the air.

"Got you." He tugged her to him.

"Wow," she whispered breathlessly when her feet touched the stage next to him. "That was . . . Wow."

The audience erupted in applause once again, and the curtains began to draw close.

"Who are you?" he asked quickly, suddenly worried to waste any time, as if she were about to disappear out of his life again.

"Me?" Her big eyes, the colour of strong coffee, glistened wild with adrenaline that must've been pumping through her. The face flushed a lovely shade of pink. "Apparently, I'm a crazy girl who believes in magic," she laughed on an exhale, her chest rising high with her accelerated breathing.

"What's your name?"

"Angela," she answered, looking both dazed and delighted.

"Angela? Like an angel? I can remember it."

"There is nothing of an angel in me." She snorted a soft laugh. "Trust me."

"We'll see."

Somebody touched his shoulder. "Marcus, encore?" asked one of the production crew.

The growing roar of the crowd going wild registered with him, and he nodded his agreement. Angela's hand was still in his. He squeezed it tighter, leading her back to the centre of the stage.

"They want to see us once more," he explained, meeting her questioning gaze.

The curtains were slowly opening again.

He leaned to her ear. "What's your last name?"

"Why?" She glanced up at him.

"In case you run away again. It'd be much easier to find you if I knew your full name."

"McAllister," she replied softly, possibly subdued by the bright light and noise ripping through the widening gap between the curtains. "Were you really looking for *me*?"

As if he hadn't made it clear to everyone out there by now.

"Nice to meet you, Angela McAllister." He smiled wider. When was the last time he'd smiled so much? Or the last time he smiled at all?

As if the crowd on the other side suddenly no longer existed, she gaped at him for a moment.

"You did this whole thing just for some distant chance to find me?" The dark pools of her eyes seemed enormous. He was afraid he'd lose himself in them if he stared for too long. "What if I didn't come?"

"But you did."

"Marcus . . . That's crazy."

"So was confronting me in Vegas, wasn't it?"

"But—"

Spotlight burst over them, cutting her off. Blinding. The noise rose tenfold, deafening and intoxicating, thick with adoration of the crowd.

Head tilted back, he soaked it all in, grounded only by the sensation of Angela's hand in his.

"Maybe it's the crazy in both of us that made this miracle possible."

Chapter 13

ROARING NOISE OF THE theater filled with people.

Bright light in my face.

Blood pumping through me at lightning speed by my heart still racing from flying.

Yes, I'd just been flying over the heads of hundreds of witnesses.

My head was spinning from it all, the stage lights blurring into long fuzzy lines.

As the curtains closed for the final time, however, the awareness of Marcus's hand holding mine had gradually took over everything else.

"Did you like the show?" he asked softly.

"Did I? Are you kidding?" I stared at his face obscured by the mask and the shadows, now that the light was gone. "Marcus, it was simply amazing! That final act . . ." I shook my head, unable to come up with a single word to accurately describe it—none seemed to be good enough.

"Is the only act that doesn't suck," Marcus finished for me.

"None of them do!"

He shrugged a shoulder. "Nah. The rest have been done a million times by others." A corner of his mouth lifted up in a smile then, and his voice lowered by a notch or two. "My favourite part was your flying."

With the curtains closed and the spotlight off, his eyes seemed darker, almost black. His skin flushed from performing, a healthy glow spreading up to his high cheekbones.

Marcus was very much a man of flesh and blood, no longer an unembodied image on my computer screen. My heart skipped a beat at this realization, and my stomach flipped with something else than mere adrenaline rush.

"Thank you for that." My own voice came out unintentionally raspy. "For making me fly."

Unable to deal with the dark heat that seemed to be building up in his gaze, I lowered mine, which brought his bare chest in my line of sight.

Just like on the bus months ago, I believed I sensed the warmth emanating from him again. The heat wave rushed from him to me, flushing me head to toe, surging through my stomach and tingling my skin.

My breasts felt heavier, and I realized with a stab of horror that my hardened nipples were poking through my lace bra and the thin material of the costume Marcus had dressed me in.

Mortified, I yanked my hand from his and crossed both arms in front of my chest.

"Can I have my clothes back?"

"Are you sure?" His voice was deep and husky. "I love seeing my show colours on you."

"Yours have changed," I pointed out, noticing just now that his usual leather pants and boots had replaced the gold silk of his stage costume.

He stepped closer, sliding his hands up my arms. Big and warm, his palms felt at once comforting and exciting against my chilled skin. A small shudder rippled through me.

"You cold, Angela?" Concern softened his voice. "Costumes are not the most comfortable of clothing."

The next moment, I felt the material of my own dress around my body again, rough and solid, compared to the delicate silk of the costume.

As if finally taking mercy on me, the air between us shimmered briefly and a black t-shirt stretched over the ridges of his wide chest, too, allowing me to focus once again.

"You . . . um, wanted to talk," I reminded.

The noise of someone dropping something backstage burst the surrounding bubble of semi-darkness and white noise of the audience behind the curtains, reminding me we were still standing in the middle of the stage. The crew must have started to pack up the props and equipment.

Evan would be around, too.

Did he see me float through the theater? Did I want my brother finding me here, with Marcus gripping my upper arms, staring at me this intently?

"We should get out of here." Marcus seemed to have guessed my state of mind. He slid his hands down my arms and found my hand again. "My dressing room is this way." He moved off the stage, tugging me along.

"Dressing room?"

He paused for a moment.

"You're right, dressing room wouldn't do. Would you prefer a hotel?"

A hotel? Would I?

Another wave of anticipation ran through me, tickling my skin with tiny shivers. Wouldn't spending the night in his hotel room be a perfect culmination of this magical evening?

The long series of images of him with numerous other women raced through my mind. Simply becoming another face in that line-up would hardly be magical.

"Can't we talk somewhere here?" I protested as he dragged me through some long corridors backstage and then outside through the back door, sneaking by the crew loading equipment into a truck.

The cool October breeze prickled my skin through the wool fabric of my dress.

Marcus slipped around the corner and into the shadows with me. "It's too cold to talk outside, and there are too many people all over that place." He tipped his chin at the theater. "I have a limo waiting here. It'll take us anywhere you want."

Anywhere I wanted to go with him.

His eyes glistened wildly in the faint glow of the streetlights, as he slid his gaze from the side of my face to my lips then along my neck down to the neckline of my dress. It felt almost tangible, like a caress, leaving a scorching sensation on my skin in its wake.

Heat spread through my body—a liquid fire in my veins—tugging at my nipples with a sweet ache and swelling hot between my legs. Yet, he hardly even touched me.

My whole body sang under his gaze when all he did was simply hold my hand. It didn't really matter where we went. I had a feeling I would not be able to resist him even if he wanted to take me right here against the wall.

The women I've seen clinging to him in the pictures appeared as if they didn't mind warming his bed for one night. Or maybe they used him, gaining memories and bragging rights of sleeping with a celebrity.

No matter what would happen between us tonight, sooner or later he'd leave, going back to his glamorous life.

Since the bragging rights of celebrity hookup didn't mean much to me, I'd be left with nothing but my memories.

Suddenly, I realized that I didn't want to remember him as just a guy who had sex with me and left me. Neither did I want to become another faceless woman in the long string of those who'd been in his bed over the years.

I needed Marcus to remain in my mind only as the man who made me fly. Those would be the memories I could cherish forever. My very own miracle, unspoiled by anything.

"Home," I said quickly, not trusting myself to keep burning for another minute under his exploring gaze. "I need to go home, please." I swallowed hard and added, "alone."

"Alone?" he echoed. Even half-hidden behind the mask, his expression of utter shock was still readable. Then the corners of this mouth hardened, and his eye narrowed. "I'll take you there."

Not letting go of my hand, he stomped in the direction of the limo parked between the theater building and the restaurant next door. My heels clicking against the pavement, I could barely keep up with his long determined strides.

"Marcus!" A shadow peeled from the wall, emerging as a middle-aged man with receding hair pulled into a ponytail. He headed towards us.

Marcus stepped in front of me promptly.

"I don't sign autographs," he said gruffly. Peeking from around his bicep, I noticed a piece of paper in the newcomer's hand.

My fingers on Marcus's forearm, I felt him tense as the man approached.

"Not even for your *biggest fan*?" The man smiled.

He seemed friendly enough, possibly a little eccentric, judging by his flamboyant clothes—silver pin-stripe suite and a purple satin shirt.

Something about the smirk on his thin lips, however, didn't sit well with me. Especially, when his unsmiling gaze slid my way, and the focus in his eyes sharpened.

"No." Marcus shifted, angling his torso to shield more of me from view. "Not for anyone."

We were mere feet away from King Street, with its bright lights, throngs of pedestrians, and busy traffic. I could see it from where we stood, yet the night shadows between the two buildings kept us hidden.

Marcus's body stiff against mine, I sensed his apprehension.

"There is autographed merchandise for sale in the lobby," I offered, in an attempt to ease the tension hanging over us heavier than the surrounding darkness.

"Lovely." The stranger's smile failed to camouflage the thick sarcasm in his tone. "But as someone who put people out of their jobs, Marcus could be a little more accommodating when asked for merely a signature, don't you think, miss?"

"What are you talking about? I employ dozens if not hundreds of people." Marcus squeezed my hand tighter, and I sensed his unease more acutely. Surely, he wouldn't be this concerned about any harm coming to him from this man, older and smaller than himself.

Was he worried he'd be the one forced to do the harm?

From the corner of my eye, I noticed the blond man, Simon, rush along the sidewalk on King Street. He was accompanied by two beefy men in black suits.

Marcus spotted them, too.

"Simon!" There was an obvious relief in his voice.

"Marcus?" Simon shook his head, squinting into the shadows between the buildings. "Why the hell would you sneak out like that?"

"Come here." Marcus ignored his question. "I want you to meet my *biggest fan*."

With Simon coming our way now, Marcus headed for the limo again, tossing over his shoulder to the man in the purple shirt, "Simon is a great source of information. He'll know the exact number of people I employ if you're still interested. Right, Simon?" He nudged his friend with an elbow as we passed by him and the two men in suits.

"Here." Simon shoved a cell phone in Marcus's free hand. "Take this at least. My job is hard enough without having to chase you all over the damn city."

His gaze stopped on me briefly, a glimmer of curiosity flickered in his expression, but he didn't voice it. Marcus left him no time for questions.

Without waiting for the driver, who had jumped out of the limo, Marcus opened the door for me and gently but urgently all but shoved me in then followed me into the vehicle and shut the door.

Chapter 14

<u>*MARCUS*</u>

Alone.

The word still rang through his brain. Not used to rejections from women, he hadn't even considered the possibility that his *girl in the red dress* might not want to have anything to do with him once he'd found her.

He'd offered her the ride in a desperate attempt to delay the inevitable goodbye. He realized he'd do anything to prolong this evening, go anywhere she went, as long as she let him tag along. Fuck, he'd agree to braid each other's hair and discuss celebrity gossip if that meant to stay in Angela's company for just a little bit longer.

This sudden attraction to her was odd, especially since he sensed it was not purely sexual. Sure, he could come up with a number of amazing things to do to that body of hers, but simply having sex with her didn't feel like it would be enough. He wanted something else, something more.

How was he supposed to drive her home now and never see her again?

The limo driver got her address and raised the partition, giving them privacy. Just before the vehicle moved on its way, Angela made a move for the door again. "I left my jacket at the coat check."

"What does it look like?"

She stared at him for a moment before the understanding spread on her face, lighting up her eyes.

"Really? Can you . . . um, conjure it out of nothing?"

"Sure. But I'd rather just get it from the coat check for you."

"Like, teleport?"

He nodded, loving the expression of wonder on her face. For once, he realized, he didn't need to hold back or pretend to be *normal*. With Angela, he had a chance to be himself.

"So?" he tilted his head. "The jacket? What is it?"

"Oh, sorry." She blinked and wrinkled her nose in visible concentration. "It's a short, black coat, double-breasted. And it has a red and orange butterfly pin on the lapel . . . Oh!" she made a soft noise of surprise as he'd put the coat on her that very instant.

"Is that it?" He made its buttons close all the way up. The neckline of her dress, he decided, was a little too low, which he found extremely distracting—his pants felt too tight in the crotch all of a sudden.

It appeared his self-imposed celibacy of late was turning him into a horndog at the most inconvenient of times. Obviously, jerking off alone in the ranch house was not enough.

"Yep. This is mine." Angela slid her hands up and down her chest, as if to make sure this was indeed her coat. He forced himself not to follow the movements of her hands with his eyes, focusing on her face instead. She met his gaze. "Is there a limit to what you can do?"

He shrugged. "If there is, I haven't discovered it yet."

The pulse of energy in him that had completely disappeared during the show had returned slowly, building up with a persistent, incessant hum beneath his skin.

"Wow." She exhaled, her eyes wide as though she tried to take all of him in at once. "This is . . . an incredible power to have, Marcus." She paused, as if considering something for a moment. "Yet, I believe you were scared when that man approached us. Why?"

There it was, another question no one had ever asked him, because no one ever knew. With Angela, he should've been prepared to explain things he hardly knew how to explain himself.

He paused, gathering his thoughts.

"What you call *the power*, Angela, is hardly a blessing, more like a nuisance and often a huge responsibility. It's a real struggle sometimes, to keep it in check."

"You were afraid you'd have to hurt that man? All he wanted was a signature."

"Fans' behaviour is unpredictable. Simon implemented the no-autograph rule after one of them tried to chop off a chunk of my hair."

"What?" There was a shock and a laugh in her exclamation, both at the same time.

"As a souvenir," he deadpanned.

"That's just insane." The tension of her expression clued him in she was straining to hold back another laugh, trying hard to look horrified for him over his crazy fan experience.

Back then it did feel terrifying. It took all he had not to combust in the middle of the mob swarming him. The fear that he'd annihilate the whole crowd of innocent people with one wrong thought was still deep inside him somewhere.

However, taking the narrowly avoided mass-murder out of the equation, the whole thing could be viewed as rather funny.

He recalled the image of the adoring female fan who brandished a pair of sewing scissors in the air with the expression of firm determination on her face, dead set to snap a chunk of his hair before the security pulled her away.

The hilarity of it made some light feeling bubble inside him. He wanted to see Angela relax and set her laugh free.

"Crazy," he agreed with an easy smile. "Why would anyone want a chunk of someone's hair? What would you do with it? Stuff a pin cushion?"

His light expression snapped her restraint.

"Sell on eBay!" She burst out laughing at last.

He sat back, enjoying the sound of it, sunny and carefree. And, as it turned out, extremely contagious—in a second, he was unable to hold his own chuckle back.

"Well," she squeezed out around the bouts of laughter. "To be completely honest, I could understand that fan's fascination. In a way." Her gaze moved to the thick strand of hair over his shoulder and she raised her hand as if to touch it.

Her laughter stopped abruptly. Her eyes grew darker, glistening in the semi-darkness of the limo, and her lips parted slightly, drawing his attention to them.

Full and red.

He fought the sudden urge to lean in and kiss them, to learn her taste.

"Thank you for making me fly," her whisper reached him, and instead of touching his hair, she covered his hand with hers on the seat between them.

His attention snapped to that point of contact. Incredibly, the incessant restless hum of the energy inside him quieted under her touch, the heat extinguished by the fresh, cooling sensation of Angela's hand on his.

So far, there had only been two ways for him to get rid of the fiery pain.

One was to release the magic into the crowd while performing, to share it with as many people as possible.

The other was to make himself come. His orgasms came at a price, though, as he had discovered. The first time he jerked off in the shower as a teenager, he caused a mandatory evacuation of the small town where he lived.

Had he just found a third way in Angela's touch?

He inhaled a lungful of air, savoring the blissful lightness of unexpected relief.

Angela must have misunderstood his sigh, as she removed her hand promptly and straightened in her seat.

"Sorry. It probably wasn't something to laugh about. I must be still high on adrenaline after your show."

Her voice was no longer husky and her eyes had lost their luster.

The moment was gone, but he needed to make sure that what he felt when she touched him was real. Ignoring her questioning look, he took her hand in his again.

To his dismay, the calming feeling was no longer there. It felt nice to hold her hand, but the cooling sensation was gone.

"Right there." She pointed out through the window unexpectedly. "The second high-rise from the corner is my building."

He followed her gesture then swept the area with his gaze.

"This is a rather eclectic mix." He raised his eyebrow under the mask.

In addition to the two visibly poorly-maintained apartment buildings that Angela pointed at, the intersection had a couple of seemingly abandoned factories and a posh-looking glass high-rise.

She laughed. "Yeah. It wasn't the best of the neighbourhoods when my roommate and I first moved in here years ago, but it has come up since. The condo building is new. The factories have been bought by a developer and are being converted into expensive lofts now."

"Is it safe to live here?" The question was unexpected, but the genuine concern that prompted him to ask surprised him more.

"Much safer than it used to be," she replied with a carefree smile, but it melted away the moment the limo stopped in front of the entrance to her building. "It was a truly magical evening, Marcus." Her voice sounded low. "I'll never forget it."

The sight of her hand on the door sent a shot of panic through his system. No way he was gong to let her leave just like that this time.

"Can I have your phone number?" he asked quickly and added, dreading another rejection, "The conversation, remember? I'd love to talk to you."

A wrinkle of concentration appeared between her eyebrows. She left the door of the limo ajar but removed her hand from the handle.

"About what?"

Anything and everything.

"No particular topic," he confessed. "Just would like to see you again."

She kept staring at him with those huge coffee-coloured eyes of hers.

He sensed some doubt warring inside her, and rushed to help her fight it. "There is really no one else out there with whom I could do *this.*"

He tipped his chin at the bright brooch on her coat, making it turn into a large live butterfly.

Pressing her hands to her chest, Angela gasped and followed it with her gaze, smile returning to her face. The butterfly fluttered past her—its wings shimmering with red and orange—then flew out through the gap left by the half-open door.

"Wow," Angela exhaled with a short laugh and turned back to him. "I could never get used to this."

"It can be fun." He grinned, soaking in the glowing expression on her face, then took his cell phone out and glanced at her expectantly.

She squinted at the phone in his hand. "Sure." She spoke, sounding as if she was trying to convince herself. "We can talk, can't we?"

He was able to release the breath he held when she told him the number.

"You can call me," she said somewhat mechanically, as if testing a new idea by saying it out loud. Her gaze then returned to him, lingering on his face a little. "Good night, Marcus." She went for the door again.

"Good night, Angela," he echoed, clutching his phone as though it were a trophy, some pirate booty he'd snatched and was not going to part with now.

Through the tinted window, Marcus watched her as she walked to the front door of her apartment building.

Expertly balancing on her sky-high heels, Angela hopped up the crumbling front steps. With a complete disregard for his best intentions, his eyes immediately went to her fantastic ass tightly wrapped in the grey fabric of her dress.

With a groan, he threw his head back. Simply *talking* with her might prove much harder than he'd thought.

Chapter 15

I WOKE UP IN MY APARTMENT, slowly drifting from sleep to reality.

Like floating on air . . .

Recalling the effervescent sensation that had coursed through my body when I was flying to the stage, I smiled through the last remnants of my sleep. The whole experience of last night was pure magic. A dream . . .

"Good morning, beautiful." *His* voice. Was I still dreaming? "Sleep well?"

What on earth!

Shocked wide awake, I sat up in bed then grabbed the sheet from my lap to cover my naked boobs. Because that's how I always slept—in the nude. Save for an occasional boyfriend, there was normally no one around when I had to get out of bed in the morning.

Today, there was Marcus.

Reclining in the orange armchair in the corner of my bedroom, he looked fantastic, as always, in his mask, leather pants and a dark-grey Metallica t-shirt, ink-black hair streaming down his shoulders.

No amount of his handsomeness, however, could calm my indignation at this moment.

"Are you out of your ever-loving mind?"

I struggled to calm my thundering heart, my hands clutching the sheet to my chest. In addition to the gazillion things that were wrong with his sudden appearance in my bedroom, he nearly scared me to death, too.

Not that I believed he would harm me—not physically anyway. The initial fear was from the shock of surprise finding him here and from the mortification at being seen naked.

"Marcus!" I raised my voice since he hadn't replied. "What are you doing here?"

Instead of an explanation, I was suddenly lifted up and hurled through the air with what felt like the speed of a bullet then deposited into his lap.

"What on earth . . ." was all I could manage, as all air left my lungs.

"I want you close," he rasped, his voice very different from his cheerful greeting moments earlier.

I caught a glimpse of the stormy blue of his eyes as he cupped the back of my neck and yanked me to him. His lips brushed by mine, and I turned my head, escaping his kiss.

His mouth landed on the side of my neck instead, and his chest rose with a deep inhale as he nibbled my skin.

My thoughts scrambled, my senses overwhelmed from being this near to the man I'd dreamed about all this time.

His now familiar, tantalizing scent drove me wild again, making my control slip. The warmth of his lips on my neck teased me with a promise of more. He pressed me closer. My arms holding the sheet to my front slammed into the hardness of his chest.

He slid his hands up my sides. The sensation of his fingers tugging at the edge of the sheet, in his obvious attempt to take it off me, yanked me back to my senses.

Calling on whatever common sense I still possessed, I shoved against his chest with one hand.

"Marcus."

His arms tensed around me, holding me in place.

"That's not how it works," I insisted. There was a note of plea in my voice, because I knew it would be so much easier for me to give in than to resist. I needed him to stop before I ended up doing something I was sure to regret tomorrow.

His forehead on mine, he panted, his hands clutching my hips through the sheet.

"It's not how it's done," I whispered slowly, as if calming a dangerous animal, and felt with relief his rugged breathing even out and his grip on me relax a little.

"How *is* it done then?" he asked, without moving.

I lifted my head to see his face. The dark heat still smoldered deep in his eyes, but I managed to catch something else flicker through them, something that reminded me of the brittle expression I glimpsed on the bus in Vegas that day. It appeared but for a fraction of a moment, then the line of his mouth hardened and he leaned back in the chair, away from me. "Tell me."

The mask obscuring his features made it hard for me to read him, but that brief flicker of vulnerability in his gaze tugged at my heart.

"It depends." Only half-aware of my actions, I lifted my hand to remove a long strand of his hair that had fallen across his face. "I gave you my phone number and the permission to call me." I brushed his hair back and couldn't resist running my fingers through the whole length of his mane over his shoulder.

It was much softer than I had imagined it would be. Thick and silky, his hair slid through my fingers like fine sand, tickling my skin.

He stilled completely under my touch. Even his breathing all but stopped.

"You never asked to come over," I continued quietly. "You can't show up in my bedroom at this hour. Uninvited and unexpected."

With a considerable effort, I removed my hand from his hair then shifted my hips from his lap, ready to get up. Slowly, he dropped his hands away from me, setting me free, and I hurried for the bathrobe on the hook on my bedroom door.

"You should've called first."

The lingering sensation of his lips on my skin and his hands on my body still burned dangerously hot through me. I desperately needed to put some distance and another layer of clothing between Marcus and I, to protect me from the fire burning low in his eyes and from my own temptation to respond to it.

"I called," his voice reached me from behind.

"When?" I glanced over my shoulder, getting into the bathrobe.

"An hour ago."

"My phone is off." I let the sheet drop only when I was dressed. Promptly, I tied the belt of the bathrobe in a double knot. Only then I turned around to face him again. "An hour ago I was still asleep. My alarm is set for seven, by the way."

He closed his eyes for a moment and heaved a deep breath.

"In my defence," he stated, his voice dropping down a notch. "I didn't know you slept naked. I expected you to wear something, like maybe an old t-shirt to bed."

"That's hardly a defence, Marcus." I laughed. "It's my home and my choice of how I sleep. The point is you shouldn't show up like this. Could you call beforehand, please, and wait until I pick it up? Or at least use a doorbell? Anything to let me know you're coming, next time."

Was there going to be a next time?

Had I just invited him over?

I rubbed my forehead, trying to get my thoughts together. They still seemed to be scattered by this rude, odd and I had to admit, hot awakening.

"I need some coffee," I mumbled.

"I'll make you some," Marcus volunteered quickly then added quietly, "Now that you've securely concealed yourself in that robe, will you let me stay?"

Giving him a stern look, I tilted my head to the side.

"I don't know. Can I trust you to respect the boundaries at this point?" His subdued expression at my words immediately made me wish to lighten the atmosphere between us. I could hardly stand the tension lingering in the room and smiled, adding in a lighter, teasing tone, "I have a concern about your manners. Someone with your vast dating experience surely knows there should be at least a dinner and some flowers before you get to see another person naked."

It was meant as a joke, but it came with a reminder of his scorching gaze on my naked breasts, which flushed me with heat all over again. Turning around quickly, I headed to the kitchen, mumbling, "Let's see about that coffee now—"

I paused before entering.

My tiny Ikea table was piled high with a whole lot of breakfast food. I spotted two Starbucks cups of coffee, eggs and bacon, a mound of pancakes, muffins, and a restaurant-style rack with spreads and butter.

"What the . . ." I turned around to find Marcus right behind me. He was holding a huge bouquet of blood-red roses that came seemingly from nowhere.

"I know nothing about dating," he said. "I've never been with a woman long enough to call it that." He winced at his own words, shaking his head. "That didn't come out right. Anyway. I'm sorry." He shoved the roses my way. "Flowers?"

"For me?" I knew he could do impossible things, but the sudden appearance of things still shocked me, although not as much as my discovering him in my bedroom did.

He thrust the roses into my arms. "I'm trying to rectify the situation here and work on my manners, too. Will you take breakfast instead of dinner?"

I pressed the prickly bouquet to my chest and stared at him with suspicion.

"Why? What would you want for it? You've already seen me naked . . ."

"I want to see you again," he said firmly.

"Naked?"

"Well." He huffed a laugh, and I considered using the roses to whack him over the head. "That would be a bonus, but I'll settle for this fuzzy bathrobe or whatever else you like wearing in the morning."

My knees gave in finally, and I plopped on a chair by the table, crushing the poor flowers in my arms.

"Why?"

"Because I can come over mostly in the mornings. I assume you work through the day, right? I have shows every day for four weeks straight, with the fifth week off. The last show of the day finishes late. And with the time difference between Vegas and Toronto—"

"No, hold on," I interrupted. "I meant why do you want to come over?"

Marcus calmly walked around the table and took a seat across from me. Unlike me, he now appeared collected and in control. A man on a mission.

"To have conversations, remember?"

He smiled.

Many things about him were familiar, but I was still getting used to his smile. The skin around the corners of his mouth crinkled, giving him a bright, happy expression, so new to me. I wondered if he had the matching laugh lines in the corners of his eyes under the mask, too.

I couldn't hold back my own smile in return, grinning at him like an idiot.

"What would we be talking about?"

He shrugged a shoulder.

"Honestly, I don't really care." He tilted his head to the side, in a way I found utterly adorable.

And that was alarming. Everything about Marcus appeared hot, cute, and simply amazing to me. Somehow, in my heart I'd already completely forgiven him for showing up in my bedroom uninvited. His lack of manners seemed almost endearing at this point, which was rather disturbing.

A sudden concern prompted me to ask, "Can you manipulate human emotions? Influence people's thoughts and actions?"

"That's what I've been trying to do here, Angela." Marcus exhaled a short laugh. "I'm trying to convince you to let me see you again. Obviously, I suck at it—you still haven't said yes."

"I meant through your magic. Can you manipulate human emotions by using your abilities?"

"No. Sometimes I really wish I could. But I'm unable to do anything human related—read their minds, influence their behaviour, or manipulate their physical bodies in any way. Except for levitating them, of course."

"I see." So, I couldn't blame my feelings for him on any mind control tricks. I had no one to hold responsible here but myself.

In which case, I didn't have much in me to resist him. The way the air between us sizzled whenever he looked at me like he did in the bedroom earlier, if I allowed him to visit me in the mornings, and he tried to kiss me again . . .

Hot tingles flickered in my lower stomach at the mere thought of having Marcus's hands on me again.

"Um, I have to ask," I cleared my throat, needing to bring it all in the open, to avoid any kind of misunderstanding later. "This is not about sex, right?"

Marcus placed his hands on the table and leaned forward to me, his eyes peering intensely through the slits of his mask.

"It could be if you want it."

My breath hitched in my throat. The temptation of the promise in his gaze rendered me speechless.

How many times had I fantasized about this man? Not even in my wildest dreams had I imagined that he would be here, sitting in my kitchen one day, offering himself to me.

Well, not *all* of himself, just a small part—a casual sexual relationship, as it sounded. After all, he'd just confessed he never was with the same woman twice. As if I didn't know that already.

"I couldn't do it . . ." I said softly.

"Why not?" His voice dulled.

His hands were on the table in front of him, clasped together so tightly that his knuckles turned white. I kept my attention on the few black and silver rings he had on his fingers, not ready to meet his eyes yet.

"Because I simply wouldn't survive it," I blurted out. "I'm not against casual sex. Generally. It works for some, and it's great. But me . . . with you." I inhaled heavily and whispered the last part, "No offence, but I simply can't be just another notch on your decimated bedpost."

My heart sped up so fast, I could hear the swishing sound of the pulse in my head as I stared at the thin leather belts with silver chains and studs coiled around his wrists.

He drummed with his thumb against the table, which betrayed that this strongly affected him, too. The fact that I knew his tell reminded me that Marcus was not a complete stranger to me. That's why it was also so difficult—with him I already had so much to lose.

After a long pause, his voice reached me, quiet and hollow. "I guess that's how one would think of me." It sounded as if he spoke to himself, until he asked, "Is that what you believe I do, Angela? Collect one-night stands like trophies?"

Still unable to meet his eyes, I slid my gaze up along the tense bulging muscles of his arms and stopped at the thin silver chain around his neck that disappeared into his t-shirt hiding whatever pendant he had on it, if any.

The chain moved rapidly with his pulse where it lay over his collarbone. It was so fast, I wondered if he could hear his blood swishing in his ears, too.

He seemed uncharacteristically tense. Nervous? Was it that important for him what I thought?

"Does it matter what I believe, Marcus? You said it yourself you don't stay with a woman long enough to even call it dating."

Granted, I might not have seen any *recent* photos of him with random girls, but then I'd been strictly limiting my time spent gawking at his pictures. During the height of my obsession, however, I'd seen enough to believe he wasn't trying to make his playboy ways a secret.

Yet Marcus meant so much to me, I realized, not as a person—I hardly knew him as a person—but as an idea of something beautiful and magical that happened to me once in a lifetime.

I wanted to protect it as much as I could.

"Marcus, it's just . . . I can't do it."

"Does it mean you don't want to see me at all?" His voice was grave. "Angela, do you want me to leave?"

That would possibly be the most prudent thing to do—ask him to go.

The thought of Marcus leaving, however, chilled me through to my bones. I imagined watching him walk away, to never see him again except in the pictures on my computer screen . . . and shuddered. I didn't think I could survive that unscathed, either.

At this point, it seemed, there was no longer any escape for me. Whether he left or stayed, I risked losing a part of myself. The only difference was whether it'd happen now or later.

"Does it have to be all or nothing?" I asked quietly, willing my voice not to shake. "If you want us to meet sometimes and talk, as friends do. I guess we could try that."

"We could?" Both disbelief and relief coloured his voice, and I sensed the pressure inside my chest easing, too.

"As long as you promise me to follow some basic rules of decency," I added, with a brief smile.

He raised both hands in the air, palms facing me.

"Promise not to barge in your bedroom uninvited."

"Better yet." I shook my head. "Don't show up in my apartment before my alarm rings at seven—"

"Six."

"What?"

"What time do you have to be at work?"

"Between eight thirty and nine."

"See? We'd hardly have any time at all if you get up at seven."

"Do you honestly expect me to wake up one hour early just for the pleasure of spending it with you?"

"Would you?" He tilted his head that way again, a light smile curving his shapely mouth. "Please?"

What was I getting myself into? How could I keep my heart safe from this man if I was unable to say "no" to him?

"Six-thirty." I forced my voice to sound as firm as I could muster. "That's my final offer."

His smile grew wider, immediately turning my insides into a smoldering pile of goo.

"And, no more kissing," I added quickly, before I lost all resolve, finding it impossible to peel my gaze away from the curve of his lips. "No touching."

No staring like you're one thought away from having my bathrobe melt away, either.

After a silent moment, he broke our eye contact with a nod. His hands linked behind his head, he leaned back in his chair.

"Friends it is then."

"Friends." I nodded, too. "Are you sure it'll work for you?"

"Well, since that's the only choice I have, I'll try to be the best friend ever." He squinted at me, with a lopsided grin. "And maybe you'll agree to re-negotiate the terms of our agreement at some point in the future?"

Honestly, I didn't have it in my heart to kill the hope in his eyes. Besides, looking at it realistically, the future of our arrangement couldn't be long. With his track record, Marcus would most likely grow bored with our friendship after a few meetings.

With him, I had to learn to live in the moment as long as the moment would last.

"Maybe." I gave him a non-committal smile. "For now, let's just have breakfast. Shall we?"

MARCUS PRODUCED A VASE, and I finally put whatever was left of the roses in the water.

"How do you take your coffee?" he asked when I reached for one of the cups on the table.

"Black," I replied before taking a drink. The coffee was black. "You?"

"Cream and sugar. One of each."

I watched him drink his coffee, too, still trying to get used to the novelty of having him in my place.

"Should I keep calling you *Marcus*? I mean is it your real name?"

"The full name is Marcus Hargrave."

Marcus the Magnificent had a last name.

"You've never considered changing it? Taking a completely different stage name, I mean? You're hiding your face. Why not the name?"

Chewing on a strip of bacon, he seemed to think about my words for a moment.

"I guess I couldn't see any particular benefit in changing it."

"What are the benefits of wearing the mask?"

"Anonymity," he replied quickly. "Now more than ever, since more people know of me. Instead of wearing a hat and some ridiculously big sunglasses when I want to go unrecognized. All I have to do is take the mask off."

"Do you do that?"

"Yes. Any time I want to be left alone in public."

"Where?"

"I like going for a walk in big cities—Paris, Berlin, London or New York—where you can be a part of the crowd without anyone paying real attention to you. I've also learned how to surf in Hawaii and went on safari in Africa once, without any hassle from fans or paparazzi."

"Wow. So, you do take it off." Still astonished from this discovery, I repeated the thought that kept bouncing in my head. "I can't believe it. I've never seen any pictures of you without the mask."

He shrugged.

"I take care not to be photographed without it. Most people are interested in Marcus the Magnificent, anyway. The mask is a huge part of what they want."

"Do you like wearing it?" I cut off a piece of the pancake on the plate next to me—its

mouth-watering smell was irresistible.

"I don't mind it. It's more like a habit now. Being without it feels like something is missing."

The quiet intensity in his voice and his gaze made me pause. I swallowed the food in my mouth and put my fork down.

"Would you let me see your face, Marcus?" I asked, fully realizing the magnitude of my request. "Without the mask?"

It was not idle curiosity that prompted me to ask, far from it. I didn't simply wish to know his appearance.

By now, I felt I knew all there was to know about Marcus the Magnificent. However, it was the tiny glimpses of the person *behind* the mask that intrigued me, making me want to learn more about him.

Marcus being here, sitting casually in my kitchen like this, made me wonder if he was ready to shed his famous personality for a moment. The fact that he searched for me in the first place told me he might yearn for someone to know the real him. And I wanted to do that for him.

"I'd love to meet you face to face." I grinned, making an effort to keep my voice light and casual, to coax him into the open. "I swear on my life." I raised a hand as if taking an oath. "No photos."

A faint smile crossed his lips, too, although the intensity in his stare did not ease.

"This would be just for you and me, Marcus," I said softly. "Another secret I promise to keep from the world."

Silent, he drummed his thumb against the coffee cup in his hand then his chest rose, as he drew in what seemed like a bracing inhale. The air in front of his face moved. The black colour of the mask seemed to be dissolving into nothing.

A moment later, Marcus stared back at me, without wearing any mask at all.

His hard features didn't hide the insecurity of his expression. Surely, it wasn't his looks that made him feel that way—mask or not, he was incredibly handsome.

Somehow, though, his face was already familiar to me. I had studied it on pictures and videos enough to know well every plane, ridge, and curve. With the mask gone, some parts simply became more apparent, filling in the blanks to complete his face. The black, long eyebrows. His high, sharp cheekbones. The slightly aquiline-looking nose that gave him a fiercely masculine expression.

Finally, the corner of his mouth lifted in the now-familiar half-smile. "Hi." He cleared his throat.

"Hello, Marcus Hargrave." I grinned back, my own smile face-splittingly wide. "It is so very nice to finally meet you."

Chapter 16

The show that night followed exactly the same program as every other night. Yet everything about it felt different to him.

In fact, the whole day since he teleported back to Vegas from Angela's apartment felt different. The colours appeared brighter, the sounds sharper, even the scents of the crypt and burning candles he evoked for his closing act seemed more intense than ever.

His heart leaped every time he thought he'd almost blew the whole thing with her. Again. This time, by dropping in on her the way he did that morning.

It might've occurred to him that giving in to his impatience to see her was not the best thing to do. However, it didn't stop him from teleporting to her bedroom in the wee hours of the morning, the moment he'd learned her apartment number from Simon.

He was fairly certain that any woman he'd ever been with before would've been delighted to find him in her bedroom. In fact, he could predict in detail how the morning would've progressed with any one of them.

With Angela, he found himself lost. She was different from anyone he'd ever known, and therefore utterly unpredictable. She made him realize how little he actually knew about women at all.

The scary thing was that with her, he didn't want to make any mistakes. For him, there was so much at stake. She drew him to her in more ways than one.

The calm breeze of her touch was just as appealing as ever. Although he noticed again that the cooling effect disappeared as soon as she had reined in her emotions.

He still got painfully hard from simply recalling her warm, fresh-out-of-bed feminine scent when she was in his arms—the feel of her soft, pliable body in his hands, the remnants of sleep giving her that unguarded, innocent expression.

His body responded to hers in every physical way, but it was the closeness that he missed the most. More than anything, he wished he could climb under the covers with her then.

His impatience almost got him kicked out of her place and her life. He still couldn't believe his luck—or more like her kind heart—that allowed him to stick around long enough to have breakfast with her.

Sitting at the miniature table of hers, he felt her tiny kitchen was the only place he wanted to be at that moment. If Angela didn't have to go to work that morning, he'd be ready to spend the whole day with her there, having coffee and talking.

She asked for his real name, and he told her the truth. *Marcus* was the only name he had and the biggest part of his identity. This was probably the reason why he never considered changing it.

His last name was not truly his. He got it shortly after he was found as a toddler, sitting alone on a pew in a small-town church, with no one to claim him as theirs.

He was told later that *Marcus* was the name he had given to the people who'd found him, being too small then to provide any useful details of where he'd come from.

Growing up, he held on to the belief that his parents were searching the world for him. As he became an adult, however, and gained a more realistic view of life, he realized that in this day and age, if his parents really wanted to find him they would've already done so. The fact that no one came forward all that time could only mean that he wasn't lost but abandoned, purposely left behind for someone else to take care of him.

At the time of this discovery, he was big enough not to let himself be affected by it. By then, he was an independent adult, comfortable in his shoes, and content behind his mask.

He didn't even realize how comfortable he'd become hiding behind it. Taking it off in front of Angela proved to be hard.

Facing her without the mask left him feeling awkwardly vulnerable and exposed. Frankly, he'd rather be frolicking in the buff in Bellagio fountains, in front of hundreds of strangers, than removing his mask again under someone else's orders.

Once it was off, however, he hardly missed it at all. Surprisingly, talking to Angela—openly like that—turned out to be simple and natural.

Spreading his wings across the span of the stage now, he thought that in a few short hours he'd get to see her again.

The realization filled him with sunny excitement, which he allowed to radiate though to the audience. As the golden flames danced along the surface of the wings, he let the memories of her feed their energy. Bright and colourful as hope itself could be.

Chapter 17

AS COULD HAVE BEEN expected, having Marcus in my life turned out to be anything but ordinary.

That morning, I had to leave for work shortly after our breakfast at my place. He left through the front door, and I assumed he teleported back to Vegas from some location in Toronto later, as his show resumed that day.

Regardless, he was at my place again the very next morning.

This time Marcus didn't materialize in my bedroom. Instead, I heard him moving in the kitchen. Judging by the sound of the clinking of dishes, he must have gotten busy with breakfast right away.

I quickly got dressed in my work clothes, brushed my hair, and even did my makeup. So when I walked out of my bedroom, I felt as ready as could be to face whatever the day might bring, or more precisely, *whomever* the day had already brought into my kitchen.

"You are a cuddly one, aren't you?" Marcus said when I walked in.

"Pardon me?" I paused in the doorway for a second then realized he was talking to my cat.

Marcus stood by the table, filling Lannister's dish with cat foot as the traitorous pet of mine purred his head off, rubbing his back against Marcus's ankle.

"He never does that to me," I said.

Marcus shrugged his shoulder. "He just wants his breakfast."

"I've been feeding him forever, but he hardly notices me at all. Do you keep catnip in your pocket or something?"

Marcus put the cat dish on the floor, and it didn't escape my attention that Lannister managed to gratefully rub his head on his hand before he moved it away.

"Traitor!" I threw at Lannister who completely ignored me—as usual.

"Animals love me, for whatever reason." Marcus handed me a cup of coffee. "Good morning."

"Thank you."

"You look great today." His voice was soft, as was the expression in his eyes.

"It's because I managed to get ready this time." I smiled.

"Nope." He grinned in response. "You look great *despite* being dressed. I'd still prefer you naked and in the sheets."

I cleared my throat, feeling blush heat up my face against my will.

"Okay," he said quickly. "That was not meant to be said out loud. Breakfast?"

He moved the chair from the table for me, and I plopped down onto it, struggling to regain my composure.

No matter how hard I tried, I couldn't force myself to stop devouring him with my eyes as he sauntered to his seat opposite of me.

Without the mask, his hair pulled back into a loose knot, he seemed different. Neither was I used to seeing him wearing jeans and being barefoot.

"You look good, too," I blurted out and hurriedly took a swig from my cup, nearly burning myself on the hot coffee. "Different."

"Good or bad different?" He cocked his head.

"Good, you always look good." It wasn't even a compliment. I simply stated the fact. "This is just more casual." I waved a hand his way. "Relaxed."

More than that, he seemed content. Comfortable.

"I've never seen you like this before."

"Not many people have." He chose the plate with scrambled eggs and bacon from the breakfast food on the table and dug in.

So, that was why I'd never found any candid shots of Marcus, because he really seemed to have no life beyond the stage.

"Has anyone ever seen you without the mask, Marcus? Friends? Family?"

He shook his head, focused on his breakfast. "Since I started performing, only Simon has."

"Is he your friend?" I've seen Simon twice already, but had yet to be introduced to him in any way.

"My manager."

I bit my bottom lip, considering his answer for a moment. If his manager was the only person who'd seen him without the mask before me, did it mean Marcus had no one closer to him than that?

"Do you ever feel lonely?" I couldn't help but ask out loud.

He met my gaze.

"Angela, I'm surrounded by people every minute of every day. Honestly, it's hard to get away most of the time."

It didn't answer my question, though. One could feel the loneliest in a crowd. Otherwise, why would he be seeking my company so persistently?

His tall body folded into the chair of mine as he devoured the plateful of eggs with gusto, he appeared to be truly content. The tension I had sensed in him while ogling his pictures or watching him perform was all but gone now.

Thinking about the pictures stirred the guilt inside me. Would Marcus still be talking to me if he knew he'd been opening up to a stalker?

The honest thing to do here would be to come clean about my obsession with him. Of course, that would give him the right to call me a psycho and leave, shutting the door on his way out, or disappearing in a puff of smoke—whatever the case might be—he was a magician after all.

My chest tightened with dread at the thought of him leaving. Today even more than yesterday I wanted him to stay.

Now that he'd let me glimpse the real Marcus, I wanted to see more of him, just like that—unmasked, in jeans, and barefoot. When I figured out his secret, I thought I had figured him out, too. Now I sensed that was only the tip of the iceberg of what the real man, Marcus Hargrave, was made of.

I needed to tell him the truth, though, sooner better than later, if just to repay for his trust.

Avoiding any eye contact with him, I set my cup on the table.

"Look, Marcus. I have a confession to make."

I heard him shove his empty plate aside.

"You don't like muffins?"

"What?" I lifted my gaze to find humour bounce in the navy-blue of his eyes.

He tipped his chin at the pastry basket on the table.

"You haven't touched any, second day in a row."

"Um, no." I fought a smile that threatened to appear in response to his playful one. "It's not about muffins. I kind of had a thing for you . . ."

"Had?" He lifted an eyebrow, teasing.

I hated to spoil his cheerful mood, but the explanation was definitely in order.

"Well, for a period of time—a few months actually—I literally was obsessed with you. I've learned everything there was to know about you on TV, internet, and social media. I Googled your name, searched for your pictures, watched all of your videos . . ." My voice trailed off. Out in the open, my obsession sounded even worse than in my head, making me feel like a real psycho-stalker.

The fact that Marcus went quiet—remnants of a faded smile on his face—only made it worse.

"What did you learn?" he asked after a moment of silence.

"Oh God, I know so much about you. Much more than a stranger should." The words poured out of me, unstoppable, although I understood that purging my shame in all its ugliness made it worse. "Sometimes, I feel I could tell your thoughts just by watching you move because I know all your gestures. The way you flip your hair behind your shoulder when you're unsure about something and take a moment to think. Or how you do that thing with your thumb when you're nervous." I mirrored the gesture on the coffee cup in front of me. "The way you tilt your head when you're curious or intrigued. And I know for a fact that you never write any of your posts or tweets on social media. Someone does them all for you. They also photoshop those azure blue eyes into all your promo pictures. Which is just stupid, by the way. Your real eyes are infinitely more beautiful."

Feeling as if I ran out of air all of a sudden I stopped, drumming my thumbs nervously, having borrowed Marcus's own twitch.

"Well, all of this is actually rather flattering," he said slowly, prompting me to frown in concentration. "In some twisted, perverted kinda way," he added, his voice more amused than angry, which gave me hope.

"You think so?" I cautiously kept any sense of relief at bay for now.

"Yes. I don't believe anyone has ever paid attention to the way I tilt my head before." He grinned, a glimmer returning to his eyes.

"So, you don't find it creepy?"

"Not really."

"Don't you think it's crazy?"

"I didn't say it's not." His teasing smile grew wider. "I just happened to like your kind of crazy, it seems."

Finally, I allowed myself to breathe in relief.

"And, in the spirit of sharing this morning," Marcus continued. "I have my own confession to make."

"You do?" I did not expect this.

"I had Simon track you in Vegas. He found your hotel, and from there your home city. That's how the show in Toronto came to be. Also, you asked me how I got here yesterday—"

"I thought you used your magic."

"Well, yes. I teleported. But before that, I gave Simon your name and street address and asked him to find out your apartment number."

"I see." While I was obsessing over his pictures, Marcus seemed to have been doing some high-tech stalking on his own. "In some twisted, perverted way," I repeated his words slowly, "it's still rather twisted and perverted, Marcus."

"You really think so?" There was a certain focus in his gaze on me, however, he didn't appear particularly remorseful.

"Any normal person would think so." I considered everything again and conceded, "Me, however? Obviously, as a self-proclaimed stalker, I can't judge."

At my words, he slacked in his chair and took another drink from his cup.

"Now we know we have another thing in common—both of us are twisted and perverted stalkers," he proclaimed brightly.

"A match made in heaven," I muttered. Marcus didn't seem to think me a horrible person because of my behaviour. I felt I could easily forgive him his, too. Really, we seemed to deserve each other, after all.

The thought made me smile at last.

"Well, at least it's all out in the open now." I inhaled deeply and changed the subject, anxious to put the awkward topic behind us.

"Thank you for the breakfast. You really shouldn't have gone to all this trouble again. I'd be happy with just a yogurt or something."

"I'll keep it in mind. But it was no trouble, as you know."

"How exactly do you do this?" I peered inside my cup, trying to spot anything unusual about my coffee. Its smell and taste were great but rather ordinary. Nothing magical. "Do you conjure it out of nothing?"

"I could." He glanced inside his cup, too, as if in search of whatever I was looking for. "I try not to, though." He put it down. "You see. Here is my other secret, Angela—I don't have the slightest idea about how it happens. If I want something done, I just think about it in a certain way, and it happens. Always. If I wish for a cup of coffee to appear—it would appear out of nowhere. But I have this theory that everything needs to stay in balance in the world. And since I can't explain where the things come from when I *conjure* them, I try not to do it. I prefer to go about it in a little more complicated, but a more conventional way."

"How?"

"Well, your coffee is from the Starbucks on Dundas West at Roncesvalles, just minutes from here."

"Did you walk there to get it?" I glanced at his bare feet.

"No. I made the coffee appear here. From there," he explained slowly. "I left some money in the till for it, too."

"You did?"

"Yes. This way I can be sure that the current balance of matter in the world has not been disturbed. Again, I have no idea if it even matters at all, but it makes me feel better about the whole thing."

"Is there something you can't do?"

"Nothing that has to do with people, their minds or their biology, as I've told you. Other than that, I haven't encountered any limits yet."

"Limitless power over the world? This is like every person's dream."

"It is, isn't it? Until you actually get it then you realize that it's more of a curse than a blessing."

"Why? You could literally get the moon from the sky."

"Yes, I'm pretty sure I could," he replied with confidence but without a trace of the excitement I felt. "I could get you the moon, Angela. The most likely consequence, I'm afraid, would be the end of the world as we know it."

"Are you saying you could single-handedly cause the world's apocalypse? With a single thought?"

He seemed to consider my words for a moment, his gaze drifting away.

"Not that I've tried, but I'm fairly sure I could."

"Wow. What if you get angry at the world and decide to end it?"

His mouth curved in a sad smile.

"That's the level of responsibility I'm talking about here, Angela. As I grew, my power got bigger. Most of my life I've been striving to restrain and control it." He must have spotted the pensive expression on my face, as his tone lightened. "Luckily, when things don't go my way, I tend to get angry at myself, not at the world around me. I've never had a notion to end it."

"What makes you so cautious then?"

"There have been a few things, which put me on guard about my power—*magic*, as you've called it. When I was a little kid, I stopped a thunderstorm once. I really wanted to stay outside and play, but the rain was coming. Being too small to know much about weather or meteorology then, instead of dispersing the clouds or turning the storm into a different direction, I just wished it gone, and it disappeared. The next morning, a tornado hit our town. Dozens of houses were completely destroyed. People were reported dead and injured."

"It might've had nothing to do with you," I protested. "Maybe the tornado was supposed to be there that day."

"Maybe. But it was a small town in Northwestern US. The last tornado reported in the area happened almost thirty years before that day. And they had none since I'd moved out." He paused. "Anyway, as much as possible, I try not to disturb the natural order of things now."

I tore off a flaky strip of a croissant. "Do you know where your magic comes from?"

"Do you mean where *I* got it from?"

"Yes. Did your parents have any? Do they know anything about *the balance of matter in the world?*"

"Maybe, but I can't ask them—they're not around."

"Why?" The piece of croissant suddenly turned dry in my mouth. "What happened? Have they passed away?"

"I don't know. I never knew my parents. I grew up in foster care. Don't you have to go to work?"

"What?" His question was so sudden, it took me a moment to catch up.

"It's well past eight." He tipped his chin at the green numbers glowing on the microwave.

"It is?" How did the time fly by this fast? "Oh my God. I'll be late!" I jumped off my chair.

"I can take you," he offered, getting up, too.

"You have a car here?" I dashed to the closet to get my coat.

It was at least forty minutes from here to my desk in the office, which meant I'd be late no matter how fast I ran to the subway.

"No," he said slowly, as if speaking to a child, following me to the hallway. "I didn't drive here."

"Right. Of course. Teleported or something. Sorry, I keep forgetting." I was running around my apartment, collecting my things—purse, keys, TTC pass for the subway.

"I've no car." Marcus leaned against the wall, watching me rush around in panic. "But I can still take you."

"Really?" I stopped in my tracks, clutching the purse to my chest. "Could you? Please? That would save me forty minutes of commute. I'd, actually, be early for once." I shoved my feet in my boots. "How does it work?"

"You have to tell me the address. Is the door to your office closed?"

I gave him the address of the building where I worked.

"But I don't have my own office. I work in a cubicle."

"Is it open?"

I nodded. Obviously, Marcus had never been in a cubicle.

"Okay. Is there a bathroom or a broom closet in the building, some kind of a closed room where no one is likely to be inside at this hour? We don't want to materialize in front of your unsuspecting coworkers and give them a heart attack."

"Right. The supply room is always locked, and I don't think anyone would be there this early. People tend to hang around the coffee maker in the kitchen first thing in the morning." I gave him the approximate location of the supply room on our floor.

"Perfect. Come here." He gestured for me to come closer.

My stomach fluttered in anticipation. I slung the strap of my purse over my shoulder and came a foot or so away from him. My back straight. My arms down at my sides.

"I'm ready."

"Closer, Angela." His voice turned warm and soft, rolling over me like a wave of honey.

I took a step forward, fully invading his personal space now. The faint smell of leather tickled my nostrils. It must have become a permanent part of him since he wasn't even wearing any leather this morning.

"A little more," he murmured, closing the distance between us. "You have to be very close to me for this to work."

He lifted my arms over his shoulders then hugged my waist, drawing me into the hard warmth of his body.

"Is this close enough?" I asked as my nose pressed to his collarbone in the opening of his shirt, then shifted my feet to perfectly align our lower bodies, too.

"Ideally," he whispered into my hair, "your legs should be wrapped around me and my mouth should be on yours—"

"Marcus!" I exclaimed, ready to lash out at him for tricking me into a hug, no matter how wonderful it felt to be held by him right now. "This is—"

A warm puff of air hit my face at that moment. It fanned my hair and made me blink. I closed my eyes for a second, and when I opened them again, we were no longer in my apartment.

My ass pressed against a box of printer paper on a shelf, and the air smelled of dust and ink cartridges.

"That's it?" I couldn't believe how fast, simple, and rather ordinary this felt.

"No. One more thing." Marcus lowered his face, his mouth unexpectedly meeting mine in a gentle kiss.

This time I wasn't fast enough to evade him, or maybe I didn't try hard enough. His kiss was warm and tender. And I melted into it, without even a thought of fighting it.

His lips brushed by mine softly, as if he tested my response. Not encountering any resistance from me, he deepened the kiss, the tip of his tongue darting out.

The heat from his mouth on mine coursed through me in waves. He flexed his arms around me, drawing me closer as the urgency of his kiss intensified. Breathless, I clung to his shoulders, letting it all happen.

Hand in my hair, he tilted my head back, prompting me to part my lips for him, and with a soft whimper, I obeyed. The warm sensation in my chest spread down, pooling somewhere in my lower stomach, with a pulsating pressure between my legs building up.

Only half-aware of what I was doing at that moment, I hooked my leg around his hips, bringing him closer. He groaned, rocking into me, his hands fervently roamed along my body finding a way under my coat. I felt him cup my breast, his thumb rubbing my hardened nipple through the fabric of my dress.

A sharp charge of desire speared through me, blinding me with need. Marcus thrust against me harder, and the box behind me shifted, causing me to lose my balance.

With a gasp, I broke the kiss and grabbed on to his arms instinctively, yanked out of the haze of lust at once.

"Marcus," I panted, my forehead pressed into his shoulder. "Stop . . . please."

He breathed hard above my ear, his body vibrating with tension, his arm muscles hard as rock under my fingers.

"I wish I could," he gritted out. "I wish I could stop wanting you, in every fucking way."

"You promised," I reminded, with no resolve whatsoever. "Just yesterday—"

Not letting me out of his arms, he leaned back, his eyes flickered between mine.

"Angela, do you really believe we could just be friends?"

The sincerity in his voice made me pause.

To be completely honest, *no*, I didn't believe we could. I knew even as I forced that promise from him that my feelings for Marcus were far from platonic. However, I still believed some distance between us would protect me.

"It's . . ." I slid my hands down to his forearms and stood taller, both feet on the ground. "It's a self-preservation thing. Around you,

I feel powerless, Marcus. And it's not because you have all the power in the world."

"I'll never hurt you," he promised firmly.

You might not even realize it if you do.

I didn't voice this thought out loud, but he must have sensed my apprehension.

"Angela, it doesn't have to happen right away." He took a step back from me, letting me breathe freely again. "We can take it slow if you want. Move at whatever pace you feel comfortable. This . . ." He reached for me and squeezed my shoulders gently. "Has never been just about sex for me, but I want to be closer than friends."

"I—" I shook my head, finding no words to reply.

"Don't say anything now." He stopped me quickly. "Just think about it. I'll come back tomorrow morning again. We'll talk." With a quick glance around, he added. "Not here."

"Not here," I echoed, the reality of the dusty supply room around us returning to me. "Definitely not here, please."

Hurriedly, I smoothed both hands over my coat and ran my fingers through my hair. With my luck, some early birds at the office could've finished their coffee already and might decide to stock up on ballpoint pens any minute, risking discovering us in here.

Thankfully, none of my coworkers were at the show on Sunday and whatever pictures or cell phone videos popped up on the internet since then didn't have my face clearly visible, due to my position above the crowd and the dim lighting in the theater at that time.

Still, finding me in the closet with Marcus would cause a lot of questions, which I wasn't ready to answer.

"Think about it, Angela," he repeated, his gaze on me.

"I will," I promised and hurried for the door, needing to escape this room where there was barely enough space for two people, unless they stood in a firm embrace. "Thank you for *the lift*, Marcus."

Chapter 18

I WOKE UP WAY BEFORE my alarm went off that morning and before Marcus was there. Fully dressed, hair and makeup done, I paced the miniscule length of my hallway, ridden with nerves in anticipation of his arrival.

'*Think about it*' he'd asked. And that was exactly what I'd been doing ever since I fled that supply room yesterday.

The problem, however, was not with what I *thought* but how I *felt*.

I missed Marcus. It'd been barely twenty-four hours, and I already couldn't wait to see him again. His scent, the feel of his arms tight around me and his mouth devouring mine stayed with me through the day and kept me up most of the night.

Marcus had crashed into my life like a hurricane of bad manners and hot kisses and turned my peaceful existence upside down.

In my mind, I realized getting too close to his fire would only mean getting burnt at the end. My heart, however, didn't care. There, I wanted more. I needed it all with him, no matter the consequences.

And that terrified me.

Staring into the kitchen, lost in my thoughts, I watched the air around the table shimmer and shift. A moment later, Marcus appeared in that spot.

"Oh!" I exhaled a nervous laugh, as an arrow of surprise shot through my chest. "I see what you meant when you spoke of giving someone a heart attack."

"Sorry, I didn't think you'd be out of the bedroom already. Normally, I try to teleport to a closet or a bathroom somewhere—"

"No," I objected quickly, afraid even to think about the implications of his sudden appearance in my bathroom, especially, if I happened to be using it at that moment. "No bathroom. Kitchen is good. It's just that it's the first time I actually saw you do it, which is a bit startling, I have to admit. I'm sure I'll get used to it, eventually."

He inclined his head, his features sharpened as if in concentration for a moment, then a rich smell of coffee filled my kitchen.

"Breakfast?" Marcus stepped aside, revealing the coffee cups, fruit, yogurt, and granola cereal on the table behind him.

"Seems so easy." I smiled at all the food.

"Using it *is* easy. Keeping it all *in* is much harder." He handed me a cup of coffee. "Hungry?"

"No." I wrapped my fingers tightly around the cup. "I'm not hungry at all, actually." My stomach had been in knots ever since I got up.

"Did you sleep well?" Marcus narrowed his eyes at me, not moving away.

"No," I confessed with a sigh.

"Have you been thinking?"

"Yes."

"Are you nervous?"

I nodded.

"Afraid?"

Not trusting myself to speak at this point, I just nodded again.

"So am I."

Shocked, I shot my gaze up to his face.

"You are?"

He stood inches away from me, his face unmasked, his expression unguarded.

"Angela." He cupped the side of my neck, running his thumb along my jawline. "I'm risking my heart here, too. Just like you are. And it scares the shit out of me to do it."

"Does it mean this much to you?" I searched his eyes for any shadow of a doubt, finding none.

Regret crossed his features, instead.

"I know what you think about me. You've seen the pictures. Everyone has. I can't change what I've done, and I won't lie to justify any of it."

I closed my eyes for a moment. The onslaught of images of him with many—now faceless to me—women on his arm rushed my memories.

"I've used women when I didn't want to be alone at night." He slid his hands to my shoulders and gave me a slight shake, prompting me to open my eyes again. "And they've used me, too, for whatever they hoped to gain from being in my bed."

He kept his gaze on mine, not letting me look away. And I struggled to breathe all of a sudden.

"Angela, I haven't been with anyone for months now."

"Why not?" I rasped, my throat dry like a desert. I wished I could take a drink of coffee from the cup still clutched in my fingers, but I was afraid I'd spill it the way my hands shook.

"I can't allow anyone to get close to me, without letting them know what I really am. Traveling from place to place made it easier to leave everything behind. Now that I've been in the same city for months—"

"Breakups would be messier?"

"In order to break up," he retorted. "One would have to have some kind of a relationship in the first place. I've never had that."

"Ever?"

He shook his head slowly.

"I've never had a second date in my life. Never shared a breakfast with a woman before you. None of them saw me without the mask. And none of them cared enough to guess what I am."

"Is that why you want this with me? Because I am the only one who knows your secret and you can be yourself around me?"

He paused for a moment.

"I'm sure that's a part of it. But is it wrong for me to want to be with someone with whom I don't need to pretend? It's definitely not *just* that, though. There is so much more." He rubbed his forehead. "What I'm saying, Angela, is that there are so many firsts for me here. And it's scary, simply terrifying to open my heart like that. But I am willing to risk it all. For you. For what I believe we could have if we try. Because I want us to try. You and I, I believe we could have it all."

I stared into the deep blue of his eyes which burned with the same intensity that vibrated through his voice. His pale skin flushed from emotions he put in his words. Their passion resonated through my chest, making me want to believe everything he said was possible.

"Everything?" I whispered.

"Yes. I want us to have it all. Please, don't make me pretend otherwise."

I suspected *everything* might have a somewhat different meaning for Marcus that it did for me. When it came to him, I was ready for a full commitment—friendship, caring, lust and love, no matter what it took.

For him, however, so much of it seemed new. I realized I couldn't demand from him what he hadn't experienced yet. But I was more than willing to give him what he'd asked for and hope for the rest to come with time.

"It's not easy. To pretend," I managed to squeeze past my tightening throat. "I want it all, too."

"More than friends?" He stepped closer, his hands sliding to my back.

"Yes, much more." My fist closed, and I realized that the cup I'd held was gone as Marcus drew me into his chest.

I tilted my head back to see his face.

"Let me do it right this time," he whispered before lowering his mouth to mine.

Slow and sensual, his kiss made my head spin as the rest of the world seemed to fall away. My heart thundered against my ribs, pumping blood and heat through my veins. Rising on my toes, I parted my lips, kissing him back.

Eager to take him in with all of my senses at once, I kept running my hands along his body—the hard ropes of the muscles in his arms, the wide planes of his back, the silk of his hair tied back. The warm, smoothly-shaved skin on his cheekbones under my thumbs as I cupped his face with both hands.

"Oh God, Marcus . . ." I panted when he let me come up for air as he nuzzled the side of my neck.

"I love the way you feel in my arms," he murmured against my skin. "It's like you belong right here." He flexed his arms, bringing me closer.

All this time, however, his hands remained at my back, not straying to explore any further.

"Breakfast?" He leaned back, catching my gaze with his. "Do you feel hungry now? You should eat something before you leave for work."

I blinked, feeling all hot and dazed from his kiss. The persistence with which he'd been pursuing this led me to believe he'd throw me on the table and take me right here the moment I agreed to be more than friends.

His sudden withdrawal confused me and, I had to admit, even disappointed me somewhat.

Slow, Angela, you wanted to take it slow.

"Sure." I nodded. "Breakfast sounds great."

"Come." He moved a chair back for me. "I want you to tell me more about yourself."

"There is really not that much to tell." I smiled, sitting down.

"How about your family?"

"Oh, no. Are you sure you want to know all about them?" My smile turned into a laugh.

"Absolutely." He took his usual seat across from me, his expression light and sunny.

And I realized that no matter what this day would bring, this breakfast with him had already become the best part of today for me.

Chapter 19

"DO YOU GET ANY TIME off at all?" Marcus asked, sitting on the floor in my living area.

With my legs on each side of his back, I sat on the couch behind him, running a hairbrush through the long strands of his hair.

"Sometimes." I rummaged through the old tin box with my hair accessories, looking for the pink crystal barrette I got for Christmas when I was sixteen. "About once a month or so I get a day off."

"And I thought *I* was a workaholic," Marcus grumped.

It was Sunday, the only day of the week when I didn't have to set my alarm early in the morning as the store didn't open until noon.

Marcus showed up at six thirty anyway. Knowing that I could spend more time with him today, he took a nap in his hotel right after his show ended in Vegas, then had a shower at my place, waiting for me to wake up.

I'd volunteered to blow dry and brush his hair but then got carried away somewhat and was now in the middle of constructing an elaborate hairdo on his head, with a ton of tiny braids held by multi-coloured elastics and hairpins.

"I'm not planning to work two jobs forever." I found the barrette and was now trying to decide on the most dramatic placement of it in my creation on Marcus's head. "You know it's just a means to an end."

As much as I'd told Marcus about my family in the past couple of weeks since he'd first appeared in my apartment, I took care to avoid mentioning the financial situation of my parents.

"A few more months. A year max, and I should be in a good place financially to quit the store job."

Actually, I didn't have any specific deadlines. After all, my job in the store wasn't supposed to last past my graduation, but here I was still working there.

"If you're having money problems—"

"No," I cut him off quickly. "No problems. Just a certain level of financial security I'd like to reach."

I'd accepted Marcus buying me breakfast almost daily. His obvious enjoyment of having it ready for me when I got up deprived me of any desire to argue about it. But that was as far as I would go. My family's financial struggles taught me to keep money matters out of any relationship as much as possible.

"I appreciate your feeding me, Marcus."

"I know you do. You keep telling it to me every morning, as if a cup of yogurt and a handful of cereal were something to gush over."

"You're forgetting the French croissants." I tugged at one of his braids playfully. "Fresh from Paris."

A few days ago, I wondered out loud if croissants tasted any different in France than the ones we got in Toronto. Marcus disappeared for a few minutes then came back with a basket of them fresh from a café in Paris, France, he explained.

"What if I felt like Thai food one day?" I teased, remembering that morning. "Will you 'fly' to Thailand to get it?"

"Nope. I'd just get some from the Thai restaurant on Bloor Street right here, in Toronto. I've never been to Thailand and have no idea where to find good food there."

"So, you've been to Paris?" I asked then recalled his mentioning going for a walk there.

"Yes. I love Paris. I've had a coffee in the café where I got those croissants. They serve them fresh all day there."

I wondered what it would be like not having to worry about passports, visas and borders, not to mention the time and cost of travel. The absolute freedom, it seemed.

"Can't you go to Thailand just for fun? Take your time to look around. Or is it too far? Is there a distance limit for your teleportation mode of travel?"

I decided to add a few more braids, mostly because I loved running my fingers through his hair.

Marcus didn't seem to mind me taking liberty with his hairstyle. In fact, he appeared to be enjoying it, too, turning his head for me, whichever way I tugged.

"No limit." He shifted on the floor, stretching his long legs in front of him. "The problem is the landing point. I need to know where to appear, without anyone seeing me. It would help if the place was also relatively safe."

"Have you landed in a danger zone before?" I half-joked.

"As a teenager, I went through a phase of wanderlust. I researched places all over the world and then visited them whenever I had a chance."

"Sounds amazing."

"Not as much as you'd think," he laughed. "Some things are best seen on TV than in real life. Anyway, the phase ended when I decided to visit sub-Saharan Africa and landed half-a-foot away from a sleeping lion." He pulled up the pant leg of his jeans, revealing several long, parallel scars on his ankle. "In theory, I can disappear instantly. In reality, however, it took me a fraction of a second to realize what I'd got myself into. That turned out to be long enough for the lion to wake up and go for my leg."

"Oh my God, I'm so sorry." I bit my lip, refusing to let my imagination run wild with what could've happened to him had he lingered any longer.

"Don't be." Marcus shrugged. "My plan was to visit the wild forests of Amazon next. Who knows how that one would've turned out? The lion incident made me change my mind."

"Thank goodness it did." I draped the last finished braid over his shoulder, admiring my handiwork.

"All done?" Marcus turned around. "How do I look?"

"Gorgeous." I smiled at the sparkle of the pink barrette in his hair, but my smile faded quickly.

There was nothing comical about his look, despite the bright elastics and the shimmer of crystals. The hairdo, in combination with his sharp cheekbones and the fierce glint in his eyes under the ink-black eyebrows, gave him the appearance of some ancient fantasy warrior.

There was that rare type of beauty—male or female—that nothing could spoil. No matter what was done to it, it wouldn't ruin it, only enhance.

My heart squeezed with a tang of longing.

"You look breathtakingly handsome, Marcus," I said the absolute truth and re-arranged the braids on his shoulders, in hope to distract us both from the flush of heat on my face and in my chest.

"Thank you for the makeover." He rose on his knees in front of me. Arms around my waist, he slid me along the couch seat closer to him. "As much as I wish I could wear it all day, I have an image to maintain." He lifted the end of one of the braids, eyeing it with a glint of amusement in his expression. "And coral pink is not my colour."

I could disagree, admiring the contrast of the glowing pink elastic against the rich black of his hair, but I didn't argue.

"I'll take them all out before you leave," I promised, sliding my hands behind his neck.

As usual, having him this close did amazing things to me. My heart sped up, my chest seemed to be running out of space for it. Warmth from his hands tingled my skin through my clothes. Hardly realizing it myself, I leaned into him, as if following a pull of a powerful magnet.

He kissed my neck. "Don't remind me of leaving yet."

Marcus didn't seem to hold back when displaying his obvious affection for me. Every time he visited, I got warm hello hugs, tender goodbye kisses, and cuddles in between.

Neither did he shy away from my touch, readily accepting it, just like today, when he let me brush and braid his hair the moment I offered.

However, we hadn't taken it much further since the day we both agreed to be more than friends. I wasn't sure why it happened. Marcus didn't try anything more, and so far I chose to be content with what we had instead of fret over what we didn't.

I enjoyed talking to him. He turned out to be a gifted storyteller, and it was an exquisite experience to listen to the stories of his past travels and his encounters with different people.

At times, it felt as if he never had anyone to talk to all his life and was eager to catch up now. I relished the time spent with him, discovering everything about him that I always wanted to know but never thought I'd have a chance to learn.

Sometimes, though, I wondered if our lack of physical intimacy had a bigger significance than I allowed myself to believe, and then I dreaded the moment when the novelty of having a friend who listened would wear off for Marcus, and he would move on.

The mere thought of us parting our ways made me physically ill, as if I could feel my heart breaking already.

"Don't leave." I kissed the side of his neck, taking in his scent. "Not yet, we still have time."

With a light brush of his lips on my temple, he pulled away, way too soon.

"You said you clean your apartment on Sundays?" He stood up, his voice cheerful and full of energy.

"I did?" I might have mentioned it last week, but why would he remember this now. "No worries. I'll do it after work tonight."

"Let me do it for you."

Slowly, he spun around, giving my space an assessing stare.

"Just leave it," I protested, envisioning him with a broom and a mop. "You don't have to—"

"Watch this." He stopped me, hand in the air.

It appeared like the floor of the living area had peeled. A murky, cloudy layer of dirt lifted from it, hovering a few inches up in the air. Staring at it in shock, I realized it even retained the shape of the surface of my carpet.

Marcus tipped his head and the grimy layer folded in on itself then floated to the garbage bin under the sink in the kitchen.

"Voila!" Marcus flicked his wrist artistically, directing my gaze to the perfectly clean carpet on the floor.

"That's it?" I exclaimed, jumping to my feet. "That's all it took? And really." I twisted around, inspecting the floor under my feet. "Did I have *that* much dirt in here?" I glanced towards the kitchen then moved my eyes to his smiling face. "Thank you." I threw myself at him, wrapping my arms around his neck again.

"You're welcome. It was no trouble as you know." Marcus hugged my waist.

"Well then." I giggled. "Cleaning will be your chore from now on. And you can never ever leave me." I meant it as a joke, but something squeezed painfully inside me at these words. "Ever," I whispered, drawing him closer to me.

Chapter 20

"THANK YOU SO MUCH, Angela! You are a lifesaver, like always."

Even though I couldn't see her at the moment, I knew Emily was bouncing up and down as she always did when even a little bit excited. She'd called me at work, asking me to take care of their mail and houseplants while she and Mikey were away on their honeymoon.

They didn't go anywhere after their wedding in June because it was practically impossible for Mikey to take any vacation during the summer. Instead, they planned a month-long trip around the world for this fall.

Mikey and Emily were going to fly east out of Toronto, make a number of stops all around the globe, and then return to Canada from the west, landing in Vancouver to visit her family before returning to Toronto.

Both of them worked hard on the list of countries and places they wanted to see. And Emily promised to keep a detailed blog with pictures online as they went.

This was a once-in-a-lifetime adventure. I was happy for them and a little envious, in a way.

I told myself that I would have a chance to do some travelling of my own one day. Mom and Dad would get back on their feet eventually, wouldn't they? Evan's rehab loan would be paid off some day. Maybe I'd get some more free time then.

"With everything going on around here, there's so much on my mind right now," Emily continued in my ear through the receiver. "I almost forgot about the poor plants. They would've died in a month."

"Don't' worry, I have your key. I'll keep them alive," I reassured her.

"There shouldn't be that much mail. We do all of our bills electronically. Just empty the flyers in the mailbox from time to time, so that it's not that obvious from the outside that we're away. Our townhouse complex is pretty safe, but still."

"Will do."

"Sorry. I hate putting more stuff on your to-do list, Angela. Especially now that you finally have a boyfriend again!" I could have sworn she started bouncing all over again.

I had told Emily and my family about Marcus. Not everything, though, I still hadn't figured out how to work in his celebrity status. Especially, since he hadn't introduced me to anyone from his surroundings and hadn't made any attempts to make our relationship public.

"It's fine, really, Emily. I don't mind it at all. It's just a couple of times a week, I'll still have lots of time to spend with Marcus whenever he's in town."

As far as my friends and relatives were concerned for now, Marcus worked in the entertainment industry and often travelled to Toronto for business.

I attempted to prevent any further questions by stating that it was still too early in our relationship to have him meet my family and that we were taking it slow for now. Not that it stopped *all* of their questions of course.

"Just swear to me again that he is not married or going through a nasty divorce," demanded Emily for a thousandth time since I told her about Marcus.

"No, he's not married, and no, he's not going through a divorce. I swear." I placed my hand against my heart even though Emily couldn't see me over the phone.

"Why all this secrecy then? Why can't we meet him? Is he an ex-con? An axe murderer who can't behave himself in public? Why else would you keep him away from us? Oh, oh, I know. He must think he's ugly or scary as hell—like a real-live Quasimodo. You know I wouldn't care about his looks, right? Or did he get injured in a horrific accident and is now covered in scars from head to toe, avoiding all people contact on purpose?"

"God, Emily! You really should write a book or make a movie. Your imagination is bursting with some crazy ideas."

"Nah. I could never stay put long enough to write a book. But don't you change the subject on me. I need to know that I'm leaving you in good hands when I go. How can I be sure that I won't return to your dead body—all cut up and stuffed in duffel bags—if I've never even talked to the mysterious Marcus in person?"

"Oh, boy," I exhaled in exasperation. It was late in the day and the office was almost empty by now. I had about twenty minutes to kill before the start of my evening shift at the store. This conversation now threatened to take longer than that. "Okay, Emily. Just because you're leaving and I want you to enjoy your honeymoon without worrying about finding a bunch of bloodied duffel bags upon your return . . ." I covered the receiver with my hand and lowered my voice to make sure whoever was still left in the office wouldn't hear me. "Remember Marcus, the magician? I went to his show last month?"

"No way!" Emily screeched like a banshee, forcing me to yank the phone away from my aching ear. "Marcus the Magnificent is *your* Marcus?"

"Well, I wouldn't exactly call him *mine* yet—"

"You're kidding, right? I can't believe it! You're dating a celebrity? Talk about having a magical boyfriend."

"Really, Emily. It's all still very new. We just talk, mostly—"

"Don't tell me you haven't fucked yet."

"Emily!"

"Come on, Angela. They say he is truly *magnificent* in bed."

"They *who*?"

"It doesn't matter. He has to be. Why else would he have a stage name like that? It's stupid."

"Well, his kisses are magnificent," I admitted.

"That's good. You can tell a lot from a kiss. It's like a preview, or an appetizer. So when is the main course going to happen? And how come it hasn't happened yet?"

A good question. One I still couldn't answer, however.

Although, his hugs and kisses had heated at times, making me wish for more, Marcus would unfailingly pull away before anything more could happen.

Having a frank conversation about it seemed a bit too forward right now. I just hoped his hesitation didn't have something to do with me.

"Angela." Emily's voice sounded serious now, even concerned. "Just tell me he is a good guy. Do you like him?"

"I do," I said with an absolute certainty, and my heart swelled with the sweet ache that had been growing there ever since Marcus barged into my personal life like a sexy, magical avalanche of bad manners one morning. "I like him very much."

Chapter 21

"THIS IS BEAUTIFUL, Marcus." I twirled around, trying to take his suite in, all at once—silver metal, dark wood, sparkling glass, and creamy white marble. The place was at least four times the size of my apartment, and that was just the lower level—living, dining and kitchenette area.

"You think so?" He watched me with a clear amusement.

Until now, we'd mostly spent time in my place. In Toronto, we also went out for breakfast a few times. I better understood his reasons for wearing a mask when I saw how much he enjoyed simply walking down the street without it.

With his hair pulled back, wearing jeans and a leather jacket, Marcus looked like an ordinary guy, even if a really attractive one. Women shot heated glances his way, but without the mask no one seemed to recognize him.

This morning, Marcus invited me to his hotel suite in Vegas. Although I'd been seeing him for over a month now, it still took me a moment to realize that I could have breakfast in Vegas and then still make it for work in Toronto in time. Teleportation was one very convenient miracle.

Marcus had explained that he had to take care of an emergency this morning and wanted me to wait for him in his suite meanwhile.

"Why on earth would you ever want to hang out at my apartment if you have something like this to come home to?" I marveled, running a finger along the butter-soft leather on the back of the couch.

"It's not *something*. It's *someone*." He stepped closer. "I look forward seeing *you* each and every morning."

I lowered my gaze under his intense stare, warm pleasure spread inside me, ignited by his words.

"Besides, I like your apartment." He brushed a lock of stray hair from my face, moving it behind my ear. "It has character—cute, with a flair of elegance, just like you."

"Cute and elegant? Sounds like an oxymoron, Marcus. You can't be both at the same time."

"Not everyone could," he agreed, smiling. "But *you* can, and you are." He kissed the tip of my nose. "Listen, I hate to leave you here alone—even for a second—but I really need to find an elephant for tonight's show. Rosy, the one I own, seemed unwell last night, and I want her to rest after the vet's visit today. I'll have to check a few European zoos to figure out where to borrow a replacement."

"Marcus." I giggled. "Only you can say something like that and mean it literally."

"And only you can understand my life for what it truly is." His hands on my waist, he leaned in for a quick kiss.

Marcus had told me that before Vegas, he used to borrow animals from European zoos for his shows. He preferred European zoos mostly because of the time difference. After the closing hours at night, there was a smaller chance of anyone noticing that the animals disappeared for a minute or two while Marcus had them on stage in North America.

Now, with regular performances in Vegas, Marcus ended up buying several large animals to avoid unnecessary questions from the staff and management. He had a few lions, tigers, and the two horses that he used in his illusion of "sawing" a horse in two.

"Breakfast is on the table. Help yourself. I'll be back in fifteen minutes. Twenty max." He walked to the bathroom, probably simply out of habit of teleporting behind locked doors.

"Do you want anything from Europe?" he asked before closing the door behind him.

"From a zoo? Sure. Bring me some cotton candy if they have it there," I joked and heard him chuckle in response.

"For breakfast? Not the healthiest of choices, Miss McAllister!" he shouted, then he was gone and the suite became quiet.

It was a little after three in the morning in Las Vegas. The sky was still dark behind the glass doors that seemed to lead to an outdoor balcony or terrace. The many bright lights pulsed from the Strip outside, lighting up the night.

My attention turned to the dining table with breakfast dishes surrounding a huge centrepiece of white roses. As I poured myself a cup of coffee from the thermos carafe, a loud knock came from the front door.

I went still for a moment, debating whether I should answer or pretend that there was no one here. As far as anyone was concerned, Marcus could've been asleep, so I kept quiet.

The knock came again, even louder this time.

"Marcus! I know you're not sleeping," a male voice shouted. "Open up or answer your damn phone! It's kind of an emergency."

I thought I recognized the voice as Simon's. We never officially met—Marcus hadn't introduced us. Maybe he had his reasons for it. And maybe, I should have kept quiet, pretending I wasn't there, but my curiosity won over. According to Marcus, Simon had been the only one who stayed with him for years, and I was eager to meet him.

Besides, Simon mentioned an emergency, didn't he?

Putting my cup down, I went to get the door and was met with a surprised frown on Simon's face.

"Hello, Angela," he greeted, quickly schooling his features into a polite expression. "Can I speak with Marcus for a second?"

"Hi, Simon. Marcus is . . . um, in the shower. You said it was an emergency?"

"It can wait until he is out. Could you tell him to call me then?"

"Sure. Um, wait . . ." I stopped him on his way to the elevator. "Would you like to have a coffee with me? I'm having breakfast."

There was at least fifteen minutes to kill, and I had a few questions that Simon could possibly answer. He was the only person in the world who had known Marcus since childhood—the time of his life that Marcus hadn't been very talkative about.

Simon examined my face for a moment before replying, "Sure. I'd love some coffee."

Chapter 22

"WOULD YOU TELL ME ABOUT how you met Marcus, Simon? He said you've known each other for years."

We sat on the opposite ends of the white couch, each of us holding a cup of coffee.

"Would you mind if I asked you a few questions first, Angela? Before answering yours?" Simon leaned back in his seat, placing his right ankle on top of his left knee.

I recalled this as Marcus's favourite sitting position, too. They had known one another long enough to copy each other's body language, it seemed. My past speculation of them being lovers came to mind.

"You know, I wondered once if you and Marcus were a couple," I blurted out before I could stop myself. Somehow, it seemed like a good enough icebreaker. I realized that it wasn't as soon as the words left my mouth, and I stared at Simon, mortified.

To my relief, he laughed.

"Ha! It would've made life so much simpler if we were. It certainly would've made my job infinitely easier. Too bad we're both too much into women for that idea to stick."

I smiled, glad he didn't seem to be offended by my words.

"Is it your first time here, Angela?"

"No." I shook my head. "My first time in Vegas was in May of this year—"

"I meant here, in Marcus's suite?"

"Ah. Yes. It is."

"I see." He put his cup on the coffee table by the couch and smoothed the material of his expensive looking dress pants over his knee. "Have you been seeing Marcus regularly since the show in Toronto?"

"Um." I hesitated.

I'd just told Simon that it was my first time in the suite. If I admitted to seeing Marcus, it would imply he'd been coming to Toronto. Surely, Simon was aware that Marcus hadn't done any conventional travelling to Canada in the past several weeks. If I told Simon now that I *saw* Marcus regularly, he would question how it was happening.

I realized it had been a mistake to invite Simon in. I'd hoped to hear more about Marcus's childhood from him. However, he caught me completely unprepared to answer any questions about us. I didn't want to lie to Simon. However, knowing from Marcus that he hadn't shared his secret with him, I had to be careful about my replies.

Simon misunderstood my hesitation.

"Sorry if my question seemed too personal. I don't need any details. To be honest, I'm just trying to gauge how much information I can reveal to you by assessing how close you and Marcus are. He doesn't speak much about you. Not that he's been around much lately to talk with me at all."

I didn't catch any complaint or reproach in his voice. He seemed to be simply stating the fact. The expression on his lightly tanned face remained open and friendly.

I studied him for a moment while considering my answer.

Simon's flax-blond hair was fashionably cut and neatly styled. His smooth, even tan must have originated in a salon, not from the exposure to the desert sun. The fine lines around the corners of his eyes and mouth told me that he laughed wholeheartedly and often, even if he appeared rather serious at the moment.

He met my gaze straight on, and I decided to be honest with him in return, as much as I dared.

"We talk regularly, Marcus and I. He calls me and texts me daily."

This wasn't a lie. Marcus called me often before I went to bed. He also texted me through the day between his shows.

Simon tilted his head, his piercing grey eyes focused on me.

"Are you his girlfriend?"

I inhaled sharply, Marcus never actually called me *that*.

"Well." I forced my voice to sound more confident than I felt. "We're sort of dating."

"Marcus doesn't date. Pardon me, but you're the first woman I've seen fully clothed in his room." He didn't sound like he was mocking me, but there was a challenge in his voice, daring me to prove him wrong.

"There is a first time for everything." I managed an awkward smile, chasing the images of an army of naked women out of my head. "We've both agreed to give it a try."

"And how has it been so far?" Simon was smiling now, too, and I physically felt the tension between us dissipate.

"Wonderful." The thoughts of the time I'd spent together with Marcus immediately brought about that fuzzy, warm feeling inside me.

"Marcus is a great guy." Simon nodded, folding his arms across his chest. "He doesn't always come across as the friendly social type, but it's not because of his personality, mostly because of the lifestyle he leads. He can't let people get too close, even though he likes having them around."

Simon may not have been in on Marcus's secret, but he obviously wasn't blind or stupid. He'd been around long enough to know more than he let on.

"He doesn't have many friends," I said carefully. "Just you."

"Well, I try to keep him safe and make sure he has everything he needs to perform."

"You knew him as a child."

"He told you how we met?"

"A little. He doesn't speak much about his childhood."

"Those were not the happiest times for either of us." Simon gave me a long penetrating look as if assessing whether I was worthy of his story. "My mom drank a lot," he continued. "Dad wasn't around. Marcus's foster parents at that time . . . well, they weren't the greatest out there, either. As kids, we spent a lot of time outside, neither one of us in a rush to get home. We used to hang out on an abandoned property. Marcus always had pop and chips lying around, and I was always hungry." He shrugged and smiled again, but it didn't reach his eyes this time. "Marcus didn't stay at that foster home for long. They moved him before the end of the school year."

"Do you know why?"

"There was an incident—an accident. Marcus didn't tell you about it?"

I shook my head in reply, worrying he wouldn't tell me, either.

"He doesn't talk about it, but maybe he should—he clams up at any mentioning of that night." Simon frowned. "I remember waking up from flashing lights and noise outside. There were fire trucks, police and ambulances on our street. The next day, Marcus was gone."

"What happened?" I urged him, my breath slowed in apprehension.

"I'm still not sure. I was too young for anyone to explain anything to me, but I overheard adults talk about a fire inside the home. It started in the bathroom. This was what puzzled everyone—most of house fires start in the kitchen or near the furnace. Marcus's foster dad was taken to the hospital that night with burns to most of his body. All kids in their care were moved to other homes. The foster dad survived, but I think he ended up in a home somewhere. The foster mom got some insurance money for the house and left, too. The next time I saw Marcus, it was in the parking lot where he was doing one of his magic shows. Did he tell you about that?"

"Yes," I confessed. "He was in high school then."

"I'm about a year older than he is, and I'd already spent months doing random jobs whenever I could get them. Shoplifted when there was no work. Ran some questionable errands for the local MC club . . . Anyway, it wouldn't have ended good for me, I know that much."

Hands on his knee, he leaned my way.

"The reason I'm telling this to you now, Angela, is because Marcus often makes people believe I've been instrumental to his success. It may be true, but it was *he* who really saved me. Without Marcus, my life would've been vastly different now." He paused for a moment, as if to add more gravity to the words that followed. "I won't let any harm come his way. Do you understand?"

"I do," I replied honestly under his piercing stare. "I want him happy, too."

"Good. He deserves some true happiness." Simon reclined again. "From the moment I saw Marcus perform for the first time, I knew he could do better than that parking lot. *We* could do better. I bought a rusty van from my mom's boyfriend of the month, and we drove all over the state. Through some buddies of mine, I got him the few first gigs in bars. We were too young to drink yet, but they would let Marcus do his show as long as it brought people and money in. We did everything we could then—supermarket openings, country fairs, birthday parties . . . " Simon's voice trailed off and his gaze focused somewhere past me as his mind must have returned to those early days of their beginnings.

I tried to imagine what it had been like for them. Two young men—still practically boys—taking on the world, all on their own. I felt grateful that Simon was there for Marcus all this time.

"You've done well." I smiled at him.

"We're doing okay," he agreed. "We both got what we deserve, it seems. He has you waiting for him here, and I . . . " His tone changed as he exhaled a sharp laugh and got up to his feet. "Well, I have a whole bunch of showgirls waiting for me in the party room downstairs. Can you let Marcus know, please, that we may need a replacement for Rosy, the elephant, tonight?" He winked at me, adding, "Whenever he gets out of the shower."

I winced—there was no sound of running water upstairs. Surely, Simon had noticed it, too, when I walked him past the closed door of the downstairs bathroom and towards the exit from the suite.

"Actually, Marcus already knows about Rosy. He's . . . um, going to do something about it," I said as the bathroom door opened, and Marcus stepped out, right in front of us, with a pink cloud of cotton candy on a stick in his hand.

"Simon?" His eyebrows shot up in an obvious surprise.

"Oh," was all I could say at that moment.

"Hi, Marcus," Simon greeted him cheerfully, seemingly completely unfazed by Marcus's sudden appearance. "I was just leaving. I came to tell you about Rosy, but Angela said you were going to handle it. So, we had some coffee instead."

He lightly punched Marcus on the arm on his way to the exit.

"Good night to you. And have a good morning, Angela." Simon winked at me over his shoulder again. His gaze flickered to the cotton candy in Marcus's hand for a second. "And all I get are a bunch of complimentary soaps in my bathroom." He laughed, closing the door behind him.

Chapter 23

MARCUS

It was clear that sleep wasn't happening tonight. He tossed the covers aside and got out of bed then staggered to the bathroom.

The skin on his hand appeared to be almost as white as the tub when he reached for the faucet. The agony that spread through him, however, made it feel like his entire body should be black and shriveled, burnt to a crisp.

Everything hurt—his skin, his muscles. Even his insides felt like molten lava, churning and bubbling in his belly as the fire consumed him whole.

The cold water from the faucet hit the back of his hand. With a hiss, most of the icy flow immediately turned to steam, with mere drops reaching the tub.

Useless.

Both hands on the sink, he leaned forward, avoiding the glossy, bloodshot eyes of his reflection in the mirror.

He had no one to blame but himself for letting it go this far. It was the end of his week off, and he spent most of it working on a new opening act for his show.

It was supposed to be his own original work, just like the Phoenix act. He got the inspiration for it from Angela, and they even did some planning together, but he wanted to keep this part a secret from her for now, planning to reveal it in a few days.

He'd been so deep into the work with his production crew, he realized he hadn't seen Angela for at least three days now.

No, more like five.

They talked on the phone through the day. But after working twelve hours straight at the venue then going over the financials with Simon at night, rushing to finish most of the planning process before his regular shows resumed on Monday, Marcus would collapse into his bed for a few hours—utterly exhausted—only to start it all over again the next day.

He glanced back at the cold water filling the tub, knowing perfectly well he'd only steam up the bathroom if he got in. The ice bath wouldn't help. It offered but an illusion of relief, nothing else.

To calm the fiery monster inside, he'd either have to share his magic with as many people as possible or to make himself come in some safe place.

It was just an hour or two past midnight. In Vegas, any time was a good time for an impromptu show. Except that he had forfeited his right to do them as part of the concessions demanded by the venue in exchange for the Toronto show.

That left sex only now.

He willed his cell phone to appear in his hand.

'Are those cars still there?' he sent a text to Simon, who had informed him of some suspicious vehicles parked around his property. They had been there on and off for days. Paparazzi, most likely. Marcus chose to stay away from the house for a while, in hopes that they'd eventually lose interest and move on to chase bigger stars.

The way the fire raged through his system, however, he couldn't care less about being caught on camera at this moment. All he wanted was a relief from this pain. A cool, fresh escape from the agony tormenting him.

There was a third way, though. Wasn't there?

Angela.

Over the weeks they'd spent together, he studied his body's reaction to her. Not the one that made his dick twitch in his pants every time her sweet, warm scent reached him or her gaze caressed him, her eyes dark and dreamy.

Every time she touched him, in passing or deliberately, he learned more about the calming effect of her hands on him. It was not a fluke, he determined, but she had to touch him in a certain way. Angela had to be turned on, sexually, for the inferno raging inside him to calm under her hands.

Blood rushed to his groin the moment he thought about that now, a different kind of fire licking up his inner thighs.

He glanced at the screen on his phone. No reply from Simon. The party boy must have finally turned in for the night.

It was too early for Angela to get up. But he didn't need her up. He wanted her just the way she would be right now—tucked in her bed, warm and soft.

Naked.

His memory immediately presented him with the image of her full breasts he'd managed to glimpse the one and only time he'd ever been in her bedroom. Dark, pebbled nipples, begging for his attention. His hard-on jolted to full mast, throbbing painfully, to add to his agony.

Now, Angela was the biggest cause of his torture.

She could also be the cure.

There were so many things to consider, too many reasons for him *not* to go to her tonight.

First of all, showing up in her bedroom again would be a blatant violation of her request. She told him she didn't want him there.

But that was before she let him kiss her, wasn't it? Way before she kissed him back and kept kissing him many times since.

Their platonic friendship lasted for less than a day. Actually, it never even was platonic in the first place. From the moment he made her fly across the old theater to him, he should have known he'd need more. From the way she'd gazed at him many times since—eyelids dropped, chest rising—he was certain she wanted more, too.

He hadn't taken her to his ranch house out of plain fear. In the isolated place like that without the risk of hurting the innocents, he was afraid his self-control would finally snap, and there was no guarantee she wouldn't run then.

Angela already knew so much about him, more than anyone ever did, and she'd accepted it all so far. However, he couldn't risk even the slightest possibility of her pushing him away now.

He needed her in his life, more than he needed to fuck her.

If he went to her now, it didn't have to go all the way, though, he reasoned with the desperation of a man possessed. He didn't need to come as much as he wanted to have her hands on him. After all, he had years of practice, years of reining his lust in by the sheer force of willpower.

The sweet memories of her body in his arms made his chest tighten. He remembered the way she pressed herself to him every time he hugged her, returning his every kiss and caress.

He'd make it all about her, he decided. The thought of having her come on his tongue made his hands tremble with anticipation.

The need to be with her took over and crushed through every reason of common sense.

Chapter 24

I WOKE UP, HOT AND sweaty, and kicked the covers off. Slowly, the top sheet crawled back over my legs and up to my waist. Too sleepy to fully comprehend what was happening, I sat up in my bed.

"What the . . ." I pulled the knees up to my chest, shrinking away from the creepy bedding.

It seemed to be still night. The room was dark, lit only by the ever-present glow of the streetlights from the window.

"Angela," came the familiar voice from the orange armchair in the corner.

"Marcus?"

God, I'd missed him! So much, my heart tightened with longing at the sight of his shape—more like a pale shadow in this lighting.

"Yes. Don't be scared." His voice sounded rough and dry.

"Are you okay? What are you doing here?" Suddenly aware of my nudity, I reached for the cover after all and tugged it all the way up to my chin.

"I . . ." He seemed to be lost for words for a moment. "I missed you," he said softly, as if recognizing the vulnerability in his honesty.

"I missed you, too," I confessed.

It had been nearly a week of nothing more but phone calls and texts. He claimed he'd been busy, and I longed to believe him. But the worry that he might be getting bored in my apartment and maybe found something else in Vegas or elsewhere to keep his attention—that it might indeed be the beginning of the end for us—kept lurking in my mind.

Clutching the cover to my chest, I lowered my feet to the floor, ready to get up.

"Is it time for breakfast already?" I longed to be closer to him, expecting my usual good-morning kiss. But he lifted his hand, stopping me on my way to him.

"Don't," he rasped. "Not yet—I'm afraid I'd singe your skin."

His words made me pause.

"What are you talking about?"

Initially blinded by the pure joy at seeing him again, I slowly became aware of how different this visit of his was.

Marcus didn't seem himself. The heat in the room that woke me up appeared to be emanating from him.

"Are you okay?"

"No. But I will be." He remained unnaturally still in the chair. "Let me do a show for you first."

Before I could reply, I felt being lifted in the air again. Flailing my arms, in an attempt to keep my balance—not an easy task when one was weightless—I accidentally let the cover drop from my hands.

Marcus groaned low then the top sheet rose from the bed, coiling around me quickly, until I was literally swaddled in it, like in a cocoon.

"Better," he stated. "Now watch."

Tentatively, I rocked a little side to side to test my balance. Being suspended in the air by Marcus, however, didn't seem the same as I imagined weightlessness in space would be. I didn't tumble through the room, following the momentum of my movements. Instead, it felt very much as if I was placed in an invisible hammock, about three feet above the bed. Without any obvious support for my body, my position still appeared stable enough for me to remain where Marcus wanted me to be.

A ribbon of silvery light slithered from between the parted curtains on my bedroom window.

"What is that?" I whispered as it shimmered and curled through the air, forming a wide circle around me.

"Moonlight," Marcus explained, his tone even. "I can't get you the moon, for the fear of apocalypse, but I can *borrow* its light for you."

The ribbon curled slowly, twisting in fantastic shapes and ever-changing patterns. The room illuminated in its pale glow, casting low highlights on Marcus's pale skin and ink-black hair over his shoulders.

He was absolutely naked, I realized, but couldn't give my full attention to this fact, mesmerized by the fantastic light show he was creating for me.

A string of yellow sparks, brighter and warmer than the moon glow in my room, entered through the window.

"From street lights," Marcus commented as they joined the silver ribbon in the spellbound dance around me.

The whole spectacle shifted, like a swell of a wave, and the fresh scent of the ocean saturated the air. Filling my lungs with it, I threw my head back in delight, as the fine mist of the surf seemed to caress my face.

"You said you have no time for vacation." Marcus's tone was softer now, filled with warmth, despite the unfamiliar rusty quality to his voice. "I brought the ocean here for you."

The soft sound of waves hitting a sandy shore filtered through the walls of my apartment, its rhythm perfectly synced with the pulsating glow of the moonlight ocean around me, the undulating waves crested with luminescent shimmer.

With an expansive swirl, the tiny golden sparks aligned themselves into star constellations above me.

"This is . . . beyond beautiful, Marcus," I whispered, staring at the tropical night sky he'd created on my bedroom ceiling for me. My very soul seemed to have curled into a warm smile inside me.

"It is," he echoed, from somewhere much closer to me this time.

Following his voice, I found his tall figure standing in front of my bed. His strong, naked body awash with moonlight, the glossy mass of his hair streaked with shimmering silver, he could have been an ocean spirit—beautiful and fiercely powerful.

The sheet came loose around me, and I caught the edge of it at my chest.

"I want you, Angela," he stated simply.

The clear yearning in his voice resonated with everything inside me. My throat seemed to have closed in, and I swallowed hard, searching for the words to reply. Finding none, I let go of the sheet, allowing it to slide down my naked body and pool on the bed below me.

He heaved a sigh, and I floated through the air to him. The heat wave radiating from him enveloped me even as he halted my movement, with about a foot of space between us.

I felt the cool bedding under my knees and realized I was no longer in the air. Now I was kneeling on the edge of the mattress, almost eye level with Marcus.

His eyes glistened wildly in the shimmering glow surrounding us. Arms tensed at his sides, his hands fisted tight, he wouldn't touch me.

The need to feel him burned through me, though. I had to make sure he was really physically here again after the torturously long days of absence. I reached for him, to cup his face, and immediately jerked my hand away with a hiss.

"You're burning," I gasped.

"I know." He exhaled—the hot air hit my face like a blast from an opened furnace. "I need you." The rough, scratchy half-whisper, I realized, must have been the only way he could talk at the moment.

His skin appeared papery dry. On the contrary, his hairline must have been soaked with sweat—the long, slick strands of his hair plastered his temples and forehead.

The wild glint in his dark eyes now seemed feverish and definitely unhealthy.

"Marcus, honey, you're not well." I shuffled closer on my knees,
the haze of desire rapidly evaporating under the heavy weight of worry for him.

I lifted my hand to his forehead. He stiffened as my skin came in
contact with his, but didn't move away.

"Careful," he whispered, and I knew the warning was for my benefit not his.

I splayed my hand on his forehead, this time forcing myself to
keep it there long enough to assess his temperature more accurately.

He was frighteningly hot, his skin almost unbearable to touch. I
would've never thought a human body could withstand this type of
fever. A chilly feeling of dread crept up my spine.

"You need to go to the hospital, Marcus." My voice came out hollow, matching the void inside me, which was quickly filling with fear.
"I'll call a taxi."

I made the move to get off the bed, but Marcus grabbed my
hand, keeping me in place.

"No."

"You know what, forget the taxi." I met his feverish gaze. "You
need an ambulance."

He shook his head then suddenly staggered forward, propping
his weight with a knee against the mattress. His head dropped to his
chest. The groan vibrating deep in his throat tore out as a tortured
cry in a voice I could barely recognize as his.

With his focus shifting, the moonlight glow in the room receded
then melted to nothing. Disappeared.

Crashing onto the bed, Marcus rolled to his side and curled into
himself. The next moment, he stretched head to toe, his back arched,
and every muscle in his body seemed to solidify to the hardness of

stone. Veins bulged on his forehead and along his neck, running in thick ropes under his pale skin.

"Marcus?" Fighting the all-consuming fear—not *of* him, but *for* him—I crawled on my knees closer and took his head between my hands. He let out another growl of pain, while I tried to keep his head steady for him as much as I could.

Terror seized my heart at the sight of sweat that beaded on his forehead only to immediately evaporate in small streams of steam.

How was it even possible?

"Marcus," I whispered. "What's happening to you?"

He could only groan in response, his body twisted into the grotesque arch.

I tried to think frantically through the wall of rising panic. What was one supposed to do when someone was having a seizure? Even under the best of circumstances, my medical expertise didn't reach far beyond the correct technique of applying a Band-Aid on a scraped knee.

"I'm calling 911." I made the decision and reached for my cellphone on the night table with a shaking hand.

"No!" He groaned again and yanked me back with the strength enough to make me lose my balance. I swayed towards him and crashed on his chest. It felt rock hard—with every muscle stretched tight under his skin.

"Stay with me," he breathed out, and the planes of his muscles relaxed beneath me. The seizure seemed to have passed just as suddenly as it began.

"Touch me," he panted. "Before it starts again."

He brushed my hair back from my forehead.

"You're so beautiful, Angela," he said in a coarse whisper. Hand at the back of my neck, he pulled me down to him then caught my mouth with his in an unexpected kiss.

The almost unbearable heat of his mouth seemed to have melted my worry away the moment his lips parted mine and Marcus slipped his tongue in. Sparks of desire ignited through me, the way they always did when he kissed me.

With a scorching hot groan into my mouth, he rolled us over, turning me on my back, the cloud of intense heat shrouded us both. The heat seemed to have seeped through me, relaxing my muscles, making my limbs hot and heavy. At the same time as sharp arrows of need shot through my chest to my belly.

Without breaking the kiss, Marcus slid his hand between us and palmed my breast, rolling the nipple in his fingers. Pressure throbbed between my legs in response. My hips jerked instinctively, and I let out a moan.

"Just like that . . ." Marcus murmured, letting go of my mouth and trailing burning hot kisses along the side of my neck to my collarbone.

The physical heat from the contact with his skin made every nerve in my body come to life—stirring and invigorating.

But the concern about the sound of his voice reached me through the hazy lust.

Marcus was unwell, without a doubt. For whatever reason, he was ignoring his own wellbeing in favour of . . . making love to me.

"Marcus, darling." Shifting to the side, I lifted his head with my hands, forcing him to meet my eyes. "You are very sick, honey," I spoke slowly, articulating every word, just in case he already was suffering from some fever-induced hallucinations that might have impeded his comprehension. Why else would he continue kissing me when he was obviously in pain and in dire need of antibiotics? "We have to get you help."

"You *are* my help," he insisted.

I strained my memory, digging through everything I knew about fighting a fever.

"Can I at least run you a cold bath then, please?" I begged. "To bring your temperature down?" I made a move towards the bathroom in hope that he would follow me.

His words stopped me. "Bath won't help. Water evaporates. I've tried."

I froze at his words.

Was that true? Or did he really get delusional from the fever?

Both thoughts seemed equally terrifying.

He must have read the horror on my face.

"No, Angela. Please. Don't be scared. You're *fearless*. Please don't be afraid of me."

"I'm scared *for* you, Marcus. You don't look very good, honey. Please let me help you somehow. Tell me what I can do."

Placing his hands on my shoulders, he lowered me back to the mattress.

"You can do everything," he murmured, his eyes the colour of deep indigo in the darkness of the night. "You can make it all go away. All you need to do is let me give you pleasure. And don't take your hands off me. That's all."

Worried, I couldn't stop staring at his ashen face. He dipped his head to my ear.

"Close your eyes," he whispered softly. "Don't think, just feel."

I obeyed by lowering my eyelids. However, the *not-thinking* part was much harder to follow.

His hand touched my breast, kneading it gently. The heat of his mouth skirted my nipple, making my thighs tremble from anticipation. Slowly, he circled the tip of my breast with his tongue then sucked the nipple in.

Arching my back, I let out a small cry from the shock of the intense heat. When he released my nipple, however, the sensation of the cool air against it flared the need between my legs.

I exhaled sharply, rocking my core against his lower stomach.

"That's it," he breathed into my skin, trailing kisses down to my belly button—the flickering of his tongue, like licks of liquid fire along my body. "This is perfect."

"You will need a doctor . . ." I whispered, in the last attempt to bring us both to our senses, even as I was stretching, arching in the hot languid waves that rolled through me under his fiery touch.

"I need *you*," he replied between the kisses. "Only you. Don't fight this." The heat of his tongue trailed down my inner thigh, nearing the most sensitive part of my body. "You are like a breath of fresh air." He slid both hands down my hips, leaving the sensation of molten lava in their wake. "A cool breeze to my fire."

"Ice queen." I huffed a brief laugh that turned to a moan when he pushed my knees apart.

"*My* queen," he corrected before diving in between my thighs.

I screamed from the almost unbearable heat of his tongue sliding along my sensitive flesh. Pressing my backside into the mattress, I jerked away from his touch, just like one would from a hot stove.

Marcus gripped my hips, keeping me in place. He stilled for a second, letting me adjust to the heat and then began to glide the tip of his tongue in slow little circles.

Soon, I could no longer tell if the waves of the intense heat that consumed me were coming from his tongue or from inside me.

"Oh, it's good . . ." I whimpered.

Just like that, he made me forget about everything around us. Nothing mattered anymore, only that tiny little petal of fire that was beginning to grow inside of me under the magical sliding of his tongue.

Slowly, he fanned the spark into a raging inferno until the powerful waves of concentrated heat exploded through me with the force of an erupting volcano.

Through the fog of the rushing orgasm, I felt his hand search for mine and I grabbed it, holding tight as the scorching waves of pleasure rocked through me.

My eyes still closed, I tried to catch my breath. My body felt as if it had melted into a puddle. Marcus slid up to me, and I pressed the side of my face to his temple.

Was it just an illusion or he really didn't feel as hot anymore?

My eyes snapped open at the thought, and I caught Marcus gaze at me. He shifted to my side, propping himself with an elbow.

"Are you . . .?" I cupped his face. His skin felt warmer than usual but no longer near as scorching hot as before. "Are you really feeling better?"

"Much better." He smiled at me brightly.

The unhealthy shine in his eyes had been replaced by a happy glimmer.

"How?" I whispered bewildered. "What was that?"

"I don't know." He shrugged, covering my hand with his. "Energy? Magic? One thing is certain, it needs to be released regularly either through me giving a show in public, to share it with as many people as possible, or . . . through having sex. I was hoping to make it until the show tomorrow night—"

"But it hurt you."

"It burned," he agreed.

"It was terrible to watch. I could only imagine . . ." I shuddered, the image of his body being twisted in agony rose in my mind.

"Don't." Marcus moved a strand of my hair behind my ear. "Don't imagine it. I'm fine now. Thanks to you."

"How?" I repeated, trying to wrap my head around all of this.

"When you touch me, it's like a blast of minty-cool air. It calms the fire under my skin. I noticed it the first time when you held my hand in the limo the night I took you home, then again every time we kissed. It has to be a certain type of touch, though."

"Like what?"

"Well." His mouth curved in a grin. "Let's say the friendly, platonic type wouldn't do it."

"So, like this then?" I lifted my hand and traced the well-defined edge of his pectoral with the tips of my fingers. My thumb brushed by his nipple, and his breath hitched.

"Just like that." He stilled.

I moved my hand lower, exploring the hard ridges of his six-pack. His muscles under my fingers rippled and flexed.

"This makes the fire go away?" I murmured, thrilled to finally have the chance to explore his body, with no clothes in our way.

"There is a side effect, though." The dry rasp was gone from his voice, replaced by a deep sexy rumble. "This kind of touch makes another type of fire build up elsewhere."

"So." I slowly traced the thin trail of ink-black hair from his navel down his lower belly. "The trick is then to keep them in balance. To cool off one, without igniting the other one."

"Yeah. Except . . ." he cleared his throat, "you make it . . . *harder*."

I glanced down the length of his torso to find him fully erect—thick and long, and pointing my way.

"I can see that." I licked my lips and continued sliding my finger downwards, all the way to the raven-black curls in his groin.

"Much harder." He exhaled sharply and grabbed my wrist, putting a stop to my exploration.

I snapped my gaze to his, surprised by his sudden gesture that felt too much like rejection. The sudden concern that I might have done something wrong dulled my mood.

"That's a good thing. Isn't it?" I asked tentatively.

"It is." Marcus lifted my hand for a kiss in the middle of my palm. The warmth in his eyes on me didn't cool, and the smile on his face remained bright. However, he kept hold of my hand, lest it stray south again, I guessed. "But I find this better." He moved his hand down the side of my body, along the curve of my hip and then around to my backside. "And this." He squeezed my ass, yanking my hips closer to his. "This right here." He kissed my lips. "Is the best." He placed another kiss on the side of my neck.

"Marcus . . ." I whispered, melting into him all over again.

"It's impossible to stay away from you." He kissed down the valley between my breasts. "Now that you're in my life, I don't know how I've ever been without you. I need you like the air I breathe."

He hooked his arm under my knee and lifted my leg over his hip. I felt his hardness press against my thigh and flexed my leg around him to bring us closer.

"There's no need to stay away from me," I whispered. "I need you, too, Marcus. More than anything."

He groaned and rocked his hips against me. "Condom?"

"What?" With my focus on his mouth at my breast and on his hand sliding between my legs, any logical thought proved difficult already.

"Do you have a condom?" Marcus rasped, letting go of my nipple for a second. "Or should I get some from my hotel?"

"Oh. Yeah." I rummaged blindly in my nightstand drawer, fishing out one of the few condoms left from the time of my relationship with Matt.

God, it's been so long since I had a man in my bed.

"Here you go." I handed it to Marcus.

He rose to his knees over me. His gaze dark and heavy as he rolled the condom on and fisted his thick dick, sliding his hand up and down its length.

His chest heaved with heavy breaths. The coal-black mane draped over his wide shoulders. His eyes flashed wild from behind the few tresses hanging over his face.

Unable to break our eye contact, I lay before him, my legs open wide, the need for him pulsing hot between my thighs.

"Come here." He covered my body with his. "I need to be inside you even if it kills me."

I felt his tip at my entrance and bucked my hips, meeting his thrust and taking him all in. "Oh God, yes."

Pleasure spread inside me like melting butter, teasing me with promise for more.

I writhed under him, entreating him to move. Harder. Faster. But he pressed his hips down, pinning me in place and held still, his forehead at my shoulder.

"I can't," he exhaled with a pained groan. "With you. Right now. I won't last a second."

"It's okay." I nuzzled his ear impatiently. "Let it go, Marcus."

His shoulders stiffened under my hands. His body trembled with an obvious effort to control himself. I couldn't understand why he would restrain himself like that.

"It's all good, honey," I slid my hands up and down his back, willing his muscles to relax.

He lifted his head and met my gaze.

"You mean so much to me, Angela. So, so much." His eyes fixed on mine with alarming intensity. "I don't ever want to be without you."

"You don't ever have to, Marcus. I'm right here." I patted his cheek and traced one thick eyebrow with my thumb. His expression was too severe, as if some profound emotions were churning inside him. "What is it, Marcus? What is bothering you?"

He blinked and looked away.

"Nothing." He kissed my nose, my forehead, my cheekbones. "You're right. You're here. It's all that matters."

His arms circled around me, he rolled us over as he continued to pepper my skin with warm kisses—inch by inch—ripping to pieces any defences I had ever built around my heart—layer by layer.

At some point, I didn't notice exactly when, he slipped out of me. His hand took the place of his erection between my thighs, and his deft fingers expertly worked my body inside and out, reaping orgasm after orgasm from me in a seemingly endless, blissful torment.

Chapter 25

I WOKE UP TO THE BLARING noise of the heavy metal song I used for my alarm. My eyes still closed, I patted the top of my night-stand in search of the phone then turned the damn thing off.

Somebody's leg was draped across my hip.

Marcus.

He'd stayed the night.

The realization of having him next to me slowly trickled though to my half-awake brain, bringing a warming sensation to my chest.

I opened my eyes, loving the sight of him in my bed, his long body stretched under my covers, the black mass of his hair spread over my pillow, as if he truly belonged here.

'One more minute,' I decided, snuggling back in, closer to him.

"Coffee?" he mumbled groggily in my hair a moment later, his arm coming around my middle to draw me closer.

"Shh. You sleep. I'll make some." I moved to get up.

"Why would you *make* it if I can just *make it happen*?" He opened one eye and peered at me through the dark curtain of tangled hair in front of his face.

"I thought you might want to sleep in this morning." I sat up and moved the hair away from his face. "If you do get up, I'll need to spend at least an hour to properly brush this mess on your head."

His eyes flickered to my nightstand briefly, and a delicious smell of fresh coffee filled the room.

"Thank you." I picked up the paper cup from the nightstand and took a sip. "Mmm. So good. You know," I added as a random thought entered my mind. "I don't understand how you don't weigh like a thousand pounds by now. If you don't even need to get up to make a coffee, what stops you from sitting on the couch, *making things happen* for yourself, doing absolutely nothing?"

"When your magic can do everything for you, it's the things that you can do on your own that become important," he replied quickly, making me think he'd already answered this question to himself. "Sure, I could teleport anywhere, but it's often more enjoyable just to walk down the street in the traditional way, by putting one foot in front of the other. Magic or not, anyone can make coffee at home, cheaper and faster than going out, right? Why are there still so many coffee shops then?"

Without waiting for my answer to his obviously rhetorical question, he stretched in bed one last time then got up. "Well, I'm not sleepy any more. I think I'll take you up on your offer to brush my hair."

He lifted his arm and the second cup floated from the nightstand into his hand.

"It wasn't an offer. It was a threat!" I laughed, jumping out of bed, too.

Something crinkled under my foot, and I picked up the ripped condom wrapper. My eyes then went to Lannister, who entered the room at that moment.

"Oh, my poor cat," I gasped, covering my mouth with my hand, at the sight of the used condom stuck to the fur on the side of my pet. "This must constitute animal abuse somewhere."

Reaching for the cat, I managed to snatch the condom as he ducked under my hand and bee-lined straight to Marcus's ankles.

"What a night of debauchery took place in your bedroom, Miss McAllister." With a teasing smile, Marcus bent over to scratch behind Lannister's ears.

"How did it even get there?"

"He slept with us."

"He did what?" I couldn't believe my ears. I had no idea where Lannister usually slept at night. It was definitely not in the pet bed I had for him and most certainly not anywhere near my bedroom—until last night, it seemed.

"He came in earlier this morning and slept on top of our feet," Marcus explained. "Purred pretty loud, too."

He glanced at the condom in my hand and reached for it across the bed. "I'll get rid of it. Sorry, no clue how I could've forgotten about it last night."

"Well, you were rather busy," I smiled. "It's fine. I'll do it."

The bathroom was right behind me. Smiling and shaking my head, I went there to get rid of the condom along with the foil wrapper. As I tossed them both in the bin, it didn't escape my attention that the condom was empty.

Apparently, during our *night of debauchery*, the pleasure was all mine.

———◉———

SINCE THAT NIGHT, MARCUS no longer bothered to wait for me in the kitchen. Whenever he showed up, he would just climb into bed with me.

More often than not, he would come over right after his last show in Vegas. He'd slip under the covers behind me quietly and hold me close.

Before long, I found myself waking up through the night, waiting for the feeling of his warm chest at my back. Only then was I able to get an uninterrupted sleep, once he was with me.

Despite him always wearing underwear to bed, I didn't change my habit of sleeping in the nude. Through his boxers, I often felt his excitement pressed hard against my back or my thigh, but he usually didn't go any further than giving me a few hugs and some gentle kisses. For the most part, he just let me sleep until my alarm went off in the morning.

Whenever we did get more intimate than just kissing, it was always all about me. Since that first night, he'd never even attempted to enter me again and skillfully evaded my tentative questions when I tried to figure out why.

If I attempted to return the favour after yet another mind-blowing orgasm he'd given me with his fingers or his mouth, he would grab my hand reaching for him or lift my face heading for his lap and then switch all attention back to me once again.

For now, I tried to convince myself not to worry and to enjoy his affection instead. He was a selfless lover, every girl's dream—there was nothing to complain about.

Chapter 26

ONE NIGHT IN EARLY December, I woke up from a deep sleep, struggling to figure out what made me awake. Marcus was not there yet, and I couldn't remember having any dreams.

Then I heard it—a scream, followed by a loud argument from outside my bedroom window. It seemed to be coming from the visitors' parking lot next to my building.

Wrapping the bed sheet around me, I got out of bed and padded to the window. I kept it ajar for the night to cool my bedroom, which often got too hot due to the excessive central heating in my building and due to Marcus's often over-heated body whenever he was next to me.

A slim blonde woman—young, probably in her late teens or early twenties—was cornered by two men in the empty lot.

"Get your hands off me! You assholes!" The girl shrieked in a high-pitched voice, loud enough to reach my place, seven floors from the ground.

In our early days of living in this apartment, Emily and I witnessed a number of fights in and around the building. We even had to call the police a few times. However, as the neighbourhood became the new up-and-coming area and developers showed interest in it, many rundown places had been repaired, rebuilt or demolished. Midnight arguments and fistfights had become the things of the past.

Was the girl one of the still remaining prostitutes in the area? Were the men fighting over a deal gone bad?

She wore high leather boots with spiky heels, and her short skirt barely covered her panties. However, something about the girl didn't fit with what I knew about women of the world's oldest profession. She lacked confidence in the situation and seemed scared and out of place in the parking lot at night.

In any case, it quickly become obvious, the two men weren't fighting each other—they were both attacking her.

The guys were visibly drunk, unsteady on their feet. Their movements clumsy and uncoordinated when they tried to grope her. The girl also appeared inebriated as she swung her purse at them and swatted their hands away, balancing shakily on her super-high heels.

I cursed under my breath and took a step back, with a full intention to call the police. My back hit a rock-hard wall of muscle, and I jumped in surprise.

"Marcus!" I exhaled with relief.

"Did I scare you?" he wrapped his arms around my waist.

"You know," I held my hand to my chest, trying to calm my racing heart, "I'm going to get you a collar with a little bell, like Lannister's, so I'd get some warning when you show up."

"Mmmm," he murmured into my hair. "If it's a black leather collar, and if you get a matching one for yourself, I might actually consider wearing it. It has possibilities—"

Another high-pitched scream came from the window, and I twisted out of his arms.

"I need to call the police, now."

"What's going on?" Marcus stepped to the window, taking in the scene below.

I already had the cell phone in my hand when he stopped me by grabbing my wrist.

"It will take them some time to get here," he said calmly, all playfulness completely gone from his tone.

"Marcus," I cautioned, attempting to be his voice of reason. "You can't intervene without revealing who you are."

"I know."

He kept his eyes on the girl as she got caught around her middle by one of her attackers, her arms pressed to her body. The second thug had ripped her jacket open and seemed to be trying to tear the front of her dress apart, except that he kept losing grip on it over and over again.

With her arms immobilized, the girl kicked her feet out randomly but had yet to hit any target.

Suddenly, her leg jerked, and she stepped down on the foot of the guy holding her, firmly planting the spiky heel of her boot through the front of his running shoe.

"Argh! You bitch!" howled the injured guy, loud enough for me to hear, and bent over in pain, letting the girl go. She stumbled away a couple of paces, blankly staring at the screaming man.

The second drunk used the moment to advance on her. Seemingly without paying attention, the girl swung her arm out, unsteadily. The tiny purse in her hand hit the attacker square in the jaw. Incredibly, the impact of the blow tossed him through the air. With a loud grunt, he hit the pavement several feet away from her.

"What the fuck!" he yelled, rolling onto his stomach. After several attempts to rise to his feet, he only managed to get on all fours.

The girl moved her bewildered stare from him to her purse then back to him again.

A small white car zoomed into the parking lot at full speed at that moment.

"Leave her alone! You scum!" A loud girlish voice rang high with emotion over the sound of screeching tires.

"You're a fucking bitch!" In a rage, the first drunk ignored the car and the fact that his white running shoe was now completely soaked with blood from the wound inflicted by the blonde. He lurched towards her again.

The door of the car swung open and another young girl, dressed in grey sweatshirt and a pair of loose pajama pants, leaped out of the driver's seat. Her strawberry blonde ponytail was swinging in the air menacingly as she ran towards the fight with the daring determination of a Chihuahua ready to attack an elephant.

"Leave her alone, I said! Get in the car, Ava!" she yelled, coming closer.

With her eyes open wide, the blonde girl—Ava—swung her tiny purse at the drunk attacking her in a half-hearted attempt to protect herself. The purse connected with the side of his head, throwing him into the bushes all the way on the edge of the parking lot.

"Holy cow, woman!" The girl with the ponytail reached Ava and grabbed her by the arm. "You'll teach me that one later. Now get in the car, and let's get out of here." She pulled her friend towards the white vehicle, chastising her all the way. "Why didn't you call me earlier? Before you left that shithole? Why would you ever go there in the first place?" She stuffed the bewildered Ava into the passenger's seat and buckled her seatbelt. "Never again, you hear me? Never again!" was the last she said before getting into the driver's seat herself and driving away.

One of the drunks finally managed to get up to his feet and stood in the parking lot alone, watching the white car disappear around the corner. The other one was still groaning loudly in the bushes somewhere.

"They'll be fine." I heard Marcus's voice just above my ear.

"You did that!" I turned to face him.

He hesitated for a second then replied with a shrug. "She obviously needed help. There was no time to wait for the police."

"I thought you couldn't manipulate human bodies. How did you use her limbs?"

"I didn't. I used her boot and her purse there."

"Look at you." Not hiding my admiration, I linked my hands behind his neck. "A sexy Vegas star by day and a crime-fighting Superman by night."

"Hardly a Superman." He scoffed and tipped his chin towards the window. "She did most of the work herself. Didn't you see?"

"You gave her strength."

"And a better aim." He chuckled. "Anyway, with a friend like that, she has a lot going for her."

My fingers at his nape, I touched the small silver chain that I'd seen him wear around his neck often. With the tip of my finger, I traced the chain to the neckline of his t-shirt and then to the middle of his chest where I felt the elongated shape of the pendant hidden under the material of the shirt.

"Does it mean something to you?" I asked finally. Some secrets he guarded more closely than others, and I could never be absolutely sure which questions he would answer.

"Maybe." He covered my hand over the pendant with his then moved them both away. "You can still get a few hours of sleep tonight. Let me take you to bed right now."

Chapter 27

SITTING AT THE TABLE, with a cup of coffee in my hands, I thought about the fight last night and about Marcus's involvement in it.

He was in the shower at the moment, allowing me to contemplate it all in peace.

As far as I understood it, his power was limitless. I called him Superman, but really, his abilities exceeded any superhero powers I knew of. His only kryptonite seemed to be his own fear to use them more.

In the movies, the best that superheroes did for humankind was prevent global disasters. Otherwise, they mostly used their abilities to fight supervillains, causing a lot of destruction along the way.

What if this could be reversed, and the special powers could be used to help deal with the consequences of the disasters that had already happened? So much suffering occurred in the world every single day. Couldn't some of Marcus's magic be used to stop the pain or at least to help with the damages?

When Marcus came out of the shower, shirtless, the black mass of his wet hair over the white towel on his shoulders, I asked if he ever thought about helping humankind on global level.

"I did." He took a cup of coffee for himself.

"And?" I asked eagerly.

"Here is the thing, Angela." He drummed his thumb against the side of the cup. "Sometimes, the more you try to fix something, the more damage you cause."

I mulled his words over in my head.

"Well, I can see this happening with big, complicated things, maybe. But what if you try to do something very straightforward?" I grabbed my laptop, opening the news page in the browser. "Here, for example. There was a flood in this region of Africa—" He inhaled, and I continued hurriedly before he could protest. "I know you avoid controlling the weather, but the flood had already happened. Now because of it, there is a disease outbreak. See, there is a very specific problem—they're short on medication. Can you make it so that they have enough?"

All it'd take for him was just one thought—and the hospital would have enough medicine to treat everyone. Right?

He rubbed the back of his neck.

"I don't want to conjure medicine."

"I know. The balance of matter—"

"It's not just that. If I get the formula wrong, people may end up dying, I wouldn't be able to fix that."

"Okay, don't conjure it." I did a few more searches on the laptop. "See, this medicine is actually produced in the United States. Can you teleport a pallet from their warehouse to the hospital in Africa?"

Marcus set the cup on the table and leaned back in his chair.

"Technically, yes."

"Great!"

"In reality, however, I can tell you exactly what would happen if I did that."

"What?" All I could see was a win-win solution here.

His gaze flickered to the computer screen briefly.

"Alright." He cleared his throat. "The medicine I'd teleport would be most likely destroyed on the spot."

"Why?"

"With the violent military conflict in the region and the high terrorist activity," he pointed at the article, "the staff wouldn't take the risk to use the medicine from an unknown source. Unable to trace it, chances are, they'd suspect it having been tainted and destroy it out of pre-caution."

"How do you know that?" The lines around his mouth hardened, and I gasped in sudden understanding. "You've done these type of things before?"

"Exactly." He nodded. "More times than I care to count."

"All with the same result?"

"Or worse." He sighed. "Once I had a disaster relief shipment stolen by a staff member, who then sold it for a huge profit to a corrupt organization I had no intentions of supporting. Another time, I erected a school building in a village overnight, only to have villagers condemn the whole place as possessed by evil spirits and burn their own homes to the ground before moving to live elsewhere."

"But couldn't it then—"

"There are more consequences than one. Always. If I take the medicine from the warehouse around here." He tipped his chin at the laptop screen. "Someone might be held responsible for the missing product. Even if I leave money for it, there would be shortages in the market for which the medicine was meant to be. As a result, people may lose their jobs, health, and even lives."

"Really . . ." My heart sank with disappointment, although I should've been able to predict this outcome—I knew Marcus had a kind heart. He supported a large number of charities. Had there been a better way to do good in the world, he would have found it by now.

"There's just no way to account for every single consequence in advance," he said softly. "There is a balance in the world, Angela, in nature and in society. It took thousands . . . millions of years to get established. No matter how strong my magic is, I am still but a man, and no man can ever know exactly how everything works in the universe. After the years of having tried and failed to solve the world's problems, I realized that the most responsible thing I could do for the humanity was to keep my magic under control."

"This is rather disheartening." I resigned with a heavy weight inside my chest. Despite my understanding of what he was saying, I couldn't help the feeling of helplessness and regret. "There is really nothing we could do without making it worse?"

Marcus reached over the table and took my hand in his.

"There is plenty anyone can do, but it works best if you do it respecting the established order of things." He produced his cell phone from the back pocket of his jeans and punched the screen while glancing at the article on the laptop screen a few times.

"Here you go." He showed me his phone with his bank's confirmation on it.

"You've just made a donation?"

"Yeah." He continued to type something into the phone. "But because I have the financial means to do more, I've just contacted the head of the charity organization responsible for the relief effort in the region." He glanced up from the screen. "As soon as the new shipment of medicine is ready to go, I'll pay for the charter to get it there within a day."

I sagged against the back of my chair.

"I'm sorry I didn't mean for my idea to cost you money."

"No big deal." He tipped his head, a smile bounced in the midnight-blue of his eyes. "Simon may still have some room for a tax write-off for me this year."

"So, if even you, with all your magic, can't solve the world's problems . . ." I gestured at the laptop screen with the news articles of today's disasters, large and small, displayed on it, "then who can?"

"Everyone." He leaned forward. "Angela, that's the best part. Everyone can do something to make this world a better place. After trying and failing so many times, I've found that small, specific problems are actually solvable. Things that everyone can do every day. If you know a hungry kid—feed him. If you see a person in need—help them. Often, you don't even need any magic or money to make the biggest difference."

He got up and came to my side.

"Come here." He wrapped his arm around my shoulders and kissed my temple. "You feel so much for others."

"That's not what I've heard," I protested. "I have a thick skin, I've been told. I'm not even a good listener as far as people's problems are concerned."

"It's because you feel the need to jump into action right away and solve all their problems as soon as you hear about them," he argued, with a conviction that surprised me as much as his words did. "You have your own way of caring, my ice queen. It may not always be with kind words and warm hugs. Yours is the way of action. You take problems of others to heart and try to solve them as if they were your own."

All this time that we'd spent together, it wasn't just me getting to know Marcus. It seemed he had learned many things about me, too, some of which I didn't even know myself.

Chapter 28

"OH MY GOD, BABY. HOW much bad luck can our family take? It doesn't stop!" My mom had always been an emotional person, but this time she seemed to be exceptionally dramatic.

"Calm down, Mom. It's not the end of the world. We'll get through it. We always have."

I stood in the stairwell of my office building, holding my cell phone to my ear. As soon as I had heard her tearful announcement that Evan had lost his job once again, I knew I shouldn't continue this phone conversation in my cubicle if I didn't want to attract unnecessary attention of my coworkers.

"It's not so bad, Mom." I kept my voice low, despite being out of earshot of everyone. "Evan will find something again. He's getting better—his last job lasted for over a year."

"They said they don't need him anymore." She either didn't hear me or simply couldn't process my replies at the moment. "He was working on a contract, as self-employed. So he is not even going to get any unemployment benefits now." She sobbed. "And Lily . . . Lily told him to start looking for a job right away, but he doesn't want to work as a stagehand again. She will break up with him!"

"Mom. She won't." I spoke in a calm, soothing tone, as if talking to a skittish animal in distress. "They'll be okay."

"You know how smart and ambitious that girl is." Mom wouldn't stop. "I honestly don't know what she sees in your brother. She will leave him now for sure . . . And then what will he do?"

"Mom, I'm sure Evan will be fine with or without Lily. But I don't think she would dump him over a job. She loves him, and he loves her, too. They will figure it out."

"I don't know, Angela. It's just too much. I can't take it anymore, it doesn't end. One thing after another. First Evan, then your dad's health, and now the house ..." Her voice cracked, and I realized that this was the first time she ever so much as alluded at their financial problems to me over the phone. Usually, she shared her fears of losing the house only in her monthly emails to me.

"It will all work out, Mom," I assured her, without having any clue if it actually would but determined to make it happen somehow.

"We can't afford another rehab, Angela," she said in a small voice that made me feel like hugging her and promising I would take care of everything. Only it would be an empty promise, one I couldn't keep. I didn't know what more I could do to help them. There were only so many hours in the day and only so many jobs I could work.

"The bank wouldn't re-mortgage our house again so soon. I asked." Mom sobbed again.

"You did? Evan is not using, Mom. He doesn't need another rehab right now. Why would you even think about it?"

"Well, you know, it doesn't hurt to ask. We always have expenses ... Money is tight."

"You don't re-mortgage your home to pay for your everyday expenses. Even I know that, and I don't own a house."

And with the way the things are going, I never will.

"Angela, I didn't call to argue with you," she said more firmly.

"I wasn't arguing, either. Didn't even raise my voice."

"See, you're arguing. You are arguing with me right now," she said in her no-nonsense mom's voice. "I just called you to ask if you could come by the house once or twice next week. Dad and I are going to Cuba for a week, and we need somebody to pick up mail and shovel the snow off the driveway if needed. Evan obviously has to worry about other things, so I can't ask him."

"You're going to Cuba? Around Christmas time? Can you afford it?" I knew she hated to talk about money, but somebody had to ask her these questions, since she obviously didn't ask them herself before booking the trip.

"Angela, your father and I deserve a break," Mom said with conviction. "Now more than ever. Don't you think?"

"It's not about whether you deserve it, Mom. It's about whether you can afford it." Talking to her was becoming excruciatingly frustrating.

"Your father could use some rest," she replied quickly. "And I just can't deal with all these problems here. We need to get away for a while. Our health and wellbeing are more important than anything and worth any money. You know Dad's blood pressure is not doing well. They may put him on a stronger medication soon. He wouldn't be able to get a travel insurance for at least half a year after that. If we don't go now, we may not be able to have a vacation for another six months."

"I haven't been on a vacation for the past two years." In fact, I worked in the store on all of the days off I got at the office last year, and I was planning to do the same with whatever vacation time I had left this year.

"You went to New York and to Las Vegas," Mom reminded. "And it's wonderful, Angela. You really should travel more. You are in the perfect stage of life for it."

"I don't have any money to spend on travelling," I confessed, breaking the taboo of not talking about my personal finances with my family.

"Well, money is always an issue for everyone, and it always will be." Mom sounded rather philosophical right now. "It doesn't mean that you should stop living your life because of it. You're young, you work hard, you deserve a vacation, and you should have one, too."

Sometimes, it felt like I was talking to an alien being from another planet, not to someone I'd known all my life. I loved my mom dearly, but it often seemed impossible to follow her logic. It was as if we had two different conversations going on at the same time—each of us talking about her own thing, without hearing what the other one was saying at all.

I stood in the stairwell long after I had said goodbye to my mother, my cellphone squeezed tight in my hand.

The news of the Cuba trip left an unpleasant aftertaste in my mouth and an uncomfortable, scratchy feeling inside.

When sending money to my parents, I didn't expect a detailed report on how it was spent, simply assuming it went towards paying down their debt. I hoped I had been helping them to dig themselves out of a hole. It gave me a purpose with an end goal in sight.

Surely, they wouldn't go on a vacation if they really couldn't afford it, would they? Maybe, their situation was not as bad as I had assumed.

But then, why didn't my parents let me know that my help was no longer required? Why would my mother continue sending me emails, asking for help?

True, I'd never complained. It appeared my silence didn't do me any favours. If I wanted to know for sure what was going on, I had to overcome my family's aversion to money matter discussions and somehow make sure that we had a conversation about it.

If my parents really didn't need my help any more, maybe I could reduce the hours I worked at the store or even quit my part-time job altogether.

The possibility of having my nights and weekends free soon ignited a spark of excitement in me. Among all the things I could do with the extra time, spending some more of it with Marcus came up on top.

I imagined having a day when neither of us had to watch the clock, when we could relax and just enjoy each other, and promised myself to talk to my parents as soon as I could, whenever they were back from their vacation.

Chapter 29

I DIDN'T MAKE IT TO my parents' house until Saturday morning to pick up the mail and to shovel the snow. My shift at the store wasn't starting until the afternoon that day. Marcus appeared at my apartment around nine in the morning and volunteered to go to my parents' house with me.

His offer made me happy in more ways than one. As much as I enjoyed his company, I also appreciated saving the time and money by teleporting with him instead of taking the bus. Having a magical boyfriend had a lot of practical benefits.

Despite it being December, we hardly had any snow yet. Whatever fell over night on my parents' driveway had almost melted already. By the time I got the shovel from the garage to clear the rest of it off, Marcus had gotten rid of every single snowflake for me already.

"Why did I even bother?" I laughed, gesturing with the shovel at the perfectly clean driveway.

"Really, why did you?" He grinned, taking the shovel from me and making it disappear back into the garage.

"This was supposed to be my only exercise for the week."

"You get enough exercise, running up and down the ladders in the store." He came closer and wrapped his arms around me. "Besides." He cupped my backside through my winter coat. "I couldn't risk you losing this."

"Oh, don't you worry." I giggled. "*This* is not going anywhere. Trust me, I've tried everything to get rid of it. My ass is here to stay."

"Good," he murmured, then covered my mouth with his in a most delicious kiss. "Are we done here? Can we go somewhere more private than your parents' driveway?" he whispered in my ear when we both came up for air.

"Just a minute." I tried to catch my breath and organize my thoughts that had been scattered by his kiss. "I need to get their mail."

"Done." He held up several envelopes and flyers that weren't in his hand just a moment ago. "Let's go. Your place or mine? To be honest, there are way too many coats between us for my liking right now. Winter clothes are irritating."

"Oh, stop complaining. It's not like you have to wear them often . . . " I glanced at the envelopes I had taken from him and went quiet.

There were about half a dozen of them, from different financial institutions and utility companies. All had a big red stamp with words *Overdue* or *Final Notice* on the front.

My parents were "taking a break" in Cuba—meanwhile it seemed like the power at their house was under the threat of being cut off for unpaid bills.

"Give me a minute, please." My heart pounded as I ran back into the house, leaving Marcus standing on the driveway.

The blue recycling box was in the laundry room, and I dropped to my knees in front of it rummaging through the old newspapers and last week's grocery flyers. Sure enough, there was a bunch of other envelopes with angry-red *Overdue* and *Final Notice* printed on them. All of them unopened.

This was the way my mom dealt with problems. She buried them in the trash and pretended they didn't exist.

I wondered if Dad knew about it, or if he preferred not to know anything.

Frozen in shock over the recycling box, with the envelopes in my hands, I didn't hear his footsteps and didn't realize that Marcus followed me into the house until I heard his voice behind me.

"Is this news for you?"

"What?" I had trouble processing anything at the moment.

"Did you know they were having money problems?" He sat on the floor next to me.

"Yes. Um . . . No. I mean I knew that they were struggling financially. A little. I just had no idea it was this bad."

"Your family doesn't talk about it?"

I shook my head.

"Do you think your mom wanted you to find out when she asked you to get the mail?"

I shook my head again.

"No. I don't think it even crossed her mind. She just ignores the problem. Obviously!" I tossed the envelopes back into the blue box. A hot flush of anger burned my cheeks now. "She must be thinking if she pretends it never happened, then it will eventually go away."

My shoulders slumped, a new emotion was rising in me—guilt. I should have known. Somehow, I'd missed the signs.

"How about your dad?" Marcus asked.

"Dad thinks that personal finance matters are boring and talking about money is vulgar—a sign of extremely bad manners. He lets Mom do whatever she wants because she "deserves" to have what she wants. The problem is that Mom always wants a little more than they can afford."

It was not his business. None of it concerned Marcus in any way. He didn't need to hear it, but I *needed* to finally be able to talk about this.

"It's not easy to spot. My parents don't make any extravagant purchases that would raise red flags. They simply live a little above their means every day. Mom goes shopping just a little too often. They take vacations one trip too many. We all get big Christmas gifts from them." I clasped my hands in my lap, unable to stop talking now. "My mom worked low-paying retail and clerical jobs all her life, most of them part-time. So there aren't any benefits or company pension from that, except for whatever comes from the government. My dad has a good pension from the teaching job he had, but it's not enough, obviously. They're going to lose the house. This is the house I grew up in . . ." I sensed my voice breaking and went quiet, afraid of having a full-on meltdown in front of Marcus.

"Is that why you need to work two jobs? Have you been giving them money?" His voice was hard. His questions felt invasive, uncomfortable but necessary, like a syringe with life-saving medicine inserted in my vein.

I nodded, keeping my gaze on my hands.

"It was supposed to be temporary," I whispered. "I offered to help when I finished school and got a full-time job. My brother went to rehab. My parents paid for it, but I felt like I needed to help, too. It was a family matter. It was supposed to be a shared responsibility . . . Now they rely on monthly checks from me to make ends meet."

"Is your brother helping, too?"

"I don't know. I don't think so."

"Then why do *you*?"

It was not idle curiosity on his part, I reminded myself. He cared about me. His concern was genuine. Still, my irritation rose at his questions because he was the one who finally made me bring it all to the surface.

"I don't know. Why do people do things they do? Because I'm the oldest, because I'm strong, because I have to be the responsible one."

"Your parents are twice your age and should know how to manage their own finances by now," he pointed out calmly.

"They're my family. *We* are a family. We're supposed to help each other out."

"Do they give you money, too?"

"They used to. When I was in school. When things were better for them."

"Is that why you're doing it now? You feel you have a debt to pay back? Or do you like to be the victim? You thrive on sacrifice?"

He just wouldn't stop.

"No! Of course not." I hardly ever thought about my reasons. Every time I sent money to my mom, I didn't think about *why*. For the past two years, my main focus was on *how*—how to come up with the money.

His stare burrowed into me, as if he were searching for an answer, urging me to explain.

"Why?" I yelled, unnerved by this intensity. "Because it's the right thing to do! Aren't we supposed to help our family and support our parents?"

"Yeah, when they're old and fragile and can't take care of themselves, not when they go away to Cuba at your expense—" he cut himself short, possibly realizing he had crossed the line.

I didn't reply.

Hot anger and resentment were rising inside me. I was angry with Evan and my parents for putting all of us in this situation. I was angry with Marcus for dragging it all out in the open and making me face it. But most of all, I was angry with myself for letting it go this far.

The absolute truth was that I liked the feeling of being needed, being the responsible daughter. I loved doing what I thought was right. It gave me a purpose, a common goal with my family. We were sharing the burden, going through tough times together.

Except that somewhere along the way it had changed, it wasn't *us* anymore. Now it was just me, shouldering it all alone. It wasn't temporary, either. And it wasn't going to get better unless I did something about it.

"Can I help?" Marcus asked unexpectedly, and I shrank from his words, as if he had physically struck me. It felt like my very soul shriveled and died.

Please don't offer me money. Don't make it worse.

"You are helping, Marcus." My voice came out strained and hollow. "You are the first person I ever talked to about it. Thank you for listening."

To my relief, he must have sensed how I felt and didn't push.

Instead, he took my hand from my lap and squeezed it gently in his. "It may be not my business, but sometimes it's hard to see the big picture if you're personally involved—the way you are right now. So I feel I should say it. What you're doing feels too much like enabling to me. Your parents have a problem. Or at least your mom clearly does." He tipped his chin at the red-marked envelopes. "You're not doing anyone any favours by supporting her spending habit. Would you give a bottle to an alcoholic?"

Deep inside, I knew he had a point.

"What can I do? I can't stop giving them money just like that—they'd go bankrupt." My chest felt tight. It hurt to breathe. "My dad's health is not great. Evan's problems gave them a lot of grief. I need to be strong for them. But I'm scared."

"You don't ever get scared, Angela. You're fearless." He drew me into a hug, the confidence in his voice shielding me from my own self-doubt, giving me the courage to open the deepest corners of my soul to him.

"Oh, I do get scared, Marcus. I'm just very good at hiding it, because more than anything in the world, I'm scared to be weak."

Chapter 30

WITH MY PARENTS AWAY on holidays, I called Evan asking him to meet me for lunch the next day. I'd figured the best way to get an accurate account of what was going on in his life was to talk to him myself.

He met me in a parkette near my office. I brought my sandwich, and he bought a hotdog from the food truck parked on the side of the street.

Brushing the light dusting of snow from a bench, we both sat down.

"Mom said you lost your job. Sorry I didn't call you earlier," I started.

"It kinda was a perfect timing. I was going to quit anyway." He shrugged.

"I know you were planning to look for something else."

I bit into my sandwich, watching him from the corner of my eye.

"Yep. I'd been thinking about changing it for a while. But you know how it is? You have a job—you get lazy. Now I have no choice but to find something." He took a huge bite of the hotdog in his hand.

I was relieved to discover Evan didn't seem to view his current situation as devastating as my mom had presented it. It was more like my brother, actually, to take everything in stride.

"What are you going to do now?" I asked.

"I want to work as a sound engineer one day." His voice lifted.

"That's what you studied for in college, isn't it?"

He nodded.

"I had a second interview for a sound technician position yesterday. They pretty much told me the job is mine. They just need a couple of days to check references and stuff." A happy grin lit up his face.

"Really? Evan, that's so great!" I hugged my sandwich to my chest, glad for him and for all of us for that matter.

"Yeah. It'd be cool," he agreed. "Money's much better, too. Oh, by the way, can you keep a secret?"

"Well, if you don't know by now—" I teased.

He didn't let me finish. "I'm saving for a ring for Lily."

"What?" A warm feeling of surprise, delight, and unexpected sadness filled me, all at once. "You're getting married?"

"Well, I'm gonna give her the ring and ask her to marry me. The rest is up to her."

"Wow! My baby brother is all grown up." I bit my lip, determined not to tear up. We both had grown up, Evan and I. We both had our own lives to live now. "I'm so happy for you."

"Not yet, butthead!" Even laughed, brushing the few snowflakes off his jeans. "She hasn't said yes yet."

"She will. Lily loves you, doesn't she?"

He nodded, the grin on his face getting bigger.

"She does. And I love her, too." His said firmly. "She's my rock. Lily has helped me so much and she believes in me, Angela, more than I believe in myself. Just her being there for me makes me feel like I could do anything. I want to be the best man I could be. For her. You know?"

Now, he sounded like he was about to tear up himself.

I put the rest of my sandwich into the plastic container on the bench next to me, and hugged my brother's shoulders. He didn't shrug my arms away as he normally would. Instead, his arms went around me, too, returning the hug.

"Lily doesn't always say the right thing, as you may know," he said, seemingly choosing his words with more care than usual. "But she always *does* the right thing. Especially for me. I can't wait to give her the ring. With the new job, I'll be able to buy it faster. There're just a few more payments left for me to finish paying off my rehab to Mom and Dad. After that, I'm buying it."

"You're giving them money for the rehab?" I leaned back.

"Sure," he shoved the last piece of the hotdog in his mouth.

"Did they ask you to pay them back?"

"No. You know they wouldn't. They didn't even want to talk to me about it. But it was my mess." He sighed. "My responsibility. So, I've been making payments ever since I got out and found a job. It took a while, but I'm almost done now."

Chapter 31

I WAS WALKING HOME from my parents' house—the place where I grew up, and which held so many memories.

However, things had changed with time. Slowly, the house had become a burden on our family. The cost of keeping it had put all of us under stress, straining relationships between us.

Lately, I had done a lot of thinking and realized that our happy places existed in time just as much as they existed in space. I loved my childhood home and always would, but I resented the house that cost my father's health and my mother's happiness.

Shortly after my parents returned from their trip, I insisted on delivering that month's money in person. Once there, I asked my father to get all paperwork, including whatever unopened past-due notices they had lying around that day.

As it often happened, the situation turned out to be even worse than I'd feared. I still had to tell them that I decided to quit my retail job and that I wouldn't be able to help them financially as much as I had been.

It physically hurt me to do it. It pained me to see the worry on my father's face, the outright panic in my mother's eyes. Especially, since I acutely felt guilt for my part in their situation—I had been the enabler.

Somehow, my mother and I ended up dealing with Evan's addiction by fueling the addictions of each other. I enabled her shopping therapy, and she made me feel needed, indispensible—the feeling I seemed to crave.

"We're going to be bankrupt." My mother sobbed, reaching for a tissue. "We're going to lose the house. Where are we going to live?"

"It was inevitable, Mom. In situations like this, it's best to deal with it sooner rather than later. Some things may still be salvaged. We'll work out the budget and the financial plan for you . . ." I so hated to be the strong and the reasonable one right now—the one with *the thick skin.*

"I know, I know, baby . . . " She waved me off and turned to my father. "What are we going to do?"

He made her tea, took her upstairs, and put her to bed.

"You know she needs help," I told him when he came back down to the kitchen. "We need to find her counseling."

He nodded somberly, and I took another inhale, trying to breathe through the heavy lump that was lodged in my throat.

"We'll have to get you professional debt management advice, too." I rubbed my chest. The pain inside only seemed stronger. "I'll do some research. Are there any services available through your retirement benefits from work? Can you look into it?"

He nodded again. My usually cheerful, chatty father refused to talk to me. I believed he was not blaming me for any of it—he was just overwhelmed by the situation—but it still hurt.

"I, um, I need to go now." I gave him an awkward side hug as he stood there silently by the kitchen counter. "I'll be around to help you with packing and moving." I gestured around the kitchen. "And everything else, of course."

"Thank you," he finally replied, his voice raw and so very sad. It broke my heart.

I walked to the bus station through the sleet and cold of January—my mother's pained face and my father's somber expression hovered in front of my eyes.

It was the right thing to do, in my mind I knew it was, but the lead-heavy, dark feeling of disappointment and failure weighed on me. It squeezed my chest in a vise and made my eyes burn with unshed tears. Still, I refused to cry.

All the way back to the city, I held the tears back, no matter how much they hurt and burned me from the inside.

Then I opened the door to my apartment and saw Marcus waiting for me there.

I couldn't hide anything from him. He knew me too well. One glance at me, and he guessed I wasn't feeling right.

"Sweetheart, what's wrong?" He reached for me, and it was my undoing.

Tossing my purse to the wall, I stepped into his arms.

Warm.

Safe.

Home.

And just like that, I couldn't hold it in anymore. The floodgates opened and tears burst out.

It was an ugly crying, with body-shuddering sobs, with tissue-requiring snot, and with one horrendous, unstoppable stream of tears.

It was no longer just about today's events, either. I cried for all the things I had never allowed myself to cry for before.

I cried because my parents were getting old, because I grew up, because there was no way to ever revisit that wonderful, carefree place called childhood. Because the things in my family would be so much worse now before they could get a little bit better.

I cried, letting go of the feelings of failure, responsibility, and guilt, because I couldn't deal with them in any other way at that moment.

I let myself fall apart because I knew he was there to hold all my pieces together.

Gently stroking my hair, he kissed away my tears even as more of them came immediately after, flooding my face in one relentless, endless torrent. He called me his love, his very own ice queen.

"My fearless woman," he murmured, holding me close, his hands slowly gliding up and down my back, soothing me.

"I am, Marcus," I sobbed into his tear-soaked t-shirt. "With you, I truly am fearless. With you, I'm not even afraid to be weak."

Chapter 32

AT SOME POINT DURING my crying fit, Marcus must have taken me to the couch, because once the tears had finally subsided, I found us sitting there, his arms around my shoulders, my head on his chest.

I slid my hand up the soaking wet front of his t-shirt.

"Sorry." I exhaled. My voice sounded rough—foreign—even to my own ear. "I've ruined your shirt."

"I've more," he dismissed, the fingers of his hand sinking in the hair on the back of my head. "How are you feeling?"

I realized I never explained why I was crying, but he must have guessed it. He wasn't at my place when I left, but he knew I was going to see my parents today, and he was aware of the reasons for my visit, too.

"Better." I drew in a shaky breath. Surprisingly, some of the heavy weight over my heart must have been washed out of me by the torrent of tears. "Much better, actually."

My fingers slid over the small, hard shape under his shirt again—the pendant he wore on the silver chain around his neck.

There was something especially intimate about us sitting in the dark like this, wrapped into each other. Or maybe it was the fact that he had just witnessed me at my worst that seemed to have brought us this much closer for me.

Either way, I felt compelled to ask him again, despite remembering him brushing me off the first time I did.

"What makes this special for you?" I rubbed the elongated shape of the pendant through the wet fabric of his t-shirt.

"I never said it was special."

"But it is, isn't it?"

I held my breath in the silence that followed, waiting for his reply and dreading it'd be another brush-off.

"Would you let me see it?" I asked when it became obvious he wasn't going to answer the previous question.

He remained silent.

It wasn't a frivolous interest on my part. He'd held me through my meltdown. One of my worst fears—showing weakness in front of someone—realized and ended up being cathartic in a way.

Despite the shame I still felt thinking about my crying on his chest, I was glad it happened. If Marcus needed someone to share whatever he'd been carrying around his neck all his life, I wanted to be that person for him.

Sensing a struggle inside him, I slid the tip of my finger up the chain, whispering, "Stop me if you're not ready."

His body tensed under me, as I came close to the neckline. Hooking my finger under the chain, I tugged at it—slowly, to give him a chance to stop me.

He didn't.

Dangling on the end of the chain, the pendant slid from under his t-shirt and into the semi-darkness of the room, glistening like a dull piece of amber.

Shaped as a narrow, upside-down cone, it was slightly curved, reminding me of a claw or a canine tooth of a mystical animal. The top part of it was enclosed in a silver setting that appeared to have darkened with time. The chain was thin and delicate. However, the pendant's setting was crudely made and seemed worn and ancient.

"They said it was on me when they found me." Marcus's clear voice startled me after the long silence.

"Do you remember anything? How old were you?"

"About two or three. Too young to remember." His eyes gleamed dark. "A priest found me in the church. I was the only one sitting on a pew when everyone had left after the mass."

"Somebody just left you there? Alone? As a tiny little toddler?" My heart swelled painfully at the image of a little boy sitting alone in an empty church.

I brushed a few long, black strands of hair from his forehead. "Could your biological parents have been like you? Do you think they had your magic?"

"Hardly," he scoffed. "I'm sure the reason they got rid of me was because I was nothing like them."

"Why would you think so?"

"Because everybody else did the same, Angela. Every time one of my foster parents noted anything *freaky* about me, I was moved to another home." He stated it as a matter of fact, without bitterness in his tone, which only made it worse for me—he had accepted it as a norm that people considered him a freak.

"You wouldn't know that for sure as far as your biological parents are concerned unless you meet them face to face. Have you tried to search for them?"

"No," he replied sharply. "I never knew where to start looking. As a kid, I had no means for it, either."

"How about now? Would you like to find them now?"

All the questions I had about his *condition* surfaced to the top of my mind, bringing in the renewed wave of worry about him. Finding where Marcus came from might possibly shed some light on where his magic originated as well as how to control it better.

"Now wouldn't be good timing, don't you think?" he snapped, getting off the couch swiftly. "If *they* didn't want me as a dirty, hungry kid then, why would *I* want them now when I can take care of myself? Even if they accepted me now, how could I ever be sure it's not only because of the money and fame?"

"Knowing where you come from—"

"I don't want to know." His voice sounded strained. The muscles in his jaw flexed, but I failed to connect these signs with the anger flaring up in him.

"If it'd make it easier," I offered. "I could search for you—"

"Angela!" My name thundered through the night suddenly, and I jumped up in surprise. It was the first time Marcus had ever raised his voice at me. "I said, I don't want to know."

He paced the floor, appearing outright furious now. His eyes glistened in the dim light. The long, black hair whipped around his shoulders every time he turned on his heel, like a whirlwind of rage.

I guessed I was not the actual reason for his anger. It had been seething inside him for most of his life—the resentment towards the parents, whom he'd never met and who, he believed, had abandoned him. I'd just poked his festering wound, letting it all rush out. Still, I shifted on the couch uneasily, faced with the fury he radiated with every rugged breath he took, like a fire-breathing dragon.

"There is no problem to solve here, Angela. I'm not one of your lost shipments that has to be traced back to the warehouse or a stray cat in need of a good home. You don't have to search for a solution for me—I already have it. I've made it this far just fine."

I opened my mouth to protest—and closed it right away, not risking adding fuel to his fire.

"You can't solve every fucking problem in this goddamn world!" Marcus continued to rage. "Not every question needs an answer." He stopped in his tracks abruptly and turned to face me. His eyes focused on me, and his expression sharpened with awareness, as if he'd just remembered where he was. "Some questions are best left alone." His voice softened. He took a step closer, staring at me for a few moments.

"I don't want to argue, Angela."

"I worry about you," I replied quietly.

According to Marcus, *the energy* inside him had been growing stronger since he was a teenager. No one knew what the future held for him. What if the iron grip in which he held his power slipped, and the beast ended up eventually consuming him whole?

"I'd love to find out if there are better ways to control your magic, so it would never hurt you again."

"I've already found a way to control it." The fire-breathing dragon folded his wings, and the man crouched down in front of me. "The most delightful one ever. You."

"But we don't know why I can calm it like that or even if I'll always be able to do that. Also, what if I'm not around, or you can't come to me in time when it starts happening again?"

"I'm not planning on your not being around." His eyes focused on mine. "Are you?"

"No. Not if I can help it." I took his face in my hands and traced his long black eyebrows with my thumbs, willing the troubled crease in the middle of his forehead to disappear. "I'll always be around," I promised, realizing there was nothing more I wished for in my heart than to spent the rest of my life with him. The commitment of my promise excited me, but since he hadn't exactly expressed the same, I added, "If you'll want me, of course."

He held my gaze for a moment, as if studying something deep inside my eyes.

"Angela." He exhaled finally, sliding his hands up my thighs to my hips then drawing me to him.

Forehead pressed to my chest, he wrapped his arms around my back tightly, and I parted my knees to fit his torso between my legs.

"I always want you," he groaned. "Every fucking minute of every fucking day."

His hot breath seeped through the material of my blouse, making the skin of my breasts tingle with heat. Warm tendrils seemed to have slid under my bra, teasing my nipples.

Heat.

As my body melted into his arms around me, his hands finding their way under my blouse, my mind jolted by a sudden thought.

He was hot. Too hot. Again.

I cupped his cheeks, trying to gauge his body temperature, but he turned his face, closing his mouth over my nipple through my blouse and bra.

My palm slid to the front of his t-shirt instead, the material was bone-dry despite being drenched with my tears just minutes ago.

"Marcus? How is it happening again?" Dread smothered my arousal, despite my knowing that my lust should bring him relief. "You had two shows today."

His week off had just ended, but he was supposed to perform today, twice. He should have been fine.

"The shows had been cancelled . . . technical malfunction at the venue," Marcus rasped, after letting go of my breast to meet my eyes. "They're fixing it."

In the state I'd been in getting home, I failed to notice that he was at my place way earlier than usual, waiting for me.

"It's happening too soon." I touched his face, his neck, slid my hands under the neckline of his t-shirt, finding him disturbingly hot everywhere. "I just saw you yesterday."

"We didn't *do* anything yesterday." He lifted a teasing eyebrow at me, but it did little to ease my concern.

Yesterday, we had breakfast together then Marcus took me to work. We hadn't gone beyond a chaste kiss and a friendly hug for a while, I realized. My thoughts had been too preoccupied with my family lately, and he had respected it.

"I'm so sorry." I wrapped my arms around his neck.

"Don't be. It's not too bad yet." He smiled. "Kiss me, my ice queen."

Now that I listened, really listened, I could catch the raspy note in his voice. The memory of his seizure sent the chill of fear down my spine, despite his cheerful words. Compassion flooded my heart before the lust could ever come.

I cupped his face and gently touched his burning hot lips with mine.

"Always," I whispered, gently blowing air at his temple, as if I could extinguish the fire consuming him this way, then brushed my lips against his scorching hot cheekbone. "I'll kiss it all away, Marcus." I dipped my fingers into his hair, pulling him closer to me. "I'll make it all better. I promise."

My heart sped up as his hands slid up my back under my blouse. The metal of the rings on his fingers was almost hot enough to burn my skin. But it was the heat of his palms on me—his fingers skimming the edge of my bra—that I forced my mind to focus on.

The small buttons on the front of my blouse popped open. The material slid off my shoulders, along with the bra straps, freeing my breasts.

My nipples drew tight in the cool air of the room, and Marcus sucked one of them into the heat of his mouth. My thighs trembled, heat swelling between them under his touch.

I moaned into his hair and rocked my hips against his hard abs, as his tongue continued to play with my nipple. Needing to feel him skin to skin, even if it burned me, I tugged his t-shirt up to take it off, but it dissolved into nothing in my fingers.

His fever seemed to be subsiding already. The skin of his back under my palms was cooling off, as my own body rapidly heated up with desire. His breathing was still heavy and his heart thundered under my palms, but I suspected it was for different reasons now.

He shoved up my skirt, getting hold of my thighs just above the edge of my stockings.

"Come here," he commanded, yanking me off the couch and into his lap.

His mouth met mine in a hungry kiss. The nylon of my stockings slid easily along the leather of his pants, and I slipped closer, my pelvis flush with his. The hard bulge in his pants hit against the sensitive spot between my legs, making me moan from the pleasure of the contact.

Through the haze of my arousal, I felt his fingers flex on my thighs. Holding me in place, Marcus shifted back, putting some distance between me and the hard ridge of his erection that I desperately craved to be rubbing against me right now.

I whimpered in protest against his mouth. Breaking our kiss, he nibbled at the skin on the side of my neck. "I want you to come on my tongue." His coarse whisper in my ear vibrated through my chest with anticipation.

Hands splayed on my shoulder blades, he lowered me onto the carpet.

I spread my legs wider for him, finding my skirt already gone, as were the blouse and the bra. Under his heated gaze, my underwear melted into the air too, leaving me only in my stockings and garter belt.

He gave me a wicked grin.

"Let me hear more of those cute whimpers you make."

His midnight-blue eyes glistened from under the black hair over his forehead before he lowered his head between my legs. His tongue slid through my folds, quickly depriving me of the ability to speak.

Gasping, I rocked my hips, as he teased my clit with small tantalizing nibbles, each taking me higher and higher.

Without taking his mouth off me, he slid his hand up my body, finding my breast. His fingers pinched my nipple as the rhythm of his tongue on me intensified.

Hot pressure coiled tight inside me then exploded through my entire body in shuddering waves of orgasm.

"Just like that . . ." Marcus murmured approvingly against my sensitive skin as his thumb replaced his mouth in squeezing every single drop of pleasure out of me.

Limply, I relaxed on the carpet when he finally let me catch my breath.

"That was . . ." I started but couldn't finish, unable to find the words that would make justice to all the wonderful things he made me feel.

With a soft chuckle, he stretched on the floor next to me. I glanced down his body, noticing the soft glimmer of light bouncing off the leather of his pants stretched tight over his persistent hard-on.

This time, I didn't reach for it—all my attempts to do so in the past had been met with gentle refusal from him.

Instead, I rolled to my side, facing him.

"Was it as good for you as it was for me?" I smiled lightly, tracing a vein on his forearm with the tip of my finger.

Lying on his back, he turned his head my way.

"I'm not complaining."

"Why not?" I couldn't help asking. His behaviour of avoiding any further intimacy with me was puzzling. The fact that it was obviously deliberate on his part hurt.

His gaze flickered to my naked breasts, and he cursed softly under his breath. A sheet I recognized as part of my bedding, appeared from nowhere, covering me up to my chin.

Tonight I wouldn't have it, though.

"I'm too hot." I pouted artistically and tossed the sheet aside then arched my back, gliding my hands up my body. "You've made me all hot and sweaty," I murmured with an exaggerated moan and cupped my boobs, squishing them together.

"Fuck!" The curse shot through the air like a bullet.

Marcus grabbed my wrists and yanked my hands over my head, bringing his body over mine.

His hair fell over us, his eyes darkened to almost black as he stared at me with the intensity that threatened to incinerate me on the spot. He pressed his pelvis into me, the hard ridge in his pants pushed against my lower stomach as his arms shook with tension.

"Stop it." His voice held a warning, but I was too far gone to head it.

"I've been dying to have you inside me, Marcus," I whispered my confession to him, tossing aside any pretense.

With a shuddered exhale, he dropped his head down, pressing his forehead to mine. Contrary to his wild expression, his voice sounded soft—pained. "Please, don't do this." He shifted his lower body off me. "Not here."

He let go of me and sat on the floor, forearms on his bent knees.

"Why?" I sat up, too, tugging the sheet over my chest after all—the time for games had passed. "What is going on, Marcus?"

"Not here," he repeated, meeting my gaze. "Not now."

His pained expression, the desperate plea on his face made my heart ache.

I tucked the sheet around myself then crawled closer to him and wrapped my arms around him in a hug, with not a hint of flirting this time.

"It's okay, honey," I whispered soothingly. "One day you'll tell me. Whenever you're ready."

His chest rose with a heavy breath as he drew me in closer.

"I don't deserve you, Angela," he whispered in my hair.

"Sure you do." I smiled against his bare shoulder. "We deserve each other, remember? We established it a while back."

His hand under my chin, he lifted my face to his.

"I want to take you to my ranch house." His words didn't match the intensity in his eyes or his voice.

"Okay." I blinked.

"When do you have a day off?" he asked, with a puzzling grim determination etched in his face.

"Well, um. I was going to give my two-week notice at the store tomorrow." I tried not to wince at the sharp stab of guilt that came with the memory of the conversation with my parents again.

Marcus frowned, as if going deep into his own thoughts for a minute. "That means you'll be off the weekend after the two weeks are up?"

"Right." I nodded.

"That's when we'll go there," he announced, stern and determined, as if declaring the plan of some strategic attack. "Now let me take you to bed. We both need some sleep."

⸻ ❦ ⸻

THE SLEEP WASN'T EASY to come, though. And judging by his uneven breathing at my back as he spooned me in bed, Marcus was not sleeping, either. I wondered what kept him awake when he shifted behind me and called in a soft whisper, "Angela."

"Yes, Marcus."

"Would you prefer if I came with a family? Like parents, siblings, aunts and uncles?"

Of all the things that could be troubling him right now, this was the one that kept him awake—what *I* preferred?

"It's not about me, honey." I turned to him. "I want you, no one else, and I'll have you just the way you are." My connection with him felt permanent and unbreakable at this point.

"I can see how much your own family means to you." Curiosity tinged his voice, and I realized he had never experienced a normal family life.

"They do," I replied. "I love them all."

"Despite how much they upset you?"

"Despite all of that," I agreed. "Those who are closest to us hurt us the most, simply because they have the capacity to inflict more pain—we care more. But it doesn't mean I don't want them close because of that. My family are also the people who make me the happiest, too."

He stared at me, as if waiting for me to continue, so I did, "A family doesn't mean just your parents, Marcus. It takes a village to raise a child, they say. You didn't just appear in that church out of nowhere. There must have been a home, a place, a number of people who knew you. Not all of them may have the means to find you, but I believe some may be happy to see you if you found them."

He rose on an elbow.

"I don't think it's possible at this point to get the answers you want, Angela."

"If you decide to search, don't do it for me." I shook my head. "What would *you* hope to get out of it yourself?"

"I don't know." He let himself fall back on the bed, staring at the ceiling. "Answers? Information?" He sounded unsure.

"How about a place to belong?" I offered.

His gaze flickered to me, but he didn't reply to my question. "If you want to know more about the nature of my magic," he said instead. "It might be worth it to look into that email then."

"What email?" Surprise mixed into a heady cocktail with hope inside me.

"Someone claiming they might have some answers about me. It was sent to my public account a few months ago. I get a lot of garbage sent to that account, and Simon has an assistant to manage it, but he showed that message to me, for whatever reason."

"Maybe he thought you might be interested to know more."

"Maybe. The person who sent the email didn't seem as crazy as the rest."

"Who sent it?"

"A woman with some unusual name that I forgot." He rolled his head on the pillow to face me again. "Stacy, the assistant, keeps all this crazy shit organized in folders, in case we need to file a restraining order against some nutcase or something. Nothing gets deleted, and I'm sure that email is still there. I'll give you the password to my account."

"You will? Are you sure?"

"Trust me, there is hardly anything worth a look in there. Definitely nothing personal."

"Okay." I shifted closer until my nose pressed into his shoulder. "Thank you."

"It's nothing." Marcus threaded his arm under me then drew me into his side. "Feel free to search."

Chapter 33

I LOGGED INTO MARCUS'S account right after all shipping issues for the day had been sorted out at work.

He was right calling the majority of messages in it "garbage." There must have been thousands of them, with hundreds of new emails arriving daily. Immediately, I felt sorry for Simon's assistant who had to go through them all.

A thought flickered at the back of my mind that my own email must be here, too, somewhere, tucked neatly into a folder named *Fan Queries* or maybe *Scheduling Questions*.

After reading a number of messages from different folders, I realized many of them must have come from some rather disturbed individuals. They called on Marcus to join secret alien societies on Earth, warned about abductions by demons, and invited to exchange magic spells and potion recipes.

It was well past the end of my workday when I finally found the email I was searching for, in the folder labeled *Seen By Marcus*. The woman who sent it was called Ingeborg, a fairly unique name, especially for Northern America. She claimed to be from Switzerland.

The tone of her message set her email apart from most of the others. Simple and to the point, she was not asking Marcus for anything. Instead, she offered to connect him with people like himself if he ever felt the need to find others like him.

My heart seemed to have skipped a bit at that offer. Were there really more people like Marcus? If so, who were they and why did no one know about them? My mind remained skeptical, even as I longed to believe Ingeborg's offer was genuine.

At the very least, I decided, she sounded like a person worth having a conversation with, and I felt hopeful.

I copied down her email address to a piece of paper and was about to log off from Marcus's account when the folder marked *Current Investigations* caught my eye.

The words said by Marcus about restraining orders came to mind, and I clicked on the folder with some trepidation about what I might find inside.

The very first email I opened surpassed my worst expectations. It contained blatant death threats.

Dread rose in my chest, as I opened another email from the same folder, then another. All of them contained similar messages. Email after email, some deranged lunatic persistently described in gory details how Marcus deserved to die.

Somebody out there hated Marcus, with a passion that could only equal my love for him. Yes, the chilling fear for Marcus that froze me in place, with my fingers trembling on the keyboard, also made me realize that I loved him.

I must have loved him ever since he awkwardly asked for the permission to see me again that morning in my apartment. Or maybe I fell in love with him the day before that, when I floated through the air of the old theater into his outstretched arms. Or it might have happened even before that.

Marcus had been my miracle, my enigma, the one true magic in this world. He'd become my best friend, then my lover, and by now—the love of my life.

And here, some sick maniac was threatening to kill him.

My stomach tied in knots with worry, I closed the browser quickly to erase the offensive words from my monitor, but they had been already burnt into my brain.

With shaking hands, I dialed Marcus's cell phone number. It was afternoon in Las Vegas. He should be up already, with some time to spare before his first show of the day started.

"Marcus. Do you know there are emails with death threats in your account?" I blurted out as soon as he picked it up.

"I'm sure there are," he replied casually.

"No, listen! There are lots of them. And they all came from the same email address, which must mean the same person, or group of people." The thought that there may be several people wanting Marcus dead brought the bile up to my throat. "Who could hate you so much? Why?"

"Did you read them all?"

"No. But I did read enough to get sick with worry."

"Then you know that whoever wrote them is not well. It's an insane person, Angela. We're looking for him because he needs help. Don't think about it too much."

"The things he said . . . That you deserve to be burnt at the stake, alive, like a witch. He wants to cut up your dead body and feed it to the dogs, piece by piece . . ." I trailed off, with a sob. The horror from the evil of those words swelled painfully in my throat.

"Sweetheart, don't worry about all that nonsense," his voice turned warm and comforting, like a cozy blanket. "Sorry, I should've warned you, but I didn't think any of this stuff could be taken seriously. Do you really believe anyone could harm me?"

I knew what he meant, and he was right, in a way. Marcus—of all people—was the most capable of defending himself, from a whole army if needed.

If he *knew* about the attack, if he *saw* the people attacking him, if he was mindful of the weapons aimed at him—he was invincible.

However, a cowardly, unexpected shot in the back, I feared, would be just as damaging to him as it would be to anyone else.

"Marcus. Honey. Just, please, be careful."

"Always am, baby." I sensed a smile in his voice. "Remember? I don't even sign autographs, keeping my space."

Autographs.

The word tugged at my mind, urging me to focus on something, just out of reach at the moment. What was I missing here?

After some more of Marcus's reassurances that he and Simon were working on identifying the sender of the emails, I made him promise to be careful one more time then ended the call.

Opening the browser once again, I logged back into his account to take another look at the disturbing emails. Scrolling all the way to the end of the long list of threats in one of them, I stared at the signature at the bottom.

Your Biggest Fan.

This was obviously meant as some twisted kind of joke. Yet, the smirk of the man asking for an autograph outside of the theater, the night of Marcus's show in Toronto, floated to the surface of my mind.

⬥

AFTER FINALLY LEAVING the office that night, I ran across the street to the public library, opened an email account under a fake last name—feeling like a covert agent from a movie—and sent Ingeborg an email.

Without naming Marcus by name, I claimed to be a friend of a person whom she contacted in April of last year with a promise to answer questions about his family. I said that my friend allowed me to connect with her on his behalf, to explore the possibilities for a further conversation.

Vague and polite, I hoped my email would trigger her memory about her offer to help Marcus. At the same time, if Ingeborg turned out to be someone who sent random emails to celebrities, she would have probably forgotten all about the one she sent months ago, and my own nondescript message wouldn't cause any harm.

Chapter 34

THE REPLY FROM INGEBORG came the very next day. According to her message, she knew right away that I was referring to Marcus and was, in her own words, *delighted* that I contacted her.

She offered to meet with me in person, to tell me about her *assumptions* about Marcus's origins, but confessed that she didn't know Marcus's immediate family personally.

The fact that she made no promises of giving me any actual information filled me with disappointment, dampening my hopes.

Hesitant to meet with a complete stranger, especially since there didn't seem to be anything definite to gain from the meeting, I politely declined her offer. However, our email exchange didn't stop after that.

Over the next two weeks, Ingeborg told me a little more about herself and her family. Her emails were always exceptionally polite to the point of sounding a little old-fashioned and even courteously formal, at times.

She said she was born in Finland, but had been living in Switzerland for decades. Her husband and son passed away long ago. I suspected she must be lonely with not many people to talk to, so I continued to reply to her emails.

In passing, I mentioned our correspondence to Marcus, and he supported my decision not to get together with a stranger. In fact, he made me promise to let him know of any future meeting requests from Ingeborg, even though I could hardly imagine any harm coming from an elderly lady.

Meanwhile, my two final weeks of working at the store were coming to an end. With the very last night shift being scheduled for Saturday, I was about to have the Sunday absolutely free.

For Marcus, however, weekends meant more work, with five performances over the two days. Since the first show on Sunday wasn't starting until later in the afternoon, we agreed to get together the night before and spend the following morning at his ranch house in Vegas, where I hadn't been yet.

After handing in my nametag to the store manager and saying goodbye to her and the rest of the staff, I was practically running home from the subway that night. The uplifting feeling of freedom lit up inside me, along with the anticipation at seeing Marcus soon.

My feet were killing me in my high-heeled boots, but I hardly noticed the pain. I texted Marcus that I was on my way home as soon as I got off the subway and hoped that he was waiting for me at the apartment already.

Impatient to see him, I took a shortcut through the alley between two factory buildings recently converted into lofts.

Wondering if all the improvements to the neighbourhood would eventually result in an unscheduled rent increase for me in the future, I hopped over the ice-covered puddles, careful not to slip over in my heels. On nights like this, I worried my mom was right when she said that my weakness for impractical footwear would cost me a broken ankle one day.

Concentrating on working out a path between the ice patches, I barely noticed a male figure at the opposite end of the alley. Before a panic had a chance to get hold of me, though, I recognized it was Marcus in the yellow glow of the few streetlights.

A warm fuzzy feeling spread through me at the sight of him, making me smile. I ran faster, but then sensed my feet disconnect with the pavement. As my legs were still going through the motion of running, I had been lifted into the air.

Laughing, I threw my arms out to the sides, like imaginary wings as I flew through the air and straight into the outstretched arms of Marcus.

"Got you," he said quietly, and gently set me down on the ground, but didn't release me from his arms.

I glanced around, to make sure there were no people watching us.

"What if someone saw us?" I giggled, leaning into his warmth.

He pressed the side of his face to mine.

"I don't care. I've missed you, and you've been too slow on those monster heels."

"Still, you should be more careful."

"Trust me," he waved off my concerns. "Even if they saw us, people would sooner believe you were an Olympic long-jump champion than that I had anything to do with it."

He placed a kiss on my cheek, running his hands over my winter coat. "I hate Canadian weather," he groaned. "There are too many clothes on you all the time. Ready to go?"

"Not yet," I started. "I still need to leave some extra food for Lannister—"

"Done."

"And grab my overnight bag—"

"Already there. Anything else?"

Smiling, I went through the short to-do list in my head.

"Nope." I clasped my hands behind his neck, leaning closer. "Take me away, Marcus."

⸺◉⸺

THE HOUSE THAT MARCUS owned but, by his own confession, hardly ever lived in was a sprawling one-story building.

Marcus teleported us right to the middle of his kitchen. Actually, it felt as if the kitchen suddenly appeared around us. One minute, I was snuggling against his chest in a cold, dark alley in Toronto. The next moment, we stood in this bright, spacious room with terracotta tile floors and clean white walls.

"Ah, it's warm." I sighed with pleasure, unbuttoning my winter coat.

"Finally." He laughed, taking my coat and sweater from me. "They'll be in the hall closet." He tossed both pieces of clothing over his shoulder, and they immediately dissolved in the air.

"Well, this is it. Do you want a tour of the house?" he asked. His leather jacket disappeared as well, leaving him in a black button-down shirt and dark jeans.

I swept the kitchen with my gaze.

"It's nice here."

The pale-wood cabinets and tiled countertops, along with the dark wooden beams across the ceiling, gave the impression of a true farmhouse—spacious but cozy at the same time. And very different compared to his hotel suite in Vegas.

"Are you hungry? We could eat first." He leaned against the kitchen island.

"No, thank you." I shook my head. "I'm good for now. Show me your place, first."

The rest of the house felt light and cozy, too, like a real home. Definitely not something I would've expected from the bachelor pad of a Las Vegas magician.

"Did you decorate it yourself? Who chose all the furnishing?" I touched the white paneling in the living room then slid my fingers along the back of a striped armchair by the large brick fireplace.

"Most of it came with the house. I changed little inside. My improvements to the place aren't all visible."

"What did you do?"

"Just, um . . ." He frowned, as if struggling to find the right words. "Had a few structural reinforcements done. The house is highly resistant to earthquakes now."

"Do they happen often in Vegas?"

"Well." He cupped the back of his neck, his gaze leaving mine. "They tend to follow me around. Come." He took my hand. "I'll show you the library."

Chapter 35

THE LIBRARY WAS A LARGE office off the main hallway, with floor-to-ceiling bookshelves lining all four walls.

"Did all these come with the house, too?" I swept the room with my arm.

"No. The books are mine. I always had some, but I've bought more since I moved here—now that I have a proper place to store them."

A glance at the titles on the spines revealed everything from classics, to historical fiction, to biographies and travel guides.

"You have diverse interests," I noted. "Have you read them all?"

"Most of them, I believe." Marcus rubbed the back of his neck again. He seemed uncharacteristically self-conscious, as if by showing his books, he was exposing more of his inner world to me, and was apprehensive about my reaction.

I knew he liked reading. Marcus told me he never did well in school, but his conversations were always intelligent and his storytelling smooth and engaging. He seemed to hold a large number of facts in his head, too, leaving an impression of a knowledgeable and well-informed person when he spoke.

"I don't read as much as I used to," he said. "But before I met you, there were days I would do nothing but read. You see." He rubbed his arm. "For me, reading a book is very similar to having a conversation, except that there is no risk of personal questions for me. Instead, the authors open up their own hearts, telling their secrets to me."

My chest tightened, as I acutely understood how being different from the norm must have made leading an ordinary life difficult for him. He chose the self-imposed isolation, guarding his secret, rather than risking having more people turn their backs on him, the way many did when he was a child.

Books ended up being his loyal companion through the years.

To break the silence settling over us, I slid my finger along a few colourful spines and read the titles out loud.

"*The Greatest Shows on Earth. Cirque Du Soleil: 20 Years Under the Sun.* These are books about circus?"

He nodded.

I stopped my finger on one of the spines.

"*When Pigs Could Fly and Bears Could Dance*?" The title made me smile.

"That one is on the history of Russian circus. Circus has always been a big part of that culture."

"Have you seen it? Russian circus?"

"Many times. You know that there is a permanent circus building in almost every city in former Soviet Union? Regular shows run all season long every year, just like theater performances in North America." His expression had animated. "There are families of performers, with generations of circus artists, born and raised to continue what their parents did. Children are taught as soon as they learn to walk. They grow up performing alongside their parents—circus is their life. Many acts involve animals, too. They are as big a part of the show as people are, if not bigger. Love it or hate it, it's hard not to admire the dedication and skill of everyone involved. It's a fascinating world on its own."

"Have you ever *borrowed* circus animals for your shows?"

"I've tried." He shook his head. "But they don't make the best stage partners for me."

"Why not?" I lifted an eyebrow in surprise. "I would think they'd be comfortable on stage"

"Too comfortable!" Marcus laughed. "I need the animals on my show to just sit or stand there while I do my work. But circus animals are true professionals—they start performing their own acts as soon as they get on stage, diverting the attention to them."

"Have you been upstaged by animals?" I teased, smiling. "During your own show?"

"I have." He grinned. "Many times. Wild creatures work better for me. They tend to calm down naturally around me, so I can perform."

"Except for that lion in Africa."

"Right," he agreed with a laugh. "Except him. I must have startled him, appearing out of nowhere like that. I'm sure, if we had a little more time to get acquainted, we would've become friends, too. I just wasn't going to bet my other leg on it."

He shook his head. "Given a choice, though, I prefer to work with zoo animals. They're already used to large crowds of people, so I feel like being on stage is not such a big change for them."

I watched his eyes light up when he talked about the circus, performing, and animals. I had rarely seen so much passion in his expression when he spoke of his own work.

"What interests you the most about it?" I gestured at the shelves with circus books. "What do you like the most about circus?"

He paused for a second.

"The skills of the artists."

"Is it something you would like to replicate in your shows? Bring in some circus elements?"

"No. Absolutely not." He leaned with his shoulder against a bookshelf, his smile fading. "Circus artists achieve their level of skill through years of hard work and relentless training, pushing the limits of what a human body was designed to do. If I go out there and pretend to walk on a wire, just like that . . ." He sighed and shook his head again. "I don't care how realistic it may appear to everyone else, I would feel like an even bigger fraud than I already am."

"What if it was real?" I shifted a little closer.

"You want me to walk on the wire for real, without using magic?" He exhaled a brief laugh. "I'm afraid I'll break my neck way before the first show."

"No, not like that." I protested. "Think about what you like doing on the stage right now. What is the best part of your show for you?"

"The opening act is shaping up pretty good."

He showed me some of it the other day, and the parts that I'd seen were phenomenal. I believed it would top even his Phoenix act once it was ready.

"And Phoenix act, too. It will always be one of my favourites. I created it thinking about the girl in the red dress." He traced the red satin ribbon I had tied as a headband. "I imagined she'd see it one day and tell me I blew her mind once again."

"You sure did." I wrapped my arms around his middle. "Tell me about your work on it?"

He brushed his hand against my hair then rested it on my shoulder.

"I thought about what I wanted people to feel when they watched it, and then about how to make my use of magic less apparent. The challenge was to make it incredible but believable at the same time."

"And you managed to do exactly that. It was incredible to watch, simply breathtaking. But it was also believable, without being confusing or uncomfortable."

"I had the wings manufactured by a company that produces theater props. So the crew know there are props being used, but I modify the wings on stage, of course, by adding light and movement. The music and stage lighting are under the control of the production crew. Mostly. I just enhance brightness, colours, and intensity here and there. Bring in scents and adjust the temperature when necessary."

His enthusiasm was clearly shining through his expression now, betraying the true showman in him, passionate about discovering his own style.

"You did really well, Marcus. The end result of your work is truly spectacular. Visually, it actually reminds me of Cirque du Soleil . . . " I stopped mid-sentence, struck by a sudden idea. "What if you invited circus performers to work with you?"

His eyes narrowed, and his brow furrowed, as if he was considering my words for a moment.

"You know I don't work with people on stage. My assistants aren't part of the act."

"You don't have to be in the same acts with the other performers. Let the circus artists do their job, and only help them make it truly spectacular. Put life in their props. Infuse colours in their costumes. Add emotions to the stage and spread the magic around them."

"So it would be like a circus show?" He sounded intrigued, and it spurred me on.

"Something like that. Circus or even variety. You can add singers and dancers if you want. Marcus, with their skills and your magic, I know you can make it truly amazing. Like nothing else on Earth." My breath caught at the possibilities, sending my heart thunder with excitement against my ribs. "You won't have to copy the acts of others anymore. You'd be working with real talent, and you can create your own acts, too. Using real magic doesn't make you a fraud, by the way. It is your gift, your very own special talent. You are a great performer in your own right, honey."

His hand moved behind my back, as he drew me closer.

"You really like this idea." It came more like a statement than a question from him, still I answered.

"I do. But that's not the point. What do *you* think about it?" Snuggling in his arms, I pressed my nose to his collarbone.

Marcus slid his chin along the sateen ribbon in my hair.

"I'm pretty sure my contract won't allow for this many changes to the show—too big of a deviation from what they'd signed me up for. Simon has been working on renewing the contract for another year next month."

"Oh well . . ." My chest seemed to deflate a little—the idea of something so wonderful I was sure he could do wasn't that easy to give up.

"Of course it may take more than a year to plan the new show from scratch. So we should probably start it now."

"You want to do it?" I exclaimed, afraid to believe yet. "Your own show, without the venue to back you up? All by yourself?"

"No, not entirely by myself, of course." He grinned back at me, a happy spark in his eyes. "I'll have Simon, to do all the boring stuff. And you to help with the rest." His voice softened. "Will you help me, Angela?"

"Of course, I will." I rested my head against his chest again. Excitement already grew inside me at the mere thought of being a part of it. "I'll love to help. Will Simon be okay with a change like that?"

"He'll have questions. A lot of questions, knowing Simon. I have the creative control over the show, though. As long as he finds new ideas financially viable, he'd let me do anything I want—circus, variety . . ." His voice deepened as his hands strayed south along my back. "Striptease."

"Striptease?" I chuckled. "Would you be the one taking your clothes off?" I slid a finger across his chest, circling his nipple under the shirt.

He sucked in air sharply.

"I could bring some efficiency to the process, don't you think?" His tone dipped even lower, and I realized his shirt had disappeared—my head was leaning against his bare chest now.

"I'm afraid you got it all wrong." I moved my hands to his back, his warm smooth skin under my palms. "The point is to take your time getting rid of your clothes, to do it slowly. You just took the *tease* out of the *striptease*, mister."

Gliding my hands down his back, I discovered his pants were gone too, as was his underwear. My hands landed on his hard, rounded backside.

The realization of him being completely naked in my arms, washed over me with a hot flush.

"Not that I'm complaining," I breathed out. Pressing my nose against his chest, I inhaled a lungful of his scent, greedily as if getting a fix. "I'll take you anyway I can."

Cupping my ass, Marcus suddenly lunged forward, shoving my back against a bookcase. I felt him grow hard as he thrust his hips into mine.

"How much *can* you take?" he asked, gruff and raw.

The tension in his arms around me, the strain in his voice should have been concerning, but the restrained passion I sensed vibrating through him felt more invigorating than intimidating to me.

My own body responded to it, immediately heating from the inside with the desire for more.

"As much as you can give me, Marcus," I whispered, digging my fingers in the hard muscles of his ass. "I want it all."

"Do you?" Hands propped on the shelf behind me, he shoved away from me, searching my eyes with his gaze. "Only, you don't know what *all* means."

"Show me," I challenged, not shying away from his penetrating stare.

"Is it possible to scare away my fearless woman?" The way he asked the question sounded as if he were talking to himself now. "What if there is a limit of your acceptance?"

"What do you mean?" Concerned by the crushed expression momentarily ghosting over his features, I reached to cup his face.

He blinked and straightened in front of me abruptly. Catching my hand in the air, he said in a more casual tone, "let's go have dinner now."

All his clothes returned at once.

"What do you feel like eating?" He asked, leading me by the hand out of the library. "I can call to order anything from whatever restaurant you like then teleport to pick it up when the food is ready. It'll only take me a few minutes."

"I, um . . ." My head still reeling from the sudden change in him, I didn't even begin figuring out what'd just happened, focusing on catching up to his long strides instead. "I'll let you choose."

Chapter 36

IRONICALLY, THE MORNING I could have slept in guilt-free, I woke up at sunrise.

It wasn't even six o'clock Vegas time, but I was wide awake, staring at the wooden beams on the ceiling in Marcus's bedroom and listening to his soft, even breathing at my side.

The dinner last night was amazing, as was the long conversation we had afterwards, talking about anything and everything except for about what was really beginning to bother me, especially, since the last night in the library.

The way Marcus avoided having the actual sex with me had been concerning for a while now. His sudden, one-hundred-and-eighty degree turn last night left me with an increasingly unpleasant scratchy feeling that wouldn't go away.

Giving up on falling back asleep, I slipped from under the covers and got out of bed.

"Where are you going?" his raspy, sleepy voice stopped me.

Lying on his stomach, Marcus peered through the curtain of hair over his face at me.

"Morning." I grabbed some clean clothes from my overnight bag on the chair next to the bed. "I can't sleep, I thought I'd take a walk outside before you woke up. Are you awake now?"

"Not quite." This was about the time when he'd normally go back to bed after taking me to work. "Do you want some coffee?" he mumbled sleepily, rolling to his back with a stretch.

The top sheet tented with his morning erection, bobbing in the air as if mocking me.

"When I get back. In thirty minutes or so." I paused in buttoning my jeans, and he followed my gaze to his crotch.

"Make sure to stay inside the fence." He cleared his throat, promptly turning to his side. "We haven't noticed the cars around here since the last week, but it's best to be safe."

"Okay." I threw a long-sleeved t-shirt on and hurried out of the room, anxious to get outside as fast as possible.

The air in his bedroom was beginning to suffocate me.

———◦———

MARCUS'S HOUSE WAS surrounded by acres of land, with the wooden rail fence marking the boundaries of the large property. He'd mentioned this was a ranch some time back, but the stables and other structures had been gone by now.

The area next to the house was professionally landscaped with pretty rock gardens, desert plants, and palm trees. The rest was left the way the nature intended it.

Short, stubby trees and patches of sage-coloured shrubs interspersed the rocky ground, painted in tender shades of pink and orange by the rising sun. Sandy red mountain ridges framed the horizon as far as I could see. There were no other buildings around, no cars, and no people.

I breathed in the crisp morning air.

The pale-blue open sky above me and the wide unspoiled land around elicited the feeling of absolute freedom. Still, I couldn't shake the heavy weight pressing on my chest.

The things happening between Marcus and I—or more accurately, the things that were *not* happening—wouldn't get out of my mind.

Last night, it wasn't me who provoked him. After that one awkward attempt at seduction in my apartment, I was too self-conscious to try anything like that again. Marcus *chose* to get naked with me in the library. Yet he withdrew just as quickly before anything else had any chance of happening.

Why?

It wasn't the sexual frustration that made me anxious about this. Thanks to his wicked oral sex skills, I was thoroughly satisfied on a regular basis.

The fact that Marcus seemed to be hiding something important from me was what troubled me the most.

Stomping down the long driveway, my arms wrapped tightly around me, I tried to figure out what could be the reason for his behaviour.

I knew Marcus found me attractive—it was not some self-confident delusion on my part. The way he obviously enjoyed my company, how he sought physical contact with me at all times—be it holding hands in public, sitting next to me so that our knees touched, or spooning me in bed—told me he craved being close to me.

The passion in his eyes, dark and smoldering, just before he'd kiss me, the way he kissed me—mind-blowing and knee-weakening—left no doubt he wanted me. Marcus himself confessed that he did.

Could he be having some medical issues?

There was no doubt Marcus didn't suffer from any erectile dysfunction. I'd witnessed his numerous erections and felt them enough times against the various parts of my body to know that was not an issue.

But maybe there was some less-known health condition that would keep him away from me?

Why wouldn't he talk to me about it then?

I thought we had no more secrets between us, yet he was obviously hiding something from me, and I could no longer ignore it. Wasn't sexual intimacy supposed to be a part of a healthy relationship? Personally, I wanted it to be.

I'd promised him I'd wait until he was ready to talk about this, but why wouldn't he be ready after all this time?

I stopped, realizing that was exactly what hurt so much—his obvious lack of trust in me.

Marcus still hadn't called me his girlfriend. We never said our *I-love-yous*. But I didn't really feel the need for all that because I sensed the true connection and commitment between us. Until now, I had been under the impression that Marcus felt it, too. I'd believed he cared about me and that what we had was as important to him as it was to me.

Could our relationship be real, though, if he didn't feel he could confide in me about something like this?

Turning on my heel at the end of the driveway, I headed back to the house, determined to have a frank conversation with Marcus. I loved him too much to ignore whatever there might be between us. If he truly didn't feel he couldn't talk to me about it, at the very least, he should be able to give me valid reasons for the secrecy.

Once inside the house, I realized Marcus must have fallen asleep by now. No matter how much the anxiety and concern were digging through me from the inside, I'd have to wait with confronting him until he woke up again.

As much as the urge to get answers this very minute burned through me, taking the chance to calm down before talking to Marcus might not be a bad idea—less risk of me saying something I'd regret later.

Standing in the main hallway, I pondered what to do next when I felt the tremors.

The ground shook under my feet, and I had to grab onto the closest wall to keep my balance.

'Earthquake?' Rushed through my brain.

The floor moved again, confirming my fears. This time the vibrations were much stronger, followed by a loud screeching noise that reverberated through the walls around me.

The dishes in the kitchen rattled loudly. Through the doorway, I watched the empty wine bottle left from our dinner last night roll off the kitchen counter and explode into a million pieces from the impact with the tile floor.

The ground seemed to rise under me, knocking me off my feet. Both hands on the wall, I sank to my knees, my heart pounding high in my throat.

What now?

Everything seemed to have scrambled in my head, blanked by rising panic.

Was I supposed to dash for the basement, stand in the doorway, hide under a mattress, or run outside?

I had no practical knowledge of these things—there weren't any real earthquakes or hurricanes in Toronto to deal with. The biggest "natural disasters" I had to endure so far were electricity blackouts due to snowstorms, and overflowing garbage on the streets due to waste collectors' strikes.

Being thrown around like a rag doll now—my perception of the physical world as being stable and solid shuttered to pieces—felt simply terrifying.

The floor continued to shake. It came in waves, each one stronger than the last. The house groaned and screeched like a tortured monster from a nightmare.

Terror sent me back up to my feet. My mind focused on getting as far away from this place as possible before the whole structure would come crashing down on us.

"Marcus!" I screamed at the top of my lungs, but my voice was lost, caught in the deafening noise around me. "We need to get out of here, honey."

The ground lurched up, sending me back to the floor. I landed on my ass this time, painfully bruising my tailbone.

Refusing to give up, I got on all fours and crawled towards the bedroom as fast as I could, bracing myself against the blows to my hips and elbows, as the shockwaves threw me side to side against the walls.

Reaching the bedroom, I shoved at the door with my shoulder, sending it to fly open.

Another wailing sound rolled through the house, and I winced pressing my hands to my ears.

I never knew earthquakes could be this loud.

A blast of heat from the open bedroom hit my face.

Then all thoughts crashed to a stop in my head, confronted with the picture in front of me.

Marcus levitated in the air, a few feet above the bed. His back arched, his body tensed, like a drawn bow ready to release the arrow. Every single muscle seemed to bulge, straining against his pale skin. His head thrown back, the long hair cascaded down in an ink-black stream, the end of it pooling on the bed below him.

Heat, light, and something else—something strong and palpable—rolled off him in powerful swells, pulsating in sync with the shocks of the earthquake that kept rocking the house.

Frozen in shock, I sat in the threshold of his bedroom—hands braced on the doorframe—unable to peel my gaze from the pale muscular figure gracefully arched in the air like a marble statue of an ancient spirit.

As if suspended in time and space, Marcus held unnaturally still. . . except for his hand. Fingers wrapped around his massive hard-on, he slid his hand up and down its length with force.

Embarrassment, followed by a violent wave of arousal, flushed my face when I realized what I was witnessing.

Struggling to maintain the balance, with the ground still lurching from under me, I held on to the doorframe and climbed up to my feet. My knees shook, maybe from the tremors of the earthquake or maybe from the different type of shivers that pulsed through me now.

Marcus growled, baring his teeth, his hand pumped faster. A bright ball of white light exploded from his chest and spread through the room like a supernova.

Its impact reached me in a wave of hot, fragrant air that fanned my hair and enveloped my body like a warm embrace. It was as if the very essence of Marcus stretched out and hugged me before slowly dissipating into the air.

Flushed, confused, and turned on beyond belief, I just stood there, watching Marcus's body relax and languidly float down to the mattress.

The house no longer shook. The earthquake stopped as suddenly as it had begun.

Marcus stretched in bed, his arms and legs spread wide, like the rays of a starfish. Slowly, he rolled his head to the side and lifted his eyelids, meeting my eyes.

Surprise, fear—borderline panic—flashed across his face before he schooled his features into the expression of calm focus.

"How long have you been back?" His voice was quiet and firm, but with a slight edge to it.

"Long enough." I let go of the doorframe and took a step inside. "Why didn't you tell me before? Or . . . show me?"

He rose on his elbows, leaning back against the headboard.

"What are you going to do?" he asked instead of answering my question. "Now that you've seen it."

His posture remained seemingly relaxed, but there was something tense, haunting in the way his eyes tracked my every movement as I approached the bed. As I came closer, I caught a flash of real fear in his eyes, and my chest tightened as if squeezed by a steel band.

Marcus was scared, waiting for my reaction.

"First." I reached for a tissue from the box on his nightstand. "I'll get rid of this mess." I swiped his sticky thigh clean as he watched me. "Then." I tossed the crumbled tissue away and sat on the bed at his side. "I'll ask you again, why the hell did you not tell me before, Marcus?" My voice rose, despite my best effort to keep it calm. "I thought you knew by now that you didn't have to hide from me. Not from me."

The hurt stirred inside me, and I bit my lip to prevent it from trembling.

"How long have you been in the house?" he asked gravely.

"Why does it matter?" I rubbed my bruised elbow. "Long enough to be knocked off my feet and crawl here on my hands and knees."

"How did this whole thing make you feel?"

"Scared," I replied honestly. "Terrified, actually. I've never seen an earthquake before. Despite what you've said about the re-enforced house structure, I feared it would collapse any minute."

"I'm so sorry, Angela. I was sure you'd be a good distance from the house by now. Had I known you were inside, I'd never—"

"Why not?" I interrupted him. "Why not tell me? I know so much about you already, and I love it all. Why on earth would you not tell me?"

He sat up straight, tugging the sheet over his lap.

"Why? Think about how you felt just now. Scared. Terrified by the chaos happening around you. But now you know, *I* was the one who caused it all. I was the reason for your fear." Marcus rubbed his face with his hands. He sounded worn, tired. "You see, Angela, orgasm is a purely physical experience. For a few brief moments, my mind shuts down, and that *thing* inside me gets unleashed, having a field day while my control slips. I hate it, but I have no way to rein it in during sex. The only thing I can do is to keep a safe distance away from people when I come, including you."

"No." I shifted closer to catch his gaze. "Not me. Please."

"Staying away from you is the hardest thing I've ever had to do," he admitted with a gentle smile. "Although, being near you is often even harder." His gaze flickered to his crotch, a corner of his mouth lifted higher. "Physically painful."

"So, how long were you going to do it this way? Were you ever going to tell me?"

"I've tried . . . I mean I've thought about telling you a few times. When I invited you here, I hoped I could. Your finding it out this way certainly wasn't the plan."

His voice faltered again, and my patience thinned. I climbed on the bed next to him then threw my leg over both of his, straddling his thighs.

"Marcus." I took his head in my hands, forcing him to meet my eyes straight on. "What did you think I'd do that stopped you from telling me long ago?"

"Run." He held my gaze as he revealed his fears. "The natural reaction here would be for you to run away in panic. Turn your back on me. Never see me again. Find someone who could fuck you the way you deserve, without the risk of hurting you—"

"I don't believe you'll hurt me."

"Haven't you been hurt already?" He cupped my bruised elbow.

"That happened because I was out there, in the hallway. Things would have been different if I stayed here, with you."

"Would you really prefer to be with me?" He frowned. "In the middle of all this mess?"

"I'd be with you anywhere," I replied, puzzled how he couldn't understand what was so clear to me. "If you held me, up there . . ." I gestured to the space above the bed. "I wouldn't be thrown against that wall out there, would I?"

"Angela." He drew in a long breath, circling my waist with his arms. "Sweetheart. For a few moments, I'm really not in control of anything that happens around me. If I let it go while we're together, I can't predict what could possibly happen to you."

Suddenly, it dawned on me. "You mean you've never come inside a woman before?"

"I've never come anywhere *near* a woman," he said, adding, "or anyone else for that matter."

"So, all those girls . . ." A crazy thought flashed across my mind. "Marcus, are you a virgin? I mean were you, before you and I . . ."

He let out a short laugh. "No. I haven't been a virgin for a very long time. But no, I never came inside a woman, not once. Generally, I try to stay away from, um, penetrative sex as much as I can."

"Don't I know that," I muttered under my breath.

"The first time I got myself off, several houses collapsed in the town where I lived."

"They did?" I sat back in shock. "Did anyone get hurt?"

"Several people got injured by the falling debris. No one died, thankfully, but people lost their homes. I'm sure you can still find the news reports on *the unusual seismic activity* in that area."

"Sounds awful."

"Exactly. Needless to say, sex—real sex—has become something I've tried to avoid all my life as much as possible, using it only to release the energy building up inside when I couldn't do a magic show for any reason."

I tried to process everything I'd just heard. His past, though, could not define our future. Nothing about him—no matter how unusual or scary—would turn me away. Marcus remained the man I loved.

He had been trying to deal with, fight, and control this unknown force inside him since he was a boy—alone. But maybe there were some moments in life when his magic could be embraced instead of restrained, now that he had me?

"Well, you're safe here," I said softly. "There is no one around."

"That's exactly why I got this house, to have a safe place."

"Very smart of you." I let my voice drop, sliding closer to him. "And super convenient for us now."

I felt him harden under me and lightly rubbed myself along the ridge of his growing erection. He grabbed my hips, his fingers digging into my skin through the material of my jeans, keeping me in place.

Not anymore, honey. I'm not letting you turn me away again.

Now that I knew what to expect, having another earthquake didn't seem that scary, definitely not enough to keep us apart.

"Marcus." Sinking my hands into his hair, I leaned into him. "Did you really think an earthquake, a tsunami, a nuclear explosion or even the world's apocalypse would scare me away from you?"

"Would you really like to be in the middle of all this?" he asked in turn. "Here, in the eye of the storm with me?"

"Absolutely." I nodded.

Narrowing his eyes, he focused on me intently.

"Fearless," he whispered, an expression of disbelief and admiration spreading over his face.

"I am," I agreed. "As long as I'm with you."

"If you get hurt in any way, I'll never forgive myself."

"Here is the thing, honey." I slid my hands down the side of his neck then along his shoulders, caressing his skin. "I have no way to be sure about this, but I *know* that nothing of yours would ever hurt me." I remembered the warmth of the phantom embrace when I stood at the threshold of his bedroom. "Unless you decide to use your magic against me." He flinched at such a notion, and I continued. "I'm confident, I'll be safe."

Sliding my hands to his back, I leaned in and kissed the side of his neck. Catching a tendril of his familiar scent, I relaxed against his hard body. It felt so right to be with him, the last vestiges of any fear or apprehension of what was to come melted away.

"You're really not afraid," he murmured, still sounding bewildered, but his hands glided up my back, drawing me into him instead of pushing me away.

"I have many fears, my darling," I whispered, nibbling on his ear as his breathing accelerated. "But you're not one of them. You've already shaken my world to the core, turned my whole life upside down, and knocked everything I knew off its foundation." I ghosted my lips over his, smiling against his mouth. "What's a little earthquake now?"

His arms flexed around me.

"I love you," he rasped, catching me completely off guard, then swallowed my gasp of surprise in a kiss. My mind was reeling from his confession as my body heated up from the sensation of his lips moving against mine.

"I love you, Angela," he repeated, letting me come up for air. And I struggled to catch my breath as my heart pounded wild inside my chest. "Every single piece of you." Without releasing me from his arms, he rolled me to my back, covering my body with his. "And all of your pieces are now mine."

He rose over me on his elbows, his face just an inch or two above mine. His hair cascaded down, shrouding us in a fragrant curtain of black silk. Eyes dark and intense, his gaze reached deep into my very soul. There was nothing I wouldn't do for him at that moment. My own love for him bubbled hot inside me, swallowing me whole and rendering me speechless.

Marcus caught my mouth in a kiss again—long, tender, and caressing, it slowly grew deeper and more powerful.

My fingers in his hair, I slid my hands along the silky strands. Rotating my wrist, I wound a handful of his hair around it, anchoring myself to him.

Letting go of my mouth, he peppered kisses along my neck then down between my breasts and lower to my stomach. I whimpered in protest and tugged on the wrist with his hair wrapped around it, prompting him to meet my eyes.

"I've had enough foreplay in the past few weeks." I gently tugged again, urging him to move up to me. "Come here. I want you inside me."

In one smooth movement, he pulled himself up and pressed his forehead to mine, "I don't keep condoms here . . . "

"Since when is that a problem for you?" I huffed a brief laugh then sensed there was more to this. "What's going on, Marcus?"

"I don't want to use one with you," he said quietly.

Shocked, I dropped my arm, allowing his hair to unwind from my wrist and spill over us again.

"I'm not on the pill," I reminded.

"I know." He stared at me.

"You know the consequences—"

"I do," he replied and added firmly, "and I want it all with you. Stay with me. Forever."

Overwhelmed by the raw emotion in his eyes and the enormity of his request, I simply threw my arms around him and drew him closer, feeling his frantic heartbeat next to mine.

This was my Marcus.

He knew little about women and never had a true relationship before me. He didn't proclaim his commitment by going down on one knee, holding out a diamond ring. He did it like this, in his own way—unconventionally, maybe a bit awkwardly, but so very real.

"I love you, too, Marcus," I whispered into the side of his neck. "You're mine, all of you."

With a groan, he grabbed my hair and captured my mouth in a bruising, possessive kiss. My breath all but stopped, as a wave of intense arousal flushed through me, tingling in my breasts and flooding my core with liquid heat.

He rocked his hips into me, and I opened my legs wider, welcoming him. Slowly, he eased inside me—tight and slick—filling me whole.

With a pained groan, he began to move, and I lifted my hips to meet him, reveling in the pleasure of having him this close.

His arms tight around me, I felt us rising into the air before we hovered, suspended over the bed, a couple of feet under the wooden ceiling beams—Marcus and I, fused together as one.

The feeling of weightlessness added to the sensation of pleasure floating through my body as he angled his hips just the right way, thrusting hard inside me.

Swirls of white-hot light curled around us, caressing my skin with warmth. My senses heightened. The tease of orgasm flickered deep inside me, and I let it grow, fully surrendering to the ecstasy Marcus brought to life in me.

The hot flush of pleasure blinded me as an intense climax shuddered my entire body.

"Oh . . . Marcus," I moaned, riding its waves, my fingers digging into the hard muscles of his shoulders.

He held me tight as we rolled through the air, our arms and legs intertwined, our hair tangled together in one black-brown mass. I wrapped my legs around his hips, clinging to him. I finally had him, all of him, and I was not letting go.

Suspended in the air, I didn't feel the house shake, but I heard the earthquake rumble through it once again. The loud noise bounced between the walls and merged with the pained groan that tore from Marcus's chest as he continued to pound hard in me.

He buried his face in my shoulder, muffling his growls, as if it would stop the onslaught of pleasure I sensed was about to explode inside him along with the waves of bright light and heat radiating from him. His body tensed around me, his arms flexed as if straining not to crush me.

"Shh." I slid my hands up and down the bulging muscles on his back. "It's okay. Let it go, my love. We'll be fine. Let it go."

His roar against my shoulder resonated deep inside my chest, as he finally erupted in fierce shudders of his own climax. The deafening noise the house made as it shook violently made me believe for a moment that it would actually collapse this time.

The idea didn't scare me, though. A warm, happy feeling floated through me, not allowing for any fear or apprehension at that moment.

Marcus relaxed in my arms, all tension seemed to have seeped out of him, as we slowly descended back to the bed.

"I'm so happy right now, Angela," he whispered into my neck. "I've never felt this way in my life. *You* make me happy."

My heart swelled from the intensity of the feelings I had for him. So much love. So many beautiful emotions. And I made my own vow right then and there—I would do anything to keep him happy. For as long as I lived.

Chapter 37

"ANGELA, PLEASE, PROMISE me you'll be careful." Marcus's voice on the other end of the line sounded stern, and I knew the deep worried wrinkle must have furrowed his forehead, even if I couldn't see it.

"I've already promised you that, honey. Like, a thousand times, really." Well, definitely close to a dozen times during this one phone conversation since I'd informed him I'd agreed to meet Ingeborg in person after all. "You know I wouldn't be doing this if she seemed dangerous in any way. I'm just hoping to get some useful information from her."

Over the weeks of our correspondence, Ingeborg's emails had grown more detailed, and with it, more unbelievable. A regular person would've probably stopped any contact with her the minute she claimed to be close to two hundred years old. However, having the living, breathing proof in Marcus that anything was possible in this world, I decided to keep an open mind.

"What she wrote to me sounds too much like fiction, but I sense a lot of it may be true. I need to meet her in person, Marcus, to see her face when she answers my questions. You know she didn't lie about her identity. Aside from her age, everything about her checked out to be true."

To my embarrassment, Marcus had made me ask Ingeborg for a copy of her passport, and she sent it without questioning his request, along with her home address and phone number. Simon had a full background check done on the woman.

"I've met my share of very disturbed individuals, Angela. I'd hate to have you come anywhere near one of them."

"It's early afternoon," I argued, appreciating his concern but also getting a bit frustrated with his persistence. "Broad daylight. I'm meeting her in a public place, a five minute-walk from my home. Honestly, darling, you're overreacting here."

He huffed a sigh. "You should have waited until I could come with you." It was late morning in Vegas, and his first show of today was about to start.

All this time, Marcus had declined writing to Ingeborg or taking her calls when she phoned, letting me deal with her instead. I suspected he was either apprehensive about confronting his past or afraid to get his hopes up only to be disappointed if Ingeborg turned out to be a fraud after all.

"I couldn't wait for you, honey. It's already evening in Switzerland, and Ingeborg goes to bed early. Besides, Simon wouldn't let you go anywhere without a bunch of bodyguards in tow," I reminded.

Since last week, under Simon's strict instructions, Marcus was to be accompanied by a number of security detail whenever he set his foot outside of his hotel suite, as the last message sent by *The Biggest Fan* put everyone on high alert.

It came a few days ago. Unlike all the other emails that were long and elaborate, this one contained just one sentence.

'I'll see you soon.'

The four small, foreboding words terrified not only me. Simon hired additional security, cut Marcus's interaction with fans from the very limited to practically non-existent, and ordered him to stay indoors at all times until the person who called themselves *The Biggest Fan* could be apprehended.

"Simon would throw a fit if he heard of me walking outside in Toronto," Marcus agreed. I've heard from him that Simon had actually threatened to quit his job if Marcus didn't cooperate in his efforts to keep him safe.

All this didn't stop Marcus from sneaking out by teleporting to see me, but we stayed inside when he came over, no more going out for breakfast.

"What Simon doesn't know, though, wouldn't hurt him," Marcus continued. "If you move the meeting to later in the afternoon, I have a few hours between the shows—"

"Honey, I've explained this already. *After* the show would be too late for Ingeborg. It would be rather inconsiderate to ask her to change her bedtime to accommodate my overprotective boyfriend. You know at her age—"

"No, I don't know. I know absolutely nothing about a *typical* lifestyle of a two-hundred-year-old person."

"Exactly. And this is my chance to find out more about everything, not just her lifestyle, but her history and how it may possibly be connected with you."

It took a few more firm promises on my part to stay safe and to have a fully-charged phone on me before Marcus was finally called on stage and had to end our phone call.

"I'll be at your place right after the show," he promised before hanging up.

⸻ ◉ ⸻

THINKING ABOUT EVERYTHING Ingeborg had told me about herself, I was running along the sidewalk on my way to the coffee shop for my meeting with her.

According to her emails, Ingeborg had been living in Zürich, Switzerland for the past fifty years.

She had been married three times. Her three husbands, son, and two grandsons had passed away from old age, all of them having had much shorter lives than hers.

All three husbands had been regular humans. However, her son and his descendants, all had some form of *special* abilities, as did many others in her extended family.

Ingeborg claimed to be able to teleport. She also said that sometimes she *'knew things that nobody told her about.'*

Her son could walk through walls and closed doors. Both of her grandsons used to levitate in the air.

Magic seemed to diminish with each generation. Among Ingeborg's great-grandchildren and great-great grandchildren, there were some who could only move small objects with their mind. Others simply lived longer than was humanly possible, without having anything else *paranormal* about them at all.

Only her great-great grandniece, Cecilia, happened to have powers similar to Marcus's in strength and versatility. Like him, Cecilia could make many things happen. Unlike him, though, she needed to use actual magic spells to do it.

Intrigued and excited, I couldn't entirely shake off the apprehension while on my way to meet the woman who claimed to have lived almost eight times longer than I have.

It was March, and although we had very little snow during the winter this year, it was wet, cold, and windy outside. The outdoor patios wouldn't open for weeks, yet.

Walking inside the coffee shop, I swept the tables with my gaze.

"Angela!" A blonde woman waved at me from the booth in the corner.

Ingeborg seemed to have recognized me immediately, although she'd never seen my picture. Maybe this was one of *the things she knew even if no one told her about.*

With a small wave and a nod in greeting, I made my way to her table.

Even with her sitting down, I could tell Ingeborg was fairly tall. Her flax-blonde hair—made even lighter by strands of silver in it—was pulled back into an elegant bun.

I would've had a hard time guessing her age. From a certain distance, she could have passed for a forty-year old, despite the greys.

However, as I got closer, her incredible age became more apparent. It wasn't so much in the fine lines around her eyes and mouth, but inside her sky-blue eyes, as clear as glass. The look in them was heavy with wisdom, as if she knew *everything* and, in a way, was tired from the weight of this knowledge.

"So very lovely to finally meet you, Angela." Ingeborg gestured at the seat across the table from her.

"It's very nice to meet you, too, Ingeborg." I shook her outstretched hand. My gaze went to the round bauble on a chain around her neck.

A perfect sphere, small and unassuming, it appeared to be made from the same smoky-looking amber like Marcus's pendant.

"You can call me Inge." She smiled. "Most people do." She followed my eyes to her necklace. "I got it from my father. Most of my relatives have one. They're supposed to either ward off demons or to warn you when they're around—no one knows for sure anymore. These days, it's just a family tradition to wear them. The amulets remind us that we all belong together. Have you seen one before?" she asked quickly. "Does Marcus have one?"

I hesitated for a moment, not willing to talk about Marcus until I was certain she was being completely truthful with me.

"How did you get here, Inge?" I asked instead of answering her question. "Did you teleport from Switzerland?"

"Yes, I did." She leaned back in her seat.

"Could you show me, please?"

A smile of understanding crossed her face.

"You need to protect your man." She nodded with a quick glance around. "You want to make sure I am who I say I am."

The coffee shop was busy this Sunday afternoon. Our corner booth, however, was mostly obstructed from view of other customers and staff.

Ingeborg slid deeper inside the booth, to hide completely from any errant glance from others, I assumed.

"All right. I'll see you in a moment," she announced, cheerfully.

The echo of the familiar puff of warm air brushed by my skin then Ingeborg's face in front of me dissolved into nothing, and she disappeared. Only her smile lingered in my mind's eye, like that left behind by the Cheshire cat.

Glancing around, I made sure people hadn't noticed her disappearance. Thankfully, no one seemed to be gaping at her empty seat.

"Hello again." I turned to her voice, finding Ingeborg sitting across from me again, as if she'd never left at all. "These are for you." She placed a small box of Swiss chocolates on the table between us. "I don't normally do it— technically, it is smuggling." She chuckled. "Besides, these are so good, they should be classified as drugs."

"Thank you, Inge." I smiled back, opening the box. Unable to stop myself, I tasted one right away. "Mmmm, these are good."

Most people would have been unnerved by a sudden disappearance and then reappearance of a woman right in front of their eyes. Because of Marcus, though, magic had become such a big part of my everyday life that the familiarity of it was comforting instead of being frightening.

To me, Ingeborg's teleportation was a proof of some connection between Marcus and her, putting me at ease in her presence.

"Is it your first time in Toronto?" I asked, savoring another piece of chocolate.

"Yes, I don't come across the ocean that often."

A waitress came with another cup of tea for her, and I asked for one, too.

"I was born and raised in Finland," Ingeborg continued when we were alone again. "Back when it was still a Grand Duchy within the Russian Empire. But, I've travelled all over Europe since then. Some of it was voluntary, and some of my travels were forced on me—the last century was volatile, as you surely know."

She gave me a sad, warm smile and took a sip of her tea.

"I do go to Arizona, in The United States of America, every few years or so," Ingeborg continued in a soft, melodious voice. "One of my relatives lives there with his family. Every year, they organize a big meeting on their property near Phoenix—a family reunion of sorts—for all of us who can attend. I try to make it whenever I can. It's nice to visit and catch up with everyone. Perchance, Marcus would like to attend it this year? It's in June."

"Do you think he should?"

She put her cup down and leaned my way.

"I will be completely honest with you, Angela. I am fascinated by this boy. His abilities are phenomenal. No one I know has the magic of our ancestors manifest in them as powerfully as it does in Marcus. More so, though, I marvel how he has survived all this time on his own, without harming himself or others. Our power can be difficult to control. One needs a fair amount of practice and, most definitely, the support and guidance of a family."

"Do you have any ideas at all who his parents might be?"

"No. Sorry. I don't know anyone who had lost a toddler. If it did happen to one of us, we would have moved heaven and earth, searching for that child. Children are rare and treasured among our kind."

"Marcus believes he was abandoned."

"Poor boy!" She shook her head, seemingly genuinely distraught. It was strange to hear Marcus being referred to as *a boy* by Ingeborg. To her, however, every living human on the planet must seem as a child. "It has to be terrible to think your own parents didn't want you."

"He was tossed from one foster home to another. Often because people felt weird or scared to have him around once they caught a glimpse of his magic. He figured his parents did the same."

"Although I don't know who his parents are, I am confident that's not what happened, dear. At least one of his parents must have been one of us and in possession of the magic. In fact, considering how strong Marcus's abilities are, I'm inclined to believe that both of his parents had it."

"Yet you don't know them?"

"There is not that many of us, only a few dozen or so whom we know of. However, that doesn't mean there couldn't be more of our kind—possibly, some groups or families we haven't encountered yet. We hide our abilities from the public. It wouldn't be that simple to spot others like us if they were out there.

"In any case, his parents would not have been afraid of his magic. They'd have had it, too. Also, since Marcus has been living in plain sight all this time, if his parents were alive, they would have found him by now. Something tragic must have happened that separated them from their child. As it is, I'm afraid they are no longer alive."

It was a grave assumption, but oddly her words gave me a sense of comfort. Once upon a time, it seemed Marcus had a family who loved him. They didn't discard him. His parents couldn't be there for him, because they were dead.

"With Marcus's co-operation," continued Ingeborg, "I could look further into it, if you like. He should have some records, from government services? I'm not sure what agencies are responsible for orphaned children in the United States, but there should be a paper trail that we could explore and reference it with the known history of our people."

"I'm not sure how he'd take it. Marcus doesn't talk much about it."

"We all need to know where we came from. Having strong roots helps us spread our wings with confidence."

"Where did you all come from? I mean your people . . . Marcus's people? How came you are the ones with magic?"

"That is something no one knows for sure. Some say we are descendants of demons who came to Earth a long time ago. Yet some believe our ancestors were angels, banished from Heaven as a punishment. Many centuries ago, one of them fell in love with a human woman and gave up his immortality for her. There might have been more than one who traded it for love. In any case, we are their children's children."

I sipped my tea in silence for a moment. There were many legends in this world. Some of them seemed to have more truth to them than others. "Did demons have magic, too?"

"I don't know if they possessed it themselves, but they hailed from another world, another dimension, if you will. When I was a child, I was told that the combined life force of both worlds, theirs and ours, was what caused the unusual abilities in the offspring of these unions."

"What do you believe, Inge, personally? Who were your ancestors? Demons or angels?"

"Does it really matter?" she asked, with a delicate shrug of a shoulder. "We are what we are, and we live our lives the best we can, just like anyone else on Earth. Some things may be easier for us, but often our abilities make it only more difficult."

That I believed. Marcus's seemingly unlimited powers came with their own, often brutal, limitations.

"I lived longer than my son and both of my grandchildren," Ingeborg went on. "I knew there was a strong chance I would out-live them when I stopped aging. There was plenty of time for me to prepare inside for their passing. Only, how can you ever prepare yourself for having to bury your babies? It's unnatural for a parent or a grandparent to bury their children. No matter how much time passes, the pain of losing them doesn't go away, even when they pass of old age, after having lived long and productive lives." She inhaled deeply and took a slow drink from her teacup. "After a while, my long life had begun to feel like a burden—too many goodbyes to dear friends and family. I actually had a sense of relief when I noticed the first signs of aging a few decades ago. Now, I'm less afraid to get attached to people, knowing there is a good chance that I could go first. Now, I may not be the one saying goodbye."

"Longevity isn't as wonderful as many believe, it seems," I ventured, taken by her honesty.

"No," she agreed. "It's not about how long you live, but how fast the world moves past you. What's the point in living long if everyone you know and love dies? Another challenge all of my kind face, regardless of lifespan, is having to hide our abilities from the world."

"You haven't found a way to come clean about who you are?"

"Sadly, no. The history of centuries of violence against anyone who is different has taught us to be extremely careful. If we want to live lives as close to normal as possible, we need to hide our abilities. I have moved and changed identities many times to disguise my true age. We train our children from when they are babies to not use their magic outside our homes."

"It must be difficult to constantly suppress a part of who you are."

"We all learn to do it. Hiding becomes second nature. I'm amazed that Marcus actually found a way to display his abilities in front of everyone."

"He needs it," I explained. "He has to share his magic with other people. Otherwise it builds up inside of him, which becomes painful. I'm afraid it could potentially destroy him."

"I've never heard of it." Ingeborg tilted her head, with clear curiosity on her face. "It must have something to do with the incredible strength of his power."

Clasping my hands in front of me on the table, I leaned closer to her.

"Do you or the others from your family know of ways to control it? Could you teach him, the way you teach your children? Marcus never had the benefit of growing up with a family who could help."

"Absolutely," Ingeborg promised softly. "How often does he need to give the shows? Can he have any break at all?"

"Well. There are other ways, too." I hesitated for a second, wondering just how inappropriate it would be to talk about our sex life with a woman I had just met, who could be my many-times-great grandmother. "Well, when we . . . Um, I mean my . . . intimate touch calms him down, too." Feeling my face heat up, I focused on my hands before blurting out, "When we have sex."

Ingeborg smiled when I lifted my gaze to hers.

"No magic is more powerful than love."

"Is that why it happens? He swears other women's touch never had the same effect. Why me?"

"Well, maybe there is some demon blood in you, too?" She stared at me, inquisitively.

"Me?" I thought about my parents, either one of them was the furthest thing from what I imagined a demon's descendant would be. "Very unlikely!" I shook my head, laughing.

"In this case, don't we all have a special effect on our loved ones? Even ordinary humans? Just a touch, often a mere presence of a soulmate can calm, soothe, and comfort us. Because Marcus's magic is so strong, I wonder if your ability to comfort your soulmate has grown to match it."

Deep in my heart, I always sensed Marcus was special to me—the word *soulmate* put the name on it. It also brought a feeling of relief—my ability to calm Marcus's fire wouldn't go away one day. For as long as I loved him, I should be able to bring him comfort.

"He is waiting for you," Ingeborg said suddenly. "We should say our goodbyes for now."

"He is?" I looked around, expecting to see Marcus here, in the coffee shop. "Where?"

"Oh, no." Ingeborg laughed. "At home. I sense he is waiting for you at home. It's getting late for me, too."

She got up, and I followed.

"Well. It was very, very nice to meet you, Inge." I shook her hand, pressing the box of chocolates to my chest.

"Please give Marcus my regards. I hope so much you two can make it to the family reunion in June. I will email the address to you. Oh, and take care of the baby," she added out of the blue.

"Baby?" For a second, I thought she was referring to Marcus, having downgraded him from *the boy* to *the baby*.

"Yes, *your* baby," Ingeborg said with a warm smile. "I can't predict the future, but it's most likely a boy, considering who his father is. Boys are far more common among our kind. In the past two centuries, there were only two girls in our extended family, my great-great grandniece Cecilia and I. Goodbye."

With a small wave, Ingeborg, slid back into the corner of the booth then disappeared into the thin air, leaving me standing at our table, struck by her words as if by lightning.

"A baby?" I mumbled to myself, raising my hand to my stomach. Was it true?

Physically, I didn't feel any different. I wasn't even late yet—my period was supposed to come any day now.

But what if it was true? Since that night in January, Marcus and I hadn't used any protection. We both knew this could happen, and it felt right.

Our relationship didn't exactly follow the usual pattern. Marcus never asked me to marry him. I still didn't recall him ever referring to me as *his girlfriend*, only *his woman*. But I was truly his, body and soul. Just like he was mine.

I felt no apprehension about his reaction to the news, only elated feeling of excitement, as I ran out of the coffee shop and headed back to him.

Chapter 38

MARCUS

He sat in her apartment, on her couch, with her cat in his lap. The only thing missing was her.

She had texted him that she was on the way home from her meeting with Ingeborg, and he was trying to calm the anxiety clawing at his insides. The reason for the scratchy feeling was not just the absence of her, he realized, but also the anticipation of whatever news she might be bringing with her.

The possibility that Angela might've discovered more people like him—that he was not the only one in the world—both intrigued and unsettled him.

Carefully and painstakingly, he had crafted a way to exist in this world, being able to lead a more-or-less ordinary life. Now, he had allowed Angela to take the risk of upsetting this balance, with unpredictable consequences.

Searching for a distraction from the anxious thoughts, Marcus stroked the soft fur of the cat in his lap then playfully flicked his ear. The cat lashed his tail in obvious annoyance, but wouldn't get off his lap and wouldn't stop purring.

It was odd to be in Angela's place while she was gone. Without her, the apartment seemed lifeless, devoid of its soul. In fact, his whole life didn't feel the same without her.

Since she quit working at the store, she had been spending most of her weekends at her parents' place, first helping them sell the house then pack their belongings to move to a much smaller condo unit.

Whatever time she could spare, Angela would let him take her to his place in Vegas. He couldn't wait to return to his hotel suite after the show when he knew she was waiting for him there. Still, it wasn't enough.

He needed her to share his bed, his house, and his life. Every day. He wanted her smell on his sheets, her toothbrush in his bathroom, and all of her multicoloured shoes in his closet.

He wanted her goddamned cat curled up on *his* couch.

Needing to see her now more than anything, he gently removed the cat from his lap and got up, ready to meet Angela on her way home—Simon's instructions to stay indoors be damned.

Ear to the front door, he made sure all was quiet in the hallway on her floor, before teleporting to the other side of the locked door. That was the only unordinary thing he allowed himself to do. Mindful of possible witnesses, he made it downstairs in the conventional way, using the elevator and doors.

Shielding his face from the biting wind, he walked down the street towards the coffee shop, briefly considering turning his leather jacket into a winter parka.

Even with the spring around the corner, the weather in Toronto didn't seem to be warming up. Over time, he got to know the city well and even grew to love it. However, these freezing winds with cold moisture in the air that seemed to seep through his clothes, no matter how many layers of clothing he had on, were something he truly despised and could never get used to.

Head down against the wind, he nearly tripped over an orange construction cone blocking the sidewalk.

"All clear." A man in a hardhat picked the cone up, letting him pass.

A block down the street, Marcus strained his eyes, searching for Angela's figure in the distance. She should be coming towards him by now. However, he couldn't make out her familiar shape among the few pedestrians huddling from the wind.

Had she already passed him somehow, without neither of them noticing?

He turned around. But there was only the sole construction worker, promptly loading the traffic cones into an unmarked van.

Something nagged at the back of his mind as the van swirled around the corner, driving away. There were no signs of any actual construction having taken place in that area of the sidewalk.

It was Sunday.

Would the city do any construction work on this day, unless it was an emergency?

Or was the sole purpose of the cones to divert the pedestrian traffic? With the sidewalk closed, the only detour would be the alley between the two old factory buildings.

Heart pounding against his ribs, Marcus hurried to the turn off into the alley, an ominous premonition narrowing in on him.

Maybe he had caught the case of Simon's paranoia, but he wouldn't be able to relax now until Angela was safe back at the apartment with him.

Turning around the corner, he finally glimpsed her silhouette at the opposite end of the valley. Her back to him, she was about to exit into the street near her building.

Angela must have run up the alley while he walked down the street, and they'd ended up missing each other.

Relief spread through him like warm milk at the familiar sight of her jumping over potholes and puddles. Angela was the only person he knew, who could successfully navigate a frozen pavement covered with slush while wearing four-inch heels.

A dark figure suddenly leaped her way from the wall, and Marcus's insides turned to ice. His Angela was snatched out of sight, dragged around the corner. Gone.

A sharp noise of screeching tires. Then silence, with only the wind howling between the brick walls of the buildings.

His feet moved before his mind had a chance to absorb what had just happened. He had no chance to think about teleporting, as his feet took him off running as fast as was humanly possible.

Only he was not an ordinary human.

His thoughts finally caught up with him through the fog of utter shock clouding his mind, and he took off into the air, flying through the alley with the speed of a bullet.

He landed in a crouch, in the very spot where Angela stood just a moment ago. A small cardboard box with a few pieces of chocolate scattered over the pavement was all that remained from her.

A painful groan caught in his throat, the agony ripping his insides to shreds. Propped on one knee, he slammed both fists into the ground. An uncontrolled bolt of energy blasted out on impact, cracking the pavement. The lightning-shaped fractures spread from his fists through the alley, zigzagging between the buildings on both sides.

Frantic, Marcus shot up into the air again, searching the streets for any trace of her or the vehicle that had taken her.

The car was gone and so was Angela, lost in one of the dozen side streets and back alleys of this older part of the city.

Rising higher and higher over the trees and the rooftops, he didn't care if anyone saw him. He hovered over the city and searched the streets in vain—there was just no way of knowing which one of the hundreds of vehicles below carried his Angela.

Hot rage collided with the icy-cold fear inside him and exploded out of his chest in one raw, guttural cry of anguish.

No longer sure if he could contain the power surging inside him and afraid to unleash it on the innocents, he rose higher into the sky.

The air turned colder and harder to breathe as he ascended. It rushed by his face in icy streams, cooling his heated skin, but the sensation was nothing like the calming, soothing touch of Angela's hand.

His heart burst into a black cloud of pure pain. His woman had been taken, and he'd done nothing.

He, the man who could do everything.

Like a stab of a dagger, the pain forced him to curl into himself, but his mind began to clear.

He scanned the city below again. From this distance, the whole of the Greater Toronto Area lay beneath him in its entirety, hugging tight the horseshoe curve of the shore of Lake Ontario.

Angela was there somewhere. She needed him.

He took a couple of deep breaths. The freezing air filled his lungs, cooling him from the inside.

The list was already forming in his head. Call Simon. Track her cellphone. Security camera images from the nearby businesses to identify the car.

He was going to figure out how to find his woman. And then he would annihilate those responsible for taking her from him.

Chapter 39

THEY RIPPED OFF MY blindfold, bringing me face to face with my captor.

The watery blue eyes of Marcus's self-proclaimed *Biggest Fan* fixed on me as a condescending smile stretched across his thin lips.

"Well, it's nice to see you here, Miss McAllister," he said, his sterile, minty breath fanned across my face.

"Why are you doing this?" I croaked, my throat painfully dry as I blinked in the semi-darkness.

Where was I?

Pale light streamed through the narrow, dirty windows positioned under the high ceiling of a large building. Concrete floors. Grey walls.

A warehouse?

Although, there were no shelves or boxes in sight, just dark, open space.

"What . . ." I attempted to clear my throat, but a violent bout of coughing sent me forward. Sharp pain in my wrists immediately yanked me back into the upright position.

I was sitting on a chair, my hands tied behind its back. The place wasn't heated, I realized, shaking from cold. I vaguely remembered someone taking off my boots and coat on the way here, leaving me only in my dress and stockings.

"What do you want?" I managed to ask the man in front of me. Two others lurked in the shadows behind him.

Surprisingly, there wasn't any fear in me yet. I was cold, uncomfortable, and very confused, but not afraid.

"What do I want from you?" He scoffed. The same leering stare I remembered from our brief encounter by the theater slithered down my body. Only now, he stared openly, without the furtiveness he had then. "I could come up with a number of things to do with someone like you, *sweetie*." The endearment fell from his lips like a dirty word, lewd and patronizing.

Someone from behind me sneered, and the sound made my skin crawl with disgust.

"Who, on earth, are you?" I asked slowly.

This couldn't be real.

"Well." The man in front of me replied curtly and straightened, moving out of my personal space. I inhaled a lungful of air, grateful it was no longer tainted by his breath. "You see, you would've recognized me right away if your fucking boyfriend didn't steal what was mine."

I took a closer look at him, straining my memory.

He appeared middle aged, maybe in his fifties, but could be younger if the bags under his eyes resulted from his lifestyle choices, not just his age. His receding hair was pulled back into a thin ponytail, just like the last time I saw him. The magenta-pink shirt he wore under the purple with silver thread blazer betrayed the taste of a showman in him.

Still, aside from that one single encounter, I was positive I hadn't seen this man before.

"The name is Harold," he snapped. "Harold the Great. And I was the greatest until that lying *bastard* entered the scene."

The name didn't trigger anything in my memory.

"Sorry, still don't know who you are."

"Bitch!" The sharp insult came with a sudden blow to the side of my face. Bells rang through my head as his fist connected with it. "You're lying, too."

Disoriented from pain, with my hands tied, all I could do was gape and blink in shock.

"Shut your mouth and listen, you whore," he gritted through clenched teeth, rubbing his knuckles. "Or I'll find a better use for that hole of yours."

The threat was met with cheering and shuffling in the shadows around behind me—a clue that there were significantly more people than I could see.

"You have one purpose here. One thing to do or I'll end you." He hovered over me, as if trying to overpower me with his mere presence.

Questions crowded my brain, pushing aside the rising fear, but I kept quiet—the blow from his fist still painfully reverberated through my skull.

"I was going to make his life a living hell after what he did to me." His voice was filled with venom. Harold must be talking about Marcus, but I couldn't figure out exactly what Marcus could've done to make this man so enraged.

"I had a whole plan. Started with emails, to scare the shit out of him—"

"If you think a bunch of death threats would scare him . . ." I couldn't hold back, despite his orders to keep quiet, "you don't know who you're dealing with."

He lunged towards me, his fingers curving painfully into my shoulders.

"Is that what you think?" he spat.

The sickeningly minty breath hit my face again, and I pressed into the back of the chair in the futile effort to get away from him.

The full awareness of what was happening hit me. Tricked to turn into the deserted alley, I had been snatched on my way home and taken to this freezing warehouse, where I was now at the mercy of a nutcase.

Anger simmered inside me, boiling hot through my fear.

"You have no idea what you got yourself into," I said, forcing the words through my clenched teeth.

He narrowed his eyes at me—cold and calculating, without a hint of any warmth or empathy.

The eyes of a psychopath.

Instead of another flare-up of rage, though, his lips stretched into a mocking smile.

"Oh, yes I do, *sweetie*. I dedicated a chunk of my life to learning everything there was to know about Marcus the Magnificent when he put me out of business." He straightened in front of me once again and took a few steps back and forth. "My show crumbled the moment he came into the picture."

"How is it his fault?" I protested, my teeth chattering from cold. "Many magicians are still thriving despite Marcus. If you have your own style that draws people—"

"I don't care about the others!" he snarled, spinning on his heel to face me. "He put *me* out of a job. What was it about him that made people rush to see him instead of *me*? He didn't do anything new. I've watched his shows. There was no originality whatsoever! He stole every single trick I did."

"Many do the same tricks," I said, evenly this time. If I made him see it the way the whole world saw it, could I talk sense into him? I doubted it. Still, despite the threat of earning another blow from his fist, I had to try. "Everyone just puts their own spin on each trick."

"Bullshit!" Harold literally jumped at my words. "Not him. I've watched him, many times. I've made videos and analyzed them, frame by frame. I know what makes him different. *Magnificent,* my ass!" His face twisted in a grimace of deep disgust. "He is a fake, a fraud. He doesn't do tricks like the rest of us. There is no hard work for him."

Dread creeped up my spine, stripping me of words. Could Harold have learned the truth about Marcus? Did he figure it out the same way I did?

"Somehow, the bastard can really walk on air or water or walls. You name it," he continued, pacing the concrete floor. "He has no props, no actual assistants. There is no other way to do what he does. His shit is real."

It took a crazy, obsessed person like myself to figure out his secret.

Harold was even more crazy and obsessed than I. The reasons for our obsession with Marcus might have been different, but there was a big similarity, whether I wanted to admit it or not. Both Harold and I were obsessed enough to pay attention and crazy enough to believe in the existence of magic.

"I put time and hard work into perfecting my skill. This piece of shit just walks out there and does it all. Just like that. With no effort at all. How fair is that?" He glared my way, as if expecting me to reply, then answered his own question. "It's not fair. One can't have everything if I have nothing. So." He rubbed his hands, bouncing on his toes. "Instead of just ruining his life, I figured I could convince him to share some of what he's got with me. Which would be fair, don't you think?"

"What do you want?"

"Oh, there are many things he could do to make it up to me. I wrote a list a while back. Except that I figured Marcus wouldn't want to share, the asshole that he is."

He cupped his chin, staring at me quizzically. "Now, how do you convince someone, who had obviously made a pact with the devil to get the powers he has, to do anything for me? How would I obtain enough leverage over someone who has all the power and no weaknesses?"

Harold paused for a moment—for drama, I guessed—not actually waiting for an answer from anyone.

"That was what I shifted my focus to," he continued. "I decided to watch his every move until he made a mistake, exposed his weakness, and gave me something to work with. He was not an easy target, I have to admit. I watched his house for weeks."

"It was you," I whispered as it dawned on me.

The cars that Marcus had complained about being parked around his property weren't paparazzi. It was all this deranged man. He was the one sitting in hiding, waiting for his chance to strike.

"Me and my boys," he confirmed with obvious satisfaction, tipping his chin at someone behind my shoulder. "That didn't give us much, though. The only one we ever saw coming and going was the housekeeper. It's like Marcus had a house he never used. Ever. After weeks of time wasted, I decided to look elsewhere."

He leaned in again, this time from a little distance, hands propped on his thighs. "I'll tell you how I found you, my dear. I didn't make it to that show he had here in October of last year. I made a mistake, thinking it was just a marketing gimmick.

"Then it occurred to me—for a publicity stunt there was hardly any actual publicity. I would've expected your face to be plastered all over the media—you gushing about your *flying* or whatever shit they would've made you say. But no, there was nothing, just some shitty pictures taken by amateurs with your face obscured.

"Two things struck me about that. First, since I'd never seen Marcus use people as assistants, I realized you must be in on his secret—you knew there was no rope tied to you to haul you up into the air during that show, after all.

"Second, since there was absolutely no media coverage on you—either during the show or after—it meant he was hiding you from everyone. And only the treasured things are worth hiding that well, aren't they?

"You, Miss McAllister . . ." he pointed my way dramatically, as if he were on stage, "turned out to be Marcus's treasure and the weakness I'd been searching for. It took me awhile to figure out your identity. But once I did, I learned more about him, too. We got pictures of his face without the damn mask. I already sold those for a pretty penny. But now I know I could get so much more from him. I've seen you together. I know he'll do pretty much anything I tell him to do to keep you from harm." A sinister glimmer flashed in his eyes. He lowered his voice, and something in his tone scraped inside me, making me flinch. "Because harm is what I do best now. It's been my sole business for the past couple of years."

"Listen," I said quietly, not above begging here, except that I didn't think begging would make any difference to him. I no longer believed there was any way to reason with this maniac. "Just let me go, and I promise I'll ask Marcus not to hurt you."

He laughed in my face.

"You are one stupid bitch, aren't you? Didn't I just tell you? *I'm* the one doing all the hurting around here." His tone carried a certain level of pride with this admission. "And guess what? I'll let you in on my little plan. He gets a bullet in his head as soon as I get everything I want on my list, and then I'll make you watch what I'll do to his dead body before I kill you, too."

A wave of paralyzing terror washed over me.

"And do you know why I'm telling you this?" he asked. "Because you won't be able to warn him anyway."

He picked up a dirty rag from the floor.

"Open that pretty mouth of yours."

"Hey, boss," came a raspy voice from behind me, making me jump. The shuffling sounds grew a bit closer. "Why would we waste the bitch? Sell her like the others."

I turned my head, craning my neck to see the ones behind me over my shoulder. Several dark shapes emerged from the shadows, a faint glimmer of light reflecting off the weapons among them.

Behind them, on the far wall washed in the pale light from the dirty windows, I spotted several thick rusty chains hanging from the rings mounted at intervals. All chains ended with metal collars attached to them. Several dirty plastic buckets lined up along the wall, with filthy rags piled nearby.

What was *this place?*

"She'd fetch a good price if we don't rough her up too much," the same raspy voice said.

"Huh? Fuck that," came another voice. This one had a thick accent, the origin of which I couldn't care to figure out at the moment. "I wanna rough her up."

Who were these people?

People? Were they human at all?

"Shut up!" Harold barked at them.

"Is that your new *business*?" I shuddered more from disgust than cold or fear this time. "Are you kidnapping and selling people?"

His fist hit the side of my mouth this time. My head jerked back, my lower lip swelling with pain and heat. Something warm trickled down my chin, and the coppery taste of blood hit my tongue.

"I said shut up," he growled through his teeth, lifting the rag in his hands to my face.

Fighting a bout of nausea from the stench of the rag, I clenched my jaws together.

"Nuh-uh. Open up, buttercup." He forcefully drove his knee into my ribs then shoved the cloth between my teeth when I cried out in pain.

Anger flared anew inside me, blinding me with the need for revenge. I wanted to kick, to shove, to hurt in response to my pain. Adrenaline rushed through me, making me feel invincible. My legs were unbound, hands tied behind the chair but not to it, I could run for it.

He said himself he didn't intend for me to survive. At least I would make it difficult for him.

The baby.

The thought sliced through me like a blade of a knife. What if Ingeborg was right and I did carry another life inside me? How could I let this madman hurt it even if I didn't care about myself?

I slumped in the chair, defeated without a fight.

"Much better, isn't it?" He chuckled, tying the ends of the rag behind my head. "Think what you want, missy—I have a business, and it is successful. I've a very generous organization as a client, who's more than made up the loss of income I endured because of your boyfriend. Speaking of which. We've sent the invite. Our friend Marcus should be here any minute." He grabbed my arm, yanking me off the chair. "Up now."

Someone handed Harold a piece of thick, rusty chain, similar—if not identical—to those on the wall.

"Here we go," he murmured, his voice thick with approval, as he wrapped the chain around my waist and locked it. "Time to get closer, Miss McAllister." He threw the other end of the chain around his middle and secured it with another padlock, leaving less than a foot of the chain length between us.

"Let's hope your asshole boyfriend is smart enough to be good." One hand wrapped around my upper arm, he produced a folded knife from his pocket with his other hand. With a click, the spring blade gleamed in the dim light. "Because if not—" The cold metal of the blade pressed into my neck.

Chapter 40

I CLOSED MY EYES, SWALLOWING hard against the blade at my throat, when a sudden explosion rocked the building to its foundation.

Light filtered through my closed eyelids. Cold air blew in streams along the floor, freezing against my feet in nylon stockings.

I opened my eyes just in time to see one of the heavy loading dock doors soar through the air as if it had been hurled by the hand of an invisible giant. It crashed far behind me, the sound followed by filthy curses and screams of pain from Harold's people.

"Marcus?" Harold sounded uncertain.

Then I saw *him* walking across the vast space of the warehouse between us, his sharp, dark silhouette like an ink painting against the daylight at his back. His long hair was unbound. The loose strands whipped in the wind like a raven wing behind him.

Silent, calm, deadly.

My man. He found me.

The familiar warm feeling spread through my heart at the sight of him, melting the bone-crushing cold for a moment.

Harold recovered quickly and shifted behind me, shielding himself with my body against the approaching menace.

"Well." Thick glee coloured Harold's voice. He pressed the knife harder into the side of my neck. His other hand curled around my throat. "Nice to deal with someone who is on time, even if that someone is a piece of shit liar. Stop right there!" he ordered, but Marcus kept coming to me, paying no attention to him or to the handful of armed men who stepped from around us, pointing their guns at him.

"Stop, I said!" Harold flexed his hand on my throat, giving me a shake.

Marcus froze. There was still a fair distance between us. His gaze quickly swept over the room, then his attention was fully upon me again.

"Good." Harold shifted from foot to foot behind me, speaking over my shoulder. "Do what I say and nobody will get hurt."

Liar.

"So, I have a rather long to-do list for you, pretty boy," Harold continued. "Let's get going, shall we?"

Two more men stepped out of the shadows. One carried a small folding table, the other an open laptop computer. Cautiously, they approached Marcus and placed the table and the laptop in front of him.

"We'll start with the basics," Harold kept going. "Money. See that number on the screen? This is my bank account. I'm doing pretty good, but I want you to add three zeros to it at the end."

Marcus said nothing, and I sensed his silence unnerved Harold.

"Note, I could've asked for five zeros," he spoke quickly, likely to cover up his insecurity. "It wouldn't make any difference to someone like you, would it? But I'm not that greedy."

Harold might have guessed Marcus's secret, I realized, but he had only a vague idea of the whole extent of Marcus's powers. He'd chained me to himself to prevent Marcus from levitating me away from him, possibly hoping he'd be safer close to me. He obviously didn't know that Marcus could pulverize that chain with nothing but a thought.

At least, I was positive he could. Just as he could disable the guns pointed at him and vanish the knife at my throat. I knew he could. I've seen him do similar things many times.

Yet Marcus did nothing. He stood in the middle of the warehouse, hands fisted at his sides, his eyes on the knife in Harold's hand.

He seemed calm, but I knew him well enough to sense the extreme tension boiling just beneath the surface.

The deep crease between his dark eyebrows told me of his intense concentration. His pale skin seemed almost white, giving him the appearance of a ghostly apparition. The complete stillness of his body was unnatural, as if he were afraid to draw in a single breath.

Pain flashed in his eyes as he stared at the knife at my throat, and I understood what was stopping him.

Harold might not have known the whole power of Marcus's strength, but he had guessed his weakness correctly. Marcus could raze this whole place to the ground in seconds, but not if there was even a slightest chance of harming *me* in the process.

"What are you waiting for?" Harold prompted. "My list is long, the day is short, and the lady here," he gave me another shake, "is getting cold and uncomfortable."

Marcus glared at my abuser without dignifying him with an answer.

I tried to guess what could be going through his mind at that moment, to evaluate the whole situation from his perspective. It wasn't the guns pointed at him or the chain around my waist, not even the knife at my neck that must have concerned him.

His biggest worry must have been Harold's hand squeezing my throat. It was the only thing Marcus couldn't control. The fear of Harold crushing my windpipe must be what was paralyzing him. Even one in a billion chance of any harm coming to me because of his actions was too much for him.

I turned out to be my Superman's kryptonite.

Unable to speak with the rag in my mouth, I implored him with my eyes, trying to tell him I wanted him to act, without the fear of the consequence.

Instead, his gaze flickered to the computer. With a deep breath, he took a step towards it.

"There you go," Harold crooned with satisfaction, his mouth hovering low over my shoulder. His breath hit the side of my face. I could feel his excitement at having people bent to his will as he fidgeted behind me, obviously unable to stay still. His crotch brushed by my hands tied behind my back, and I curled my fingers, shrinking from the contact.

A sudden thought flashed through my brain. My attention zoomed in on Marcus as I waited for him to look at me again.

Standing in front of the laptop, he glanced up, and I held his gaze, willing him to understand what I was about to do.

All he needed was a moment, and I was going to give it to him.

I was not a fighter. I'd never hit a person in my life, but I called on all the anger, fear and desperation churning inside me, putting it all in one blow, as I threw my head back, aiming for Harold's nose. At the sickening sound of smashed cartilage, I grabbed his limp dick through his pants and squeezed it as hard as I could.

A loud, high-pitched wail came from his mouth. His grip around my throat loosened. The knife slid along my neck, but I felt no pain.

Shoving away from him, I let myself fall to the side. The chain stretched tight, the rusty links screeched against each other, as it yanked against my waist for a moment before being blown to pieces by Marcus's glare.

I hit the concrete floor with my side and elbow—hard—and immediately curled into myself, bracing for whatever was to come.

Harold's wailing scream was cut short with a quiet puff and a brief searing noise. A pungent stench of burnt flesh hit my nostrils. I held my breath as silvery grey streams of hot ash misted across the floor, caught by the draft.

The grey ash was all that was left of Harold, I realized. Unable to process all the horrors at once, I closed my eyes.

Warm hands reached for me. The restraints fell from my arms, and the filthy rag disappeared from my mouth. Strong arms lifted me off the floor. Marcus pressed me to his hard chest, scorching hot like a furnace, and I melted against him. It felt like heaven both to my shivering body and to my tormented soul.

I draped my arms over his shoulders, barely noticing the pain that shot through my body, and buried my nose in the side of his neck. The familiar, comforting scent of hot spice and warm leather filled my lungs, blocking the stench of the warehouse.

An array of noises raged all around us—heavy cursing, loud clunks of useless weapons, screams of pain, rapid sounds of footsteps running either towards us or away from us.

All of them were silenced one by one with puffs of air and searing sounds, and when I finally ventured to open my eyes again, more grey ash joined the dark, morbid whirlpool churning in the air around us.

Everything ended within minutes, without Marcus uttering a single word. Silent, he carried me out into the afternoon light.

The warehouse seemed plain and ordinary from the outside. I must have passed it many times on my monthly visits to our distribution centre located in the same industrial area, just north of the airport. The building stood apart from the rest, in the centre of a large lot, giving Harold enough privacy for his dark deeds.

What a vile, sinister place.

A deafening explosion shattered the still, chilly air. A wide column of fire shot thirty feet into the air from the roof of the warehouse. The blazing inferno came down like a waterfall, engulfing the whole building in flames in less than a second.

Marcus kept walking away from the blaze, quiet and seemingly calm, though I felt his strain vibrating through every fibre of his being, betraying the tremendous effort it took him to rein in the storm raging inside.

The violent manifestation of this power lay behind us. The building, as well as the criminals inside it, had been incinerated with quick, silent efficiency.

Suddenly, I understood much better why Ingeborg and her people lived in hiding and why Marcus refused to let the world know about his magic.

To me, Marcus's gift had been something wondrous, pure, and beautiful, meant to be enjoyed and shared with people.

However, this wasn't how everyone would see it. Marcus could be deemed a monster, who needed to be contained and isolated, if not destroyed. Some might find ways to exploit his gift, potentially using him as a weapon against humanity.

I slid my hands up his back. The fact that he continued to walk instead of teleporting us told me his mind was still there somewhere, in a dark place. Restless energy must be coursing through him, surging beneath his burning skin. Wanting to soothe it, I stroked his nape gently.

"It's okay, Marcus," I whispered. "We're going to be okay. You saved me."

The high-pitched wail of sirens came from the distance—the police and fire trucks must have been on their way to the scene.

"We have to get out of here, my love," I said. "It's my turn to keep you safe, and I promise I'll spend a lifetime doing it."

Chapter 41

HE TOOK ME HOME TO my apartment, drew a warm bath for both of us, and washed the ash out of my hair. Later, he carried me to bed and crawled under the covers behind me then held me close in utter silence.

The ash was off my body, but a thick layer of it still weighed heavily on my soul.

"We need to get you to the hospital," he said.

"I hate hospitals," I replied. Saying something as trivial as that brought back some sense of normality. "The wait times will kill you sooner than any emergency that brought you there."

He chuckled softly in my hair, and I turned in his arms to face him. My ribs protested, and the dull pain in my elbow spread up to my shoulder. The band-aid over the shallow cut on my neck tugged at my skin.

The injuries would take a while to heal. Meanwhile, the pain would remind me of today's events every time I moved.

Fidgeting with the ice pack that Marcus got for me, I tried to figure out the right way to ask.

"Marcus?" I started carefully, wondering if he was ready to talk about it. "Have you ever burned someone before?"

Slowly, he lifted his hand and brushed a few stray hairs away from my face. His gaze slipped behind me as I waited.

"Yes," he replied finally.

"When you were a child?"

He inhaled slowly.

"Yes."

"Was it . . . Was it an accident?"

"No." He tapped his thumb against my ice pack. "Not an accident."

A few more seconds passed before he continued, "I was eight, maybe nine. Still too young to fully understand what was going on in that foster home, but I felt something wasn't right and preferred to play outside with Simon. I shared a bedroom with two older boys, but all the younger kids had their own rooms in that house. Looking back—" He cut himself short.

Rolling on his back, he rubbed his face with both hands.

"I'm not sorry," he said softly. "How can I be? If anything, I should've done it to him earlier."

Silent, I lifted my uninjured arm and splayed my hand on his chest, right over his thundering heart.

"I got up in the middle of the night once, to use the bathroom." His jaw muscles clenched. "He happened to be awake and cornered me in there. He said if I lived under his roof, I had to be a good boy and follow the rules of his house. I was terrified when he held me down, but it was the pain that ignited the anger, and I exploded. I don't remember much after that. My mind had gone blank. I came to only after he had already passed out on the floor. His clothes had burned off, but the fire still raged all around him. I stopped the flames. I remember being afraid that he'd die. I didn't want to kill him, Angela. I just wanted him to stop."

Fighting a lump in my throat, I stroked his chest soothingly, unable to speak, not sure if he even wanted me to say anything at this point.

"He ended up dying in a care home a few years later," Marcus continued, staring at the ceiling. "He never fully recovered from his burns. So, essentially, I killed him after all."

"You stopped him from ruining the lives of other children." I finally managed to get into words some of what I felt. "Who knows if any of those he'd molested ever recovered from his abuse?" My throat tightened, and I pressed my palm to his chest firmly to stop my hand from shaking.

He took my hand and laced his fingers with mine, turning to his side to face me, his expression darkened. "It's frighteningly easy for me to hurt people, Angela. Sometimes, all I have to do is simply let it loose. But I've never wanted to harm anyone. Until today. Today, I wanted to kill them all. Those who took you? I didn't want them to exist."

His words sent a chilling sensation through my chest, but the truly scary part was that I understood him completely. If there was a judgment passed on him, I should be judged, too, because I accepted his actions as my own.

"The world may be a better place if some people didn't exist," I replied gravely.

"Does it justify a murder?" He stared at me intently.

"I don't know." I sighed. "I'm sure there are many ways to look at it, Marcus—morality, ethics, law—but I don't care. I promise you that I will never hold your past against you. Just like I would never judge you for what you did today. I used to believe that people were never all good or all bad, that they were always somewhere in-between. But today, I saw pure evil with my own eyes. Some filth just doesn't deserve to walk the earth. They deface this world with their presence."

His chest heaved as he closed his eyes and pressed his forehead to mine.

"Now that you know," he whispered. "Now that you've seen, can you still love me?"

Wrapping my uninjured arm around his shoulders, I drew him closer.

I might be his weakness, but we were also each other's strength.

"I could never *un*-love you, Marcus. You are mine, all of you. Your faults are my own, and all of your secrets are mine to keep." I reached for a kiss, but the cut on my lip made me wince.

"I can't heal." He tenderly skimmed along my lip with his thumb. "I would give up everything I have, all the magic in the world, just to be able to heal this right now."

The deep regret in his voice tightened around my heart.

"Well," I attempted a smile, lest I break into tears. "If your bargain for healing powers works out, could you please start with my elbow? It hurts the most."

My effort to lighten his mood didn't seem to work.

"I'll never forgive myself for letting them take you." He groaned.

I shook my head.

"Don't, please. What happened today was not your fault, Marcus. Maybe I shouldn't have left the apartment in the first place? We can drive ourselves insane, thinking about what we could or should have done, but Harold would've gone ahead with his plan one way or another, if not today then some other day. We did the best we could under the circumstances, and we both survived. That's what matters."

Taking in his beloved face, I traced his jawline with the tip of my finger. "He said he sold pictures of you without the mask," I warned, remembering Harold's bragging. "We'll have to find a way to stop them from being published."

To my surprise, he just shrugged. "It might be too late for that. Let them see."

"Are you ready for that? To face the world unmasked?"

"My hiding didn't keep you safe. The world may as well know it all now. I want to show everyone that you are mine. Move in with me," he said, unexpectedly.

"To Vegas?" I gaped at him, sitting up in bed.

Despite us living thousands of miles apart, thanks to his abilities, I hardly ever felt the distance. Moving in together had a bigger meaning for him than just the matter of convenience, I sensed.

"Yes. Will you do that?" He sat up, too. "You can find another job there. Something similar to what you have here. Or you can help me with the show full time, instead. Whatever you want."

His tone remained even, almost casual, but the intensity in his eyes flickering between mine betrayed his nervousness.

"Are you worried about me living on my own?"

"Maybe. But that's not the main reason. I simply want you near me, Angela. The same house, the same bed. Like a real family."

A real family.

Something he never had. Now, I could give it to him.

"I'd love to be your family, honey." I leaned closer to him, smiling. "And I may not be coming alone," I said, remembering my news. It was odd to think about myself as a woman with child yet, someone's mom in the future. "Ingeborg thinks I'm pregnant."

"Are you?" His eyes grew wider as he drew me to him by my shoulders. "Is that true?"

"I don't know. I don't feel any different, to be honest, but she seemed to be rather confident about it. I guess we should go to the hospital after all, or at least to see my doctor. Would you be happy if it turned out to be true?"

"Would I?" He gave me one of his brightest smiles, the first one today. "I'd be the happiest man on earth."

Chapter 42

"HERE WE ARE." I TOOK Marcus's hand in mine as soon as I sighted the picnic table with my family and friends gathered around it.

It was May, nearly two months since that dark Sunday in March. With Marcus and I leaving for Vegas tomorrow, most of this time had been spent in preparation.

As soon as my injuries healed enough to return to work, I ended up quitting my job. At first, it was weird to find myself without having to rush to the office on Monday mornings, but my freed time filled up fast.

Between helping my parents settle into their new condo and getting ready for my own move, I found myself as busy as ever.

In anticipation of my arrival, Marcus had been working on fortifying his ranch house with a state-of-the-art security system. He also hired a few more bodyguards and a chauffeur to drive me around.

To move me to Nevada, Marcus had also renewed his driver's licence and bought a car. Since my doctor had confirmed I was indeed going to have a baby and neither of us knew how teleportation would affect it, we decided to travel by the conventional means, at least during the pregnancy.

Everyone in my life knew about Marcus and me by now. However, today was the first time he was going to meet my family.

Holding hands, we crossed the grassy area near the waterfront of Lake Ontario where my family got together for an early spring picnic to say goodbye to us.

"Oh my God! I'm so very happy to finally meet you, Marcus!" my mom practically screamed with excitement as Marcus handed her a bouquet of red roses.

And just like that my two worlds finally collided.

Marcus shook hands with everyone. We pushed two picnic tables together end to end and took out the food from the coolers we brought with us.

I watched Mom fuss with paper plates and napkins as she set the table, and remembered how shocked the rest of us had been to discover an enormous collection of items she had bought over the years only to stash them in several hiding places all over the house.

Clothes, shoes, dishes, even children's toys piled in shopping bags and boxes in the basement and attic. Many bags had store receipts tucked inside. Almost all of the items still had their price tags.

My mother sobbed quietly, watching us load it all in Lily's car, to take back to the store what we still could. She wasn't sorry to part with her "treasures"—they'd served their purpose to her as soon as she paid for them and brought them home. She was crying from shame, having the proof of her *condition* being brought up into the open.

Surprisingly, Lily came up with the right thing to say that day.

"It's an addiction. You can never get rid of it completely, Jen, but with help, you can control it and stop it from ruining your life."

My mom exhaled a shuddered breath and gave her a small nod in reply before going back in the house. Her shoulders relaxed a little, as now she knew we weren't there to judge her.

I walked over to Lily then and hugged her. As calm as her words sounded, I knew they were heartfelt because she spoke from experience. All this time, she had been there for my brother more than any one of us had.

Lily was my family, too.

Evan had finally given her the ring. It was a princess-cut diamond in pretty gold setting, which she absolutely loved and proudly showed to everyone who cared to see.

"You know, Marcus, you should consider cutting your hair off." Lily's voice came from across the picnic table, yanking me out of my thoughts.

I threw a worried look her way—I loved his hair just the way it was, magnificently long.

"It can't be practical for a man." Lily munched on cheese and crackers, completely oblivious to my distress.

"You think so?" Marcus tilted his head, tiny sparks of amusement sprung to life in his navy-blue eyes.

"Long hair is fine for women." She touched her glossy bun, with not a hair out of place. "Your hairstyle looks impressive on stage, but it must be a pain otherwise. It's not like you can pin it up, either—a bun doesn't work for men."

"It doesn't, huh?" Marcus stretched his arm over the table and closed his empty hand into a fist. With all eyes on him, he displayed a black hair elastic in the middle of his open palm a moment later.

"Wow!" Emily laughed, clapping her hands.

"Did you have it up your sleeve?" Evan unceremoniously tugged at the cuff of Marcus's leather jacket, trying to peek in. "How did you do it?"

"If I tell you—the magic will be gone," Marcus gave him the standard answer.

Only *I* knew that his magic was much more enduring than that.

He pulled his hair back and used the elastic to twist the heavy mass into a knot quickly.

"What do you think?" he asked Lily with a cocky grin and turned his head to the side, as if inviting her to take a better look.

"Well." Furrowing her brow, she bit her bottom lip. "This is weird, but you actually can pull it off—you still look hot."

"Hey!" My brother nudged her in the arm. "He may be your brother-in-law one day."

"Honey," Lily explained patiently. "I simply stated the fact—he is hot. It doesn't mean I want to have sex with him."

My mom choked on the leaf of lettuce from her salad, and Dad quickly changed the subject. "These are beautiful roses, Marcus." He waved his plastic fork at the flowers that Mom had somehow arranged in two centerpieces by now.

"Thank you. Angela loves roses. I figured her mom would, too."

"Oh, roses *are* my favourite," Mom gushed, and I smiled to myself.

"What is it?" Marcus caught my expression.

"Well, I probably should've confessed a long time ago." I glanced up at him. "I don't really like roses that much."

"You don't?" He seemed genuinely surprised.

I shook my head. "To be completely honest, I find them prickly, flashy, and too expensive."

"Really?" He rubbed his chin. "What *are* your favourite?"

"I love wild flowers—their smell always reminds me of summer."

"Wild? You mean like the ones that grow in fields and forests?"

I nodded.

"You're kidding me, right? I don't know of any florist—either here or in Vegas—that sells them."

"You don't have to give me wild flowers." I smiled. "There are many others I like almost as much."

"No, I should be able to give you the ones you love. Except that, how would you suggest I get them? By prancing around a meadow somewhere, gathering wild flowers for you?"

I imagined Marcus *prancing* in his leather pants and boots and burst out laughing. He watched me for a few moments, a warm smile playing on his lips.

"You know." He covered my hand with his on the table. "For you, I just might do that."

I loved seeing him this relaxed and comfortable around my family. Marcus was so much more social by nature than he had allowed himself to be, sentenced to self-isolation by his extraordinary abilities.

That my family appeared to like him, too, thrilled me. I thought we should invite them all to Vegas for a visit as soon as I had settled in myself.

"Okay, Angela, Marcus, you have to tell them your news." Emily's excited voice rang over the table. "Please! I can't wait anymore. It's been killing me for the past twenty-four hours."

I told Emily about my pregnancy a day ago. To be honest, I didn't expect her to keep the secret for this long.

"Can I tell them?" Emily begged, and it literally shot out of her the moment I gave her a nod. "Angela and Marcus are having a baby!"

"Is that true?" My father leaped off his seat then plopped back down.

"Oh my God!" My mom clutched her hands to her chest, the shock on her face melted into the expression of utter happiness. "Congratulations, my baby-girl. Marcus." Mom gazed at him with pure adoration, and for a moment I wondered if she'd go on thanking him for sticking around long enough to get me pregnant. "So glad Angela's found you." Her bottom lip trembled, and she dabbed at her eyes with the napkin in her hand.

My dad hugged her shoulders.

"Really? Way to go, sis!" Evan yelled and punched Marcus in the arm.

"Congratulations!" Emily jumped up and down, looking as excited as if she'd heard the news for the first time herself.

Lily grinned and hugged Mikey for whatever reason.

I squeezed Marcus's hand tight and smiled so wide my face hurt. These were my people. Every one of them was perfectly imperfect, and all of them together made up my family, my world.

EPILOGUE

He stared at the screen mounted in the back of the seat in front of him, but had a hard time actually following the movie that was playing on it.

For what felt like a millionth time during their flight from Toronto to Vegas, his gaze strayed to Angela, who was peacefully dozing in the seat next to him.

Through the material of his pants, he patted the small, rectangular box in his pocket to make sure it was still there—the ring he was planning to give her as soon as he carried her over the threshold of his, now *theirs*, ranch house.

Over the course of the last weeks, carefully asking all the right questions, he had figured out which ring she'd want.

She could've wished for the most extravagant diamond in the world, and he would have found a way to get it for her. But she chose amber—inexpensive, understated, and warm. It reminded her of his necklace, she said, and wearing it would make her feel like she belonged into his family, even if she never met them.

Angela accepted his past, without reservations. His fearless ice queen, she was giving him the courage to try and do the same.

Listening to her stories about Ingeborg and her people had been comforting. Knowing there were other people, similar to him in many ways, made him feel like there might really be a place he belonged.

Angela had mentioned the family reunion in Phoenix in June, and the more he thought about it the more he felt they should go. Especially now, since there was no longer just himself to consider.

His gaze slid along Angela's belly, barely three months along, there were hardly any visible changes yet. Ever since the doctor confirmed the pregnancy, though, Marcus couldn't stop being apprehensive about everything.

In addition to the normal fears any new parents faced, he and Angela also had to worry about which of his powers would be passed on to their baby and what would be the implications of raising a *magical* child.

Angela's vivid imagination kept coming up with terrifying scenarios of their baby setting his crib on fire or teleporting to someplace unknown and dangerous.

He had no definite answers that would calm her down, but they were not alone. Ingeborg's people had been raising children with supernatural abilities for centuries and might have answers to many of the questions.

As if feeling his gaze on her, Angela stretched with a sweet moan and opened her eyes.

"You're not watching your movie?" she asked with a warm lazy smile then winced, rubbing her neck. "You've spoiled me with teleporting, darling. I can no longer sit on a plane for hours, even in first class. My whole body feels stiff and sore."

"It's not that long now." He reached to massage her shoulders.

"Thank you." She nuzzled his hand, leaning into his touch. "Oh, this feels good. I love you, honey."

She was meant for him, there wasn't a doubt in his heart. She was his light, his happiness, his soulmate—the only one who knew everything about him and loved him despite it all.

For the first time ever, he looked into the future with fondness and optimism, because she'd be at his side, every day and every night.

His girl in the red dress.

"I love you, too, my fearless woman."

THE END

TO LOVE A MONSTER

Chapter 1

<u>MONSTER</u>

Intruders!

He leaped out of the icy water onto the rocky riverbank and shook his hide.

Rising on his hind legs, he stretched to his full height, sniffing the air. The breeze was in the wrong direction—he didn't smell them yet. But he *felt* the trespassing. He was all the way by the river bordering his property at the east. The intruders must have entered from the road to the west.

He had no idea what date it was, but judging by the leaves falling from the trees and the frost on the ground in the morning, it must have been around October, maybe November. Either way, the hunting season would be in full swing, which could mean that the intruders were hunters.

There were plenty of *Private Property*, *No Trespassing* and even *Violators Will Be Prosecuted* signs placed all along the barbed wire marking the boundaries of the estate. However, this didn't seem to deter the occasional hunter from crossing over in a pursuit of a deer or an elk.

As long as it was the deer that they were after, he had nothing to worry about, except that people in general were a nuisance.

Maybe the cougar will get them.

The sneaky cat had been stalking him for years. Of course when he wished him to show up and chase the intruders away, the cougar wouldn't be around.

He drew in another lungful of air, searching for any foreign scent on the breeze.

Nothing.

Still, the nagging feeling of the intrusion wouldn't leave him, forcing him to move west, towards the house. It couldn't hurt to make sure the hunters stayed away from it.

He sped up until he broke into a full-on sprint, his paws hitting the leaf-covered ground soundlessly. Hot blood pounded through his veins along with the satisfaction of being alive.

Further west, an inhale of air finally brought in the scent of the strangers, bringing him to an abrupt stop so fast, he almost tumbled over his head like a clumsy puppy.

The scent wasn't what he expected.

None of the usual smell of oil and gunpowder of a hunter. Instead, the faint scent of fancy cologne and delicate, flowery perfume reached his sensitive nose. And it was the subtle, delicate scent of female bodies underneath the perfume that hit him like a punch in a gut.

His blood boiled, his vision clouded, and his cock hardened so painfully fast, it slapped his underbelly with force.

Primal need to breed forced him up onto his hind legs again. He threw his head back, his long horns pressed against the shoulder blades. Flexing his fingers, he released razor-sharp claws, and roared into the cold air around him.

The mating call of a beast reverberated through the woods, bouncing off the tree trunks in cascading echoes.

Chapter 2

"What was that?" Ashley froze in her tracks. Following closely behind her, I bumped into her.

"What the fuck?" Jason, my boyfriend of over two months, tightened his grip on the axe in his hand, his knuckles white.

I was pretty sure my face was just as pale. The deafening, blood-curling howl had made my insides turn to chilly slush.

"No clue," I replied. "But it certainly sounds vicious."

"We should go back, guys," Ashley muttered.

"It's just some wild animal. Probably a wolf." Jason seemed to have recovered quickly. "There are three of us. It won't attack in the broad daylight. Come on." He moved ahead, lifting the axe he had brought to cut through the bush in his right hand and cradling his precious camera to his chest with the other.

"There was too much roar in that howl for a wolf." Ashley pointed-ed out, not moving from her spot. "And it sounded way too loud. If it really was a wolf, it must be the size of a bull."

"I'm with Ashley on this one." I nodded, not moving either. I'd known Ashley for three days and in that time we hadn't agreed on everything, but right now we were definitely on the same page. I shivered. Our fun afternoon outing didn't feel that harmless anymore.

Last night, after a long conversation with a drunk at the bar of the hunting lodge where the three of us were staying with a group of Jason's hunter friends, he decided to go on a search of an abandoned cabin in the woods.

The drunk had described it as *'the most fucking beautiful hunting cabin that you'd ever see'*, which spiked Jason's interest as a photographer.

"I think we should go back," Ashley sounded more adamant by the moment, glancing around nervously, her hands twisting the cord of her backpack.

Unlike her boyfriend, Ashley didn't hunt, and neither did I. Bored out of our minds from waiting at the lodge for the hunting party to return every night, we tagged along with Jason for something to do.

"We're almost there, Ash," Jason insisted. "Look, if you really want, you can go back and wait in the truck."

"Uh-uh." Ashley appeared resolute. "I've watched way too many horror movies to be the one waiting in the car. If we go, we all go together." She moved ahead muttering under her breath, "At least this way I'd have a chance to get away if that thing attacks *you* first."

I hesitated for a second. The blood still ran cold in my veins, and the terrifying sound of the howling roar continued to ring in my ears.

From my limited knowledge about wild animals though, they rarely attacked unless provoked, and I had no intention of provoking anything.

Jason and Ashley started walking away so I hurried after them not wanting to be left behind.

"Aha!" I heard Jason exclaim triumphantly. "This must be the driveway the guy was talking about." He pointed at the dense, seemingly impenetrable wall of wild rose bushes to our right.

"A driveway?" I stared at the prickly shrubs, confused.

"He said the old driveway is overgrown with rose bushes, and the cabin itself is surrounded by them."

"It makes no sense. Why would the driveway be more overgrown than the woods around it? Shouldn't it be the other way around?"

"Fuck if I know." Jason shrugged. "Isn't the Wild Rose the provincial flower of Alberta? You're from Alberta, Sophie. I'm from BC. If you don't know why it grows the way it does, how am I supposed to know?"

The bushes in front of us might have been Alberta Wild Rose, but I'd never heard of them growing like this, high and dense, forming an impassable hedge.

I rolled my eyes at Jason's logic, but kept silent. Lately, I'd noticed it was best not to reply in cases like this. Jason would never miss a chance to argue simply for the sake of having an argument—just another opportunity to hear himself talk.

"Anyway," he continued. "All we have to do now is follow the rose bushes all the way to the cabin."

"Easy-peasy," chimed in Ashley, marching ahead with much more bounce in her step than could have been expected after her earlier hesitation. And I followed, trying to keep up.

It didn't take long before we ran into another wall of rose bushes. This one grew perpendicular to the one we had been following. This time of the year, the delicate pink flowers of the wild rose, had already been replaced by red, glossy fruit.

"And there it is," Jason grunted with satisfaction then started swinging his axe left and right to crush the thorny branches in our way in order to make a passage through the hedge.

Ashley squeezed by him as soon as he stopped. "Holy cow!" I heard her whistle. "Is this *the cabin*?"

"Yesss," Jason hissed triumphantly and thrust the axe back in my direction then lifted his camera as soon as I took the axe from him. "This is something else! Totally worth the trip."

I stepped around him and into the clearing. The rose bushes circled the yard of the cabin in a neat shape, like a live fence, with a spectacular building in the centre.

"I wouldn't call it a cabin." I took in the enormous structure in front of me.

Two stories high, with a third-floor glass observatory on top, the sprawling log-and-stone building looked more like a high-end estate home or a movie star's retreat.

"Who would build something like this here?" I asked in shock.

"Some rich folks who didn't know what else to do with their money." Jason already snapped busily away with his camera.

"How did they get all these rocks and logs in here?"

"Hey guys," Ashley called from the front porch. "Wanna go in? The door is open."

More By Marina Simcoe

<u>*Demons Series*</u>
Demon Mine
The Forgotten
Grand Master – 2019

<u>*Stand Alone Novels Set in Demons Universe*</u>
The Real Thing
To Love A Monster

<u>*Science-Fiction Romance*</u>
Enduring (Valos of Sonhadra)
Experiment – 2019/2020

About the Author

MARINA SIMCOE LIKES to write larger-than-life love stories with characters, who may or may not be entirely human, because she firmly believes that our contemporary world could always use a little bit of the extraordinary.

She has lots of fun exploring how her out-of-this-world characters with their own beliefs, values and aspirations fit into our everyday life.

She lives in Canada with her magically sexy husband, their three little miracles and a cat, who might be into black magic.

For more illustrations of all of her books please visit Marina Simcoe Author page on Facebook or www.marinasimcoe.com.

Please Stay in Touch

Newsletter signup: http://eepurl.com/c__RGn
Readers' Group
Marina's Reading Cave: www.facebook.com/groups/
621598474945014/
www.instagram.com/marinasimcoeauthor
www.marinasimcoe.com
www.facebook.com/MarinaSimcoeAuthor/
www.amazon.com/author/marinasimcoe
www.bookbub.com/profile/marina-simcoe
www.goodreads.com/MarinaSimcoe

www.ingramcontent.com/pod-product-compliance
Lightning Source LLC
Chambersburg PA
CBHW031630200726
48288CB00019B/611